UNDER THE KNIFE

The curtains were drawn. The apartment felt close. Mac slowly made his way through the apartment, searching as he went. He sprung the closet door near the entryway. Nothing. No one.

Methodically and quietly he entered the living room, bathroom, kitchen. They were all empty. Then Mac moved toward the darkened bedroom. The intruder had to be there. Jennifer, too.

"Jennifer." He heard a motion, maybe fifteen feet away in the far corner of the room. Mac groped for a light switch and found one. A lamp went on beside the bed. His eyes followed the noise. Beano had one hand over Jennifer's mouth, the other held a knife to her throat. There was already a streak of blood across her neck where he had cut her. Her eyes bulged in terror.

"Come any closer and I s

MORTALIT

JACK CHASE

MORTALITY RATE

A SIGNET BOOK

SIGNET
Published by the Penguin Group
Penguin Putnam Inc., 375 Hudson Street,
New York, New York 10014, U.S.A.
Penguin Books Ltd, 27 Wrights Lane,
London W8 5TZ, England
Penguin Books Australia Ltd, Ringwood,
Victoria, Australia
Penguin Books Canada Ltd, 10 Alcorn Avenue,
Toronto, Ontario, Canada M4V 3B2
Penguin Books (N.Z.) Ltd, 182–190 Wairau Road,
Auckland 10, New Zealand

Penguin Books Ltd, Registered Offices:
Harmondsworth, Middlesex, England

First published by Signet, an imprint of Dutton Signet,
a member of Penguin Putnam Inc.

First Printing, October, 1997
10 9 8 7 6 5 4 3 2 1

REGISTERED TRADEMARK—MARCA REGISTRADA

Printed in the United States of America

PUBLISHER'S NOTE
This is a work of fiction. Names, characters, places, and incidents either are the product of the author's imagination or are used fictitiously, and any resemblance to actual persons, living or dead, events, or locales is entirely coincidental.

BOOKS ARE AVAILABLE AT QUANTITY DISCOUNTS WHEN USED TO PROMOTE PRODUCTS OR SERVICES. FOR INFORMATION PLEASE WRITE TO PREMIUM MARKETING DIVISION, PENGUIN PUTNAM INC., 375 HUDSON STREET, NEW YORK, NEW YORK 10014.

I even added, "You wouldn't even have seen the fish in all that foam if you hadn't first thought he would be there." But I couldn't shake the conviction that I had seen the black back of a big fish, because, as someone often forced to think, I know that often I would not see a thing unless I thought of it first.

—Norman Maclean,
A River Runs Through It

PROLOGUE

The doors leading into the intensive care unit were tightly closed, and no amount of pushing would budge them. There were no handles to pull, no knobs to turn. But each door had a tiny window, and it was through these that she was able to glimpse the pandemonium beyond. A glass-enclosed cubicle at the far end of the unit was the epicenter of furious activity. It was as though the vast human and technological resources of the great hospital had at once been brought to bear on this single juncture of life and death. But in her current state of bewilderment it did not occur to her that the unhappy beneficiary of all this attention might be her husband.

Her name was Havlicek—like the basketball player. It hadn't meant anything to her when she first came to this country. She hardly knew what basketball was. But everyone always wanted to know, Are you related? And at the

7

beginning she had always said no, she didn't have any relatives here in America, except of course for her husband and her daughter. Still, they remembered her because of the name which they already knew, and after a while it became easier not to go into great detail when they asked. She would give a little smile, a tiny shrug of her shoulders, thinking to herself, how did she know whether or not they were related? It was an unusual name. A distant cousin perhaps—but no need to emphasize the distance.

They treated her differently then. Schoppich, the butcher, became deferential, often waiting on her out of turn or saving back some special piece of meat. And the man who delivered the heating oil, Simmons, was always wanting to know what she thought of the Celtics' chances in this game or that—the implication being that he was not averse to a small wager now and then, especially if he could improve his odds through the benefit of a little inside information. But Mrs. Havlicek refused to be drawn into that game. Gambling is a sin, she scolded him. He ought to know better. Ah, but if it's such a sin, Simmons wanted to know, why are they having weekly Bingo down at St. Anthony's? That's quite a different thing, she would say. That's for charity. And besides, she knew very well it wasn't Father Murphy who was taking Simmons' basketball bets. She would slam the door, but next month Simmons would be back, wondering once again about the Celtics.

Her husband hadn't approved of all this at first, but over the years his stance had softened somewhat. After all, he couldn't prove they *weren't* related. In later years, when they wrote his name *John* instead of *Jun*, he didn't bother to correct them. It simply seemed more American, he finally decided, written that way.

Mrs. Havlicek had been awakened very early this morning by a phone call from the hospital. Her husband, the nurse said, had taken a turn for the worse. They were moving him into intensive care. Something about his heart.

But there's nothing wrong with his heart, Mrs. Havlicek had protested. It was her husband's *mind* which was the problem—not his heart. Perhaps there had been some mistake in identification.

The patient's name is John Havlicek, the nurse said. The basketball player? Mrs. Havlicek had asked. The nurse was pretty certain the man was not a basketball player. At any rate, she said, don't get too worried. He just has a little irregularity of his heart rhythm. We're only being cautious.

Mrs. Havlicek had decided against calling her daughter and son-in-law. They both worked so hard and needed their rest. Besides, they had been out to visit Jan the night before. He didn't seem to recognize them, of course. You couldn't be sure if he even knew they were in the room. He hardly spoke at all anymore. The doctors weren't very hopeful.

Not calling her daughter meant that Mrs. Havlicek had to take the bus to the hospital—two transfers on a cold, dark winter's morning. A light snow had begun to fall, looking very gray in the dawn's first light. Menacing low clouds threatened to crash down and plunge the city back into the darkness from which it was striving so desperately to emerge. It reminded her of her former home, the one she had fled with her husband and daughter so many years ago. But the gray there had come with the industrial revolution and would not leave with the rising sun. You could escape that gray only by escaping the country.

When finally the tower of the ancient red-brick hospital once again loomed before her, it inspired the same sense of awe it always did. Years before, in Paris, she'd had exactly the same feeling as she stood before Notre Dame—an intense awareness of being in the presence of something much greater than herself.

Anna Havlicek had never had a sense of God communicating directly to her. She could sometimes feel His presence, but had never actually heard His voice. She talked to the priests; the priests talked to God. She received her instructions from the priests, whom she trusted implicitly as emissaries of God.

But if Anna felt remote from God, her separation from modern medicine was light-years greater. At least she went to Mass once a week. She hadn't been to a doctor since her daughter was born. Her husband hadn't been certain even that was necessary. So now when the doctors spoke, it was as though they were delivering the word of God. Who was she to question them? Besides, everyone said they were the best doctors in the city—probably the best doctors in the world.

There was a soft whoosh and a rush of air, and suddenly the ICU doors opened before her. A flood of people streamed out around her— technologists, doctors, nurses—all looking very young, all oblivious to the tiny white-haired lady standing in their path. Their conversation gave no hint of the struggle which was now behind them.

But as Anna headed into the vacuum, she was abruptly filled with an undefined foreboding. Every fiber of her being became relentlessly focused on the now abandoned cubicle at the far end of the ICU.

"Excuse me," a voice called from somewhere.

"Excuse me!" There it was again. "May I help you?" A very serious young lady in a white uniform was now standing in front of Anna.

"Havlicek," was all Anna said, and that barely above a whisper.

"We tried to call you, Mrs. Havlicek. You must have been on your way to the hospital."

"I had to take the bus," Anna apologized. "Two transfers."

"Your husband went into V-fib, Mrs. Havlicek. There was nothing we could do."

Anna stared at the earnest young woman. Where was this V-fib into which her husband had gone? "May I see him?" she asked.

"Let me check with his primary nurse." She turned and disappeared into the last cubicle at the end of the ICU. When she reappeared there was another very serious young woman in her wake.

"Hi, I'm Jennifer," this new nurse said. "Why don't you give me just a few minutes to straighten things up?"

"Oh, I don't mind," Anna said. "I've had to clean up after him at home these last few weeks. He can't do anything for himself anymore."

Jennifer's expression became suddenly quizzical. She threw a frustrated glance in the direction of the other nurse. "Mrs. Havlicek, perhaps you would like to sit down."

Anna shook her head.

"Mrs. Havlicek, your husband passed away a few minutes ago. I'm sorry. I thought you knew that."

Anna felt her knees weaken. She thought she might faint.

"It was his heart, Mrs. Havlicek. He went into ventricular fibrillation. We couldn't get him out of it."

Anna tried once more to make this girl understand. "But there's nothing wrong with his heart," she pleaded. "It's his mind that's the problem."

ONE

"Has it ever occurred to you," the voice asked from the shadows above, "how much money has *already* been thrown away, how many thousands of hours of precious nursing and physician time have *already* been wasted, in a futile attempt to prevent this woman from killing herself?"

Every muscle in Mac McCall's body instantly tensed. Had others experienced the same reaction to those words, or was it simply that Mac's personal insight into the case caused him to be unduly sensitive?

The diatribe continued unabated.

"We are living in an era of strictly limited resources. I could not find it possible to justify the spending of a single additional penny on this patient—much less consider authorizing the tens of thousands of dollars of public funds which would be necessary to finance yet another round of pointless cardiac surgery!"

Mac didn't need to turn his head to identify the speaker. He recognized the voice well enough. But an outsider, hearing those dogmatic words emanate from the darkened upper reaches of the dimly lit amphitheater, might well have assumed that the speaker, Austin Delacroix, was some distinguished senior professor, not—like Mac himself—a fourth-year medical student.

Everyone's attention now focused on George Williams, the student who had presented the case. He stood on the floor of the amphitheater without benefit of a lectern to hide behind or notes to prod his memory.

"The issue is quite straightforward," George said. "If she does not receive the surgery, she will die."

"We're all going to die," Delacroix responded. "The only uncertainties are *when*? and *how much is it going to cost*?"

With that the ancient amphitheater fell into a creaky silence. Mac's mind wandered momentarily, distracted by the aura of history which suffused the room. It was not at all difficult to imagine a time, perhaps a century or more ago, when another group of students occupied this very theater, not to attend an ethics seminar but rather to observe a demonstration of anatomy.

The wooden tiers of seats were banked steeply so that the room was tall rather than long. The utility of this arrangement a hundred years ago was that the seated spectator had an excellent vantage as the cadaver was dissected and various points of anatomy were demonstrated. But for a student presenting a case now, there was very much a sense of being looked down upon by those asking questions. The dim lighting contributed to a feeling of Inquisition.

A student with less self-confidence or a less sharply focused intellect than that of George Williams might well have felt intimidated. Mac supposed that it didn't hurt that George was six feet ten inches tall, destined, Mac had told him, to become the world's tallest pediatrician.

It was clearly the aura of history which had motivated Professor Arthur Sterling Law's selection of the old amphitheater for his twice-monthly ethics seminar. Professor Law often referred to the "shifting sands" of medical ethics, contrasting, for example, past eras when even the dissection of cadavers was a high crime with the current trend toward the legalization of euthanasia.

To be selected to participate in Dr. Law's seminar was a great distinction. Three junior and three senior medical students were picked each year. To be chosen as a third-year student—and thus participate in the seminar for two years—was the highest honor a student could receive.

Mac had always said that if you'd asked him

on the first day of his freshman year who would be the three juniors picked for the seminar from his class, he could have told you without a moment's hesitation: Turner Frost, Peter VanSlyke, and Austin Delacroix. From day one they had been the three everyone noticed. Wealthy, handsome, brilliant, they'd come from the "best" families, had attended the best schools. Not a hair or credential out of place.

Anyone who had failed to notice the trio on their first day of class could not have missed them on the second. A junior faculty member from the biochemistry department became hopelessly bogged down on a point in molecular genetics. The threesome guided him out of the morass in a manner aimed more at humiliating than helping the young professor. The lecturer told them that, as future physicians, they could stand to be a little more empathetic. Peter VanSlyke told the lecturer he could stand to be a little better prepared.

Today the three had George Williams in their sights. His background could not have been more different from theirs. An African-American, George had fought poverty and all the other afflictions of a big-city ghetto to get where he was today. He also had a seven-year-old son he was raising practically single-handedly.

"So, Dr. Williams . . ." It was the voice of the unflappable Professor Law which came down from on high to break the silence. During the seminar he always referred to the students as "Doctor," a common practice at the medical school. "To summarize the case you presented, the patient is a twenty-five-year-old female who is an abuser of intravenous cocaine and heroin. One year ago she was admitted to the hospital with infection of two valves in her heart—a direct result of her drug use. In addition to many weeks of antibiotic therapy, she required open-heart surgery to replace her aortic valve. She was ultimately cured of her infection, and at the time of discharge she promised not to abuse intravenous drugs in the future. Unfortunately, she was unable to keep that promise.

"Now the patient is once again admitted to the hospital, this time with infection of her new prosthetic aortic valve, again a direct result of her IV drug abuse. We are advised by her physicians that she will not survive this admission unless she receives a second cardiac surgery, this one to replace her damaged, infected aortic prosthesis. Is that an accurate summary, Dr. Williams?"

"Yes, Professor."

"I now appoint you to be her physician, Dr. Williams. What is your recommendation?"

"For me it is not a complicated question. Surgery is clearly indicated and should be performed as soon as possible. As a physician my duty is to treat my patient. I have no right—much less obligation—to decide who is or is not deserving of my care."

"And what if she returns next year with yet another infection? Would you recommend additional surgery?"

"As a practical matter, Professor Law, the cardiac surgeons have made it quite clear that a third surgery would, for technical reasons, not be possible. It is a moot point."

"Dr. VanSlyke, perhaps you would favor us with your opinion on the case."

"I don't think it will come as a complete surprise to anyone," VanSlyke said, "that I totally disagree with Dr. Williams."

A smattering of nervous laughter filtered through the amphitheater.

"I believe," VanSlyke continued, "that physicians do have a fundamental responsibility to shepherd wisely the limited resources available. This patient has demonstrated an inability to avoid the behavior which has now twice resulted in life-threatening infection. There is every reason to believe that she will continue to engage in this behavior. Additional surgery at this time would only delay the inevitable and place an additional financial burden on the community."

"Well, there you have it," Professor Law's precise voice announced from out of the darkness. "We could not wish for two more well-articulated or diametrically opposed points of view. Dr. Williams states that it is the physician's duty to treat his patient without regard to the financial burden placed on society. Dr. VanSlyke argues that our resources are finite, and that the physician must make difficult decisions regarding their allocation. I submit that this is the fundamental ethical question confronting medical practice as we approach the new millennium.

"I am reminded of the early days of kidney dialysis. We had only a very limited number of dialysis machines available, and organ transplantation was not yet a practical reality. Simply put, we had far more patients who needed dialysis than the number of available machines. Committees were formed and decisions were made. Some patients were offered life-sustaining dialysis, others were not.

"Perhaps the limitation of resources was more obvious in those cases. You had one machine; you had many patients who would die without dialysis. The problem was quite straightforward. The dilemma confronting modern society is, on the other hand, somewhat more subtle. Instead of a handful of patients, we have the health-care needs of an entire nation to deal with. And the resource we have to allocate is not just a kidney machine or two, but rather the total economic output of the United States of America—not to mention our ability to borrow against the output of untold future generations.

"This single tragic case which Dr. Williams has presented today is an apt metaphor for the dilemma faced by society as a whole. If we are unable to agree on the proper management of a single case, how can we ever hope to resolve the infinitely more complex issues facing the entire nation?"

Professor Law paused briefly for effect, but the students correctly understood that this last question was rhetorical.

"The hour has grown late," Dr. Law announced. "If there are no further questions or comments, I think it is time for us to adjourn."

"Just one question." It was George Williams who spoke. "A patient who was presented here last time—the man with Alzheimer's—I understand that he died unexpectedly. Do we have any autopsy results?"

Mac and George had been talking about the patient, John Havlicek, earlier in the day. The sudden death had taken Mac by surprise, but on the other hand, Mr. Havlicek was not a young man.

"The gross examination of the body was unrevealing," Austin Delacroix reported. "The microscopic examination is still pending."

With that, the meeting broke up. Mac folded

up his notebook and went down to the floor of the amphitheater to speak with George Williams, but the emotion in George's face warned Mac away. He took George's arm briefly and gave it a sympathetic squeeze.

George had somehow made it through the seminar without breaking. Mac had to admire him for that—even if he couldn't fully understand George's motivation for picking such a difficult case to present.

Mac watched the other students file out of the room, all apparently oblivious to the very real drama which had just taken place before them. To the best of Mac's knowledge, none of the other students had any idea that the patient George Williams had just presented—the heroin addict now battling her second episode of bacterial endocarditis, the woman who would very soon die without a second heart operation—was George's wife, the mother of his young son.

TWO

After the seminar broke up, Mac headed back to the intensive care unit. He had several more hours of work before he could even think about going home for the night. When he finally did make it back to the apartment, tired and hungry, the last thing in the world he needed was to find another envelope shoved under the door. He didn't open it. There was no need. A plain white envelope, unsealed, addressed to "Apt. 205." Jennifer hadn't paid the rent. Again.

"Jennifer!" There was no answer.

He walked into the bedroom. The bed looked as though she'd just gotten out of it. The bathroom door was closed. The shower was running.

Relax, Mac. Get hold of yourself. You've had a long, difficult day. What you really need right now is the soothing effect of a little vitamin B—on the rocks.

Bourbon on the rocks had several things to recommend it—mostly centering around instant gratification. The recipe was not complicated—Mac had never had a failure—nor was it time-consuming. And the drink had what pharmacologists called "rapid onset of action." Just a couple of sips and Mac could already begin to feel the hard edges of a difficult day begin to soften.

Of course, for any knowledgeable student of medicine there was a ready rationale for the drinking of alcohol. Cardiovascular benefits. Virtually every epidemiological study ever conducted had shown the same thing. Drinking two to four ounces of alcohol per day markedly decreased the risk of coronary artery disease. Drink less and you increased your chances of a heart attack.

And there was biochemical data to back up the clinical studies. Alcohol consumption increases the amount of HDL, the so-called "good" cholesterol which is associated with a lower incidence of coronary artery disease. Alcohol also increased the levels of tPA, a natural clot-dissolving substance.

Mac's class learned these intriguing facts during what was otherwise an extremely boring second-year lecture on cholesterol metabolism. Professor Karnof, who most people agreed was well on his way to a second Nobel prize, always talked with his back to his class so as not to be disturbed as he scribbled his endless equations on the blackboard. The combination of the professor's monotone delivery and illegible scrawl had a rather predictable sedating effect on his students. It was not unusual for Professor Karnof to finally turn around after fifty minutes of lecturing and find the classroom nearly empty. The only question was, did he even notice?

On this particular day, the 99.9 percent of the lecture hall which was not within Karnof's field of vision had been given over almost entirely to the design, manufacture, and test flight of paper airplanes. There had even been some discussion of moving on to kite flying when, completely out of the blue, an entirely unexpected and unprecedented event occurred. A student actually asked Dr. Karnof a question. The room abruptly took on the silence of an abandoned airplane hangar.

"Professor Karnof, did you say that drinking alcohol *prevents* coronary artery disease?"

The professor was clearly thrown off balance by the unexpected interruption, but he did manage to nod his head in response before turning back to the board.

But the student's thirst for knowledge was not yet fully slaked. "And the more you drink, the less likely you are to have a heart attack?"

"Well, up to a point, yes." For perhaps the first time in his forty-year-long teaching career, Karnof had the undivided attention of an entire medical school class. "It would appear," he said, "that two cocktails per day is about optimal. That is what I permit myself." This brought a brief titter from the audience.

"So," the student continued, "we should advise our patients to drink?"

"Heavens, no!" Karnof was practically apoplectic. "You can't *advise* people to drink. The potential for abuse is far too great."

Mac couldn't resist wading in at that point. "I guess then," he said, "this will just have to be our little secret."

The only person in the room who didn't laugh was Professor Karnof. He was not known for having a well-developed sense of irony.

Mac also believed that the calming effects of alcohol couldn't help but be good for the heart. It was lucky that Jennifer had been in the shower when he came home, and he hadn't been able to instantly unload on her. On the other hand, their relationship was never going to work unless Jennifer was able to get a handle on her problem. He was willing to do anything he could to help her, but she had to do her share too.

There did not *need* to be a money problem. True, like most medical students, Mac lived on loans and scholarship money. But there was enough to get by on. And Jennifer was an ICU nurse, for crying out loud. By Mac's standards, Jennifer was *wealthy*. Besides, living together saved mounds of money—not to mention the fringe benefits.

Even this modest apartment was way too expensive for Mac to afford on his own. Jennifer had to come up with her half of the rent each month. She couldn't keep spending every dime she made on new clothes and jewelry and her fancy car. It just wasn't going to work.

Mac was suddenly aware that he no longer heard the shower running. He finished his bourbon in a single swallow and headed into the bedroom. He heard Jennifer's voice from the other side of the door. At first he was confused; then he realized that she was singing softly to herself. She sounded happy, carefree—and the fact that she seemed so oblivious to their financial distress rekindled Mac's anger.

"Jennifer!" Louder and with more edge than he had intended.

The singing stopped.

"Jennifer, we have to talk." Mac was struggling very hard to bring his anger under control. "I found another envelope under the door."

The bathroom door slowly opened, releasing a cloud of warm mist. Jennifer stood there, still wet, wrapped in a towel, backlit by the bathroom lighting. She seemed unwilling to leave the safety of her bath. She stared up into his eyes, and as she did, hers filled with tears. Her shoulders began to tremble.

"Oh, Jen." An entirely different emotion now in his voice.

She came into his arms, and Mac held her tightly, stroking her wet hair while she cried. He kissed her on the temple and then very slowly on each eye. As his mouth found hers, the last residue of anger evaporated. He knew only her warmth and wetness and the fragrance of her soaps and shampoo.

Jennifer pulled back from him and began to undo the buttons of his shirt. As she did, her towel fell away.

Mac tried to steer her toward the bed, but Jennifer shook her head. With a fistful of his shirt in each hand she pulled him back into the bathroom.

"I have a better idea," she said. She almost smiled.

Fringe benefits.

THREE

The patient had now been in the emergency room for more than an hour, and still no one had the slightest idea who she was or just exactly what it was that was trying to kill her. She was in shock. She had a high fever. She was listless and unresponsive. When painful stimuli were employed—for example, by using the edge of a metal instrument to apply excruciating pressure to the base of a fingernail—the patient would groan and attempt to withdraw the threatened extremity. Except for her altered mental status, no neurologic deficit could be detected.

The emergency room staff did their best to stabilize the patient, beginning intravenous-fluid resuscitation immediately, ordering appropriate X-ray studies and blood work, and initiating broad-spectrum antibiotic therapy. Then they called the ICU. Mac's team took over management of the patient while she was still in the

ER. When it was time for the patient to be transferred upstairs, one of the ICU physicians would accompany her.

Mac's supervising resident was a rather intense young woman named Laura Rubenstein. Mac had taken to calling her Ruby, and the name had quickly caught on around the hospital. Grounds enough, she had told him, for Mac to fail his ICU rotation.

Right now Laura was examining their new patient, and since physical examination wasn't exactly a team sport, Mac decided to see if he could uncover any more history on their mystery patient. Previous experience in the ER had taught him that Elvira Long was the best place to start.

Elvira Long had been the triage nurse in the emergency room for something like three hundred years. She'd seen it all—more than once. If you wanted to learn medicine, all you had to do was shut up and listen to Nurse Long. But if a young doctor thought he already knew everything there was to know, Elvira Long would stand back and let him prove just how wrong he was.

Mac found her in the waiting room dealing with a group of teenagers who thought they should be seen out of turn.

"Yo, Mama," the big one in front said, "I got to get to an appointment for a *job* interview."

He was maybe eighteen years old; the three behind him were younger. All four wore the same uniform: black warm-up suits, unlaced leather high-top basketball shoes, baseball caps turned backward.

Elvira Long was unimpressed.

"First off, I'm not your mama. Second thing, the only *appointment* you've got coming up is with your *parole* officer."

The three younger boys started to snicker, then immediately turned their eyes to the floor to avoid the dark look their leader threw back at them over his shoulder.

"You all go ahead and find seats, now," Nurse Long told them. "When it's your turn, I'll let you know."

The boys knew they'd met a brick wall. They reluctantly shuffled off, back into the chaos of the waiting area.

The first time Mac had seen this place he'd had a very strong sense of déjà vu. Then it came to him. The bus station—on a cold, snowy winter's night. The cavernous space. The wooden benches. The milling masses, some impatient, others resigned, some simply seeking shelter. No way to get comfortable. The bus depot had never been Mac's favorite place, just the only affordable transportation home. It was either the bus or hitchhike—or stay where he was.

"Hello there, Mac. How's our girl doing?"

Elvira Long had turned to find Mac standing behind her, staring off into his past.

"Her blood pressure seems to have leveled off. Other than that she's about the same. We still don't have a clue what's going on."

"Septic shock." No doubt in Nurse Long's mind. Some infection somewhere in the patient's body had flowed over into the bloodstream and overwhelmed her ability to maintain her blood pressure.

Mac nodded agreement. "But we don't have any idea where her primary infection is." Maybe Ruby would find something on physical examination. Or maybe the lab work would turn up something. "Did you get a chance to talk to her before she cratered?"

"No." Elvira shook her head. "I noticed her when she came in. Well-dressed young woman. But she wasn't carrying a purse or anything that seemed odd. And instead of coming up to the desk to check in, she just found a place and sat down. I thought maybe she was waiting for someone, or was lost or something.

"Anyway, she sat there for maybe ten or fifteen minutes. Then I noticed her get up and walk toward me. We made eye contact, and she kind of started to smile, you know, like maybe she recognized me or something. I saw how pale she was. I mean, she was *white*. She took another step and then just collapsed."

"Any idea who she is?"

"Like I said, I had that feeling she thought she knew me. Maybe she's just the friendly type. Anyway, I don't know her. I've got a pretty good memory for faces. She's not someone I've ever met before. And there was no identification on her."

In the end, Elvira Long's observations had been more tantalizing than elucidating. Mac thanked her and headed back to check on his patient. Laura Rubenstein was off in a corner writing her admission note, so Mac would have the patient to himself for at least a few minutes.

Her blood pressure was increasing back toward normal. Her temperature was down to 102 degrees. As he examined her, she appeared to be aware of his touch—indicating much less depression of her central nervous system than she had demonstrated barely a half hour before.

Mac reviewed the portable chest X ray which had been taken in the ER and the small amount of lab data which had been completed, then sat down next to Laura.

"So, what do you think?" Laura asked. Quiz time.

"I wasn't able to get any more history, so that's still a big unknown. Her physical exam is entirely unremarkable except for her vital signs and mental status—which seem to be improving. I presume she's septic. Her white blood count is elevated. She's had a fever. But we don't have a source. Her chest X ray is negative. There's nothing to suggest urinary tract infection. Her abdomen is unremarkable."

"What about her squash?" Medicalese for *brain*.

"Her neck's supple, but that doesn't exclude meningitis. She could have a brain abscess, but there's nothing localizing on her neurological exam. We should probably do a spinal tap."

"Is that safe?"

A very important consideration. The adult human skull is quite rigid. So-called space-occupying lesions, such as brain tumors and abscesses, cause increased pressure inside the cranium. Because there is normally no route for release of this pressure, the brain becomes compressed and patients develop a variety of neurologic problems and, ultimately, coma. Performing a spinal tap in a patient with increased intracranial pressure can cause a downward movement of the brain and compression of vital centers at its base. This can be rapidly fatal.

So Mac considered Ruby's question very carefully. "Like I said, there's nothing localizing on neurological exam. There's no evidence of increased intracranial pressure. I'd say it's safe."

"I agree, but I think it can wait till we get her upstairs. You go ahead and write the admitting orders, and I'll go over them with you when you're done."

"Ruby?"

"What?"

"I love it when you give me orders."

Ruby smiled.

Ten minutes later, they went to get their patient to take her up to the ICU. Remarkably, her eyes were open and she was looking around. She clutched Mac's hand.

"Doctor, am I going to be all right?"

"You've given everybody a pretty good scare, but things are looking much better now."

She gave him a weak smile.

"Is there anyone," Mac asked, "you'd like us to notify that you're here?"

The woman settled back onto her pillow and closed her eyes. She shook her head ever so slightly, but very definitely, no.

FOUR

When they got back up to the ICU, Mac looked at his watch for the first time in a couple of hours and told Laura Rubenstein, "I'm supposed to be at a disciplinary committee meeting over at the medical school at four o'clock."

"Are you in some kind of trouble I should know about?"

Mac gave her an exasperated look. "Give me a break, Ruby. I'm one of the student members of the committee."

"How long will you be gone?"

Ah-ha! The real issue: the medical student, that cheap and nearly inexhaustible source of labor—the answer to the resident's eternal prayer for another pair of hands—for how long would the fair Laura be deprived of his assistance?

Mac put on an expression of grave concern. "You think we may be getting some confusing cases you're going to need me to help sort out?"

"It's not your mind I need, McCall."

Mac grimaced, the pain inflicted by her careless remark evident on his face. "Oh, Ruby, please say it ain't so." He walked out of the ICU shaking his head in dismay. "I can't say my father didn't warn me. He told me you women are all after the same thing."

Mac looked back just once as he pushed open the ICU door and caught the incipient smile on Laura's face.

Mac sat down just as Dr. Law called the disciplinary committee to order. The solemn faces of those gathered around the conference room table testified to the gravity of the occasion. A student had been accused of cheating during an exam. If the committee determined that the charge was true, the penalty would be summary dismissal from the school.

Professor Law had chaired the committee for as long as anyone could remember. He was remarkably adept at conducting these very difficult proceedings in a manifestly fair and unemotional manner, managing somehow to combine the empathy of a loving grandfather with the wisdom of Solomon.

Law was a man probably well into his sixties. His hairline was slightly receding, but despite his age he still sported a healthy crop of white, wavy hair. He had once been quite tall, but was now slightly stooped and carried a few extra pounds. He was a very fastidious dresser and—to the best of Mac's knowledge—had never been sighted without his trademark bow tie. His nails were always impeccably manicured. He wore a wedding ring on his left hand, a poignant reminder of the terrible sadness that pervaded his private life.

"Turner Frost, a fourth-year medical student, has brought the complaint," Dr. Law said, "and we will hear his testimony first." As he spoke, his eyes scanned the room, commanding the attention of all. They were eyes of iridescent blue, manufactured of finest crystal. And they were more than merely intelligent. They were omniscient.

Frost nodded to Professor Law as he took his seat at the head of the table. He made fleeting eye contact with Austin Delacroix, a student member of the committee who was seated next to Mac. The tall, confident Frost had chosen to wear a gray flannel suit for the meeting. Mac was pretty certain he could live for the better part of a year on the money Frost had spent for that suit.

Turner Frost's sonorous voice bore traces of an accent which, to Mac's ears, had at first seemed vaguely British. But the speech patterns of Austin Delacroix and Peter VanSlyke were nearly identical to Frost's, and Mac had come to understand that it was merely a patrician dialect that they spoke, a dialect which—like their clothes—served to distinguish them from the remainder of the student body. They might as well have been wearing crowns.

"I do not bring these charges lightly," Frost began. "I assure you that I am fully aware of their seriousness, but I am also mindful of my own obligations under the student honor code as well as my responsibilities as the physician which I soon will be. Society must be able to have confidence in the integrity of physicians, and the medical community must be willing to weed from its ranks those who would abuse the public trust. A dishonest medical student cannot reasonably be expected to become a trustworthy physician.

"On February twenty-seventh of this year, I knew that the second-year class was being given an examination in microbiology. I was therefore surprised to find a student from that class—during the very hour that the exam was scheduled to be given—talking on the telephone in a far corner of the medical school. As I approached, the student's back was to me, but I could hear him quite distinctly discussing points of microbiology. That student's name is Diego Vena . . . Vala . . . Velanu—"

"Valenzuela! *Diego* Valenzuela!" The accused student's voice trembled with rage. Then he added in a voice dripping with sarcasm, "Just like the country."

Around the table, students and faculty members attempted to suppress smiles. Karen Anderson, a third-year medical student seated directly across from Mac, covered her mouth with her hand. They exchanged glances briefly, but Mac had to force himself to look away to avoid laughing out loud.

Professor Law met the problem head-on. "Touché, Mr. Valenzuela."

"I apologize to Mr. Valenzuela," Frost said, "but my difficulty in pronouncing his name does not mitigate against the seriousness of his actions."

"Could you be more specific," Professor Law asked, "about what you overheard?"

"He was discussing bacteria which cause pneumonia, pharyngitis, and meningitis—and which antibiotics are effective against them. I subsequently learned that these issues formed a major portion of the examination which he was supposed to be taking at the exact time I overheard him talking on the phone."

There were some additional questions asked by various members of the committee, but nothing terribly relevant was elicited. Then Diego Valenzuela was asked to take a seat at the head of the table to respond to the charges. He was small in stature and quite slender. He had black hair and angry black eyes. His voice shook as he spoke.

"There is no doubt in my mind—" He paused here to take several deep breaths in an effort to control his ever rising rage and sense of indignation. "There is absolutely no doubt in my mind whatsoever that these charges are motivated by the racism that infests every corner of this institution. If I were Caucasian, I would not be here today." Again he hesitated.

"I did not cheat on this examination, nor have I ever cheated on a test in my life."

"Just so that we can be clear," Professor Law said gently, "are you saying that what Mr. Frost told us is not accurate? Are you saying that you were not talking on the telephone, or that you did not say the things he claims to have heard?"

Mac could tell that Diego was once again struggling against the flood of emotion welling up within him. It was hard to imagine the humiliation he must feel, the pressure he must be under. Diego Valenzuela was in, at least, his eighteenth year of formal education—six years beyond high school, just five more to go, counting a minimum of three years of residency. If he were to be found guilty, all that would be lost.

Mac tried to put himself in Diego's position. The first thing he thought of, was how would he be able to tell his parents? After all their sacrifices, how could he face them after being expelled from medical school for cheating?

"What I'm telling you, Dr. Law, is that I did not cheat on that exam. Also, I believe that— even as a student of this medical school—I should have a right to privacy. When I talk on the telephone, I should be entitled to the expectation that my conversations are private. I should not be at risk of having portions of what I say twisted and used against me in racist attacks."

Professor Law himself now took a deep breath and made an effort to get the student back on point. "I'm certain I can speak for the committee in saying that, at another time, we would be fully prepared to consider any charges you yourself might wish to bring related to your rights as a student. However, for now I must ask you to speak directly to the charge against you. If you have any defense, please bring it before the committee. Our only interest is to fairly evaluate the accusation. I assure you that we operate under a presumption of innocence, but you cannot hope to be acquitted of the charge unless you can help us to understand just exactly what did happen and why."

And then Diego Valenzuela did what Mac would have said—only moments before—could not be done. He made it appear possible that everything he had told the committee was true, *and* that everything Turner Frost had said was also true.

"I have two children," Valenzuela began. "On the night before the microbiology exam, my youngest developed an earache. My wife and I were up all night with the baby. I wouldn't have even come to school that day if it hadn't been for the exam. Halfway through the test I called my wife to see how the baby was doing. We discussed possible complications and what antibiotics we might use." Almost as an afterthought Valenzuela added, "My wife is a nurse." Then he sat back in his chair and folded his arms defiantly over his chest. The room was silent.

It was Dr. Law who finally spoke. "I assure you, Mr. Valenzuela that we are all quite pleased to hear such a straightforward, logical explanation for what had heretofore seemed such a bleak episode. I believe all the committee needs now is some sort of corroborative statement—perhaps the physician who treated your child could write a letter—"

Valenzuela interrupted, very clearly insulted by Law's request for proof. "We started the baby on antibiotics which we already had at home, and she was much better by that afternoon. We didn't end up having to take her to the doctor."

"Perhaps your wife could at least appear before the committee." Law was clearly attempting to be conciliatory, but Diego would have none of it.

Valenzuela abruptly brought himself to his feet and, summoning all the dignity he could muster, said, "I will not allow my wife to be humiliated before this committee as I have been. If you have come to the opinion that there are too many Hispanic students in this medical school, there is nothing I can do about it—except sue the school and the individuals serving on this committee."

And with that he left the room.

FIVE

... MORTALITY RATE

The sudden departure of Diego Valenzuela brought the disciplinary committee meeting to an abrupt close. It was decided to reconvene in a couple of days, and in the meantime to see if any more facts could be determined.

When Mac got back to the ICU, Jennifer was at the main desk preparing to leave for the evening.

"How's our new patient doing?"

Jennifer rolled her eyes. "Dr. Jordan says she'll be able to leave the ICU in the morning—sooner if we need the bed." Al Jordan, the attending physician, was the faculty member who had ultimate responsibility for all the patients in the unit as well as for supervising house staff and students.

But Jennifer's expression implied there was something unusual going on. "What's the story, Jen?"

"See for yourself. But I warn you, you may need an appointment."

"She's had a few visitors?" Was this the same woman who hadn't wanted them to notify anyone that she was in the hospital?

"You might say that."

"Does she have a name yet?"

"Sharon Bailey."

Jennifer put her coat on, shaking her head, but gave Mac a smile before she left. "See you later."

Mac always felt like he should give Jennifer a kiss when they said good-bye, an impulse which had to be resisted in the ICU. Instead, he just smiled and headed off to check on his patient. Nothing in his experience prepared him for what he found.

Sharon Bailey was sitting up, smiling, carrying on a lively telephone conversation. Her face was made up. She was wearing what Mac would describe as a negligee—certainly not the modest hospital gown most ICU patients wore. There were two other people in the room: a woman of about the same age as the patient, and a little girl perhaps five or six years old.

When Mac walked into the room, Sharon Bailey laid the telephone receiver down on the bed and asked, with a great deal of expectant enthusiasm, "Are you Dr. McCall?"

Mac smiled and held out his hand. "Actually—" he began.

"Hey, everybody! This is Dr. McCall, the man

who saved my life!" She held his hand tightly in both of hers.

"Actually," Mac began again, "I'm just a fourth-year medical student, and I really haven't had much to do with your care so far."

"You're just being modest. Everybody says you're the smartest guy in the whole hospital."

Mac couldn't imagine who *any*body would be, let alone "*every*body."

"Anyway," he said, "I'm Mac McCall, and I'm pleased to see how well you're doing." He smiled as he spoke and gently extricated his hand from her grasp.

Sharon Bailey blithely introduced the others in the room. "This beautiful little doll is my daughter Tiffany, and that's Jill, my best friend."

Mac continued to smile as he said hello to the others in the room, but his facial muscles were beginning to tire.

"I wonder if I could speak with you alone for a few minutes, Ms. Bailey? When I saw you in the ER, you still weren't able to give me very much information."

Although Sharon Bailey was eager to answer questions, none of the information she related moved Mac any closer to a diagnosis. She had felt fatigue for several weeks and had a poor appetite. This morning she had experienced nausea and vomiting, and then a severe, pounding headache. She began to feel faint. Because she had no personal physician, she had come to the ER for evaluation. The rest, as they say, was history.

Her only previous hospitalization had been when Tiffany was born. The birth had been uncomplicated. Sharon Bailey had experienced the usual childhood illnesses, but had otherwise been in good health. She had had no previous surgeries, had no known allergies, and took no medication except for an occasional aspirin.

On physical examination, she was perhaps fifteen pounds overweight. Examination of the abdomen revealed some vague areas of tenderness—of uncertain significance. The remainder of the physical examination was unrevealing.

Mac didn't have a clue what was going on, and he told his patient so. "I'm eager to hear what Dr. Rubenstein has to say. Maybe she's got some bright ideas."

"I doubt it." Sharon Bailey's chipper demeanor immediately evaporated. "I'm not sure she cares what happens to me, one way or the other."

"What makes you say that?"

"I don't know. She just didn't seem very concerned. She didn't examine me nearly as thoroughly as you did."

"Well, just for the record," Mac said, "she *is* a very concerned physician. I'd sure be happy to have her be my doctor. I think what probably happened, she examined you very carefully in the emergency room when you weren't aware of what was going on. Then, when she examined you again up here, it was just a follow-up exam that didn't need to be as thorough."

"Maybe." Sharon Bailey's reply was deliberately curt. It was clear she wasn't convinced, and Mac suspected there was something else going on. For some reason she and Ruby just hadn't hit it off.

Mac found Laura Rubenstein off in a corner writing a progress note in the chart of another patient.

"What do you think's going on with Sharon Bailey?" he asked her.

"Beats me." She signed the note she was writing and then looked up at Mac. "I think she was septic when she came in. I wasn't sure she was going to make it, but she's had a pretty dramatic response to antibiotics. It's hard to put together."

"Her abdomen's still a little tender. Maybe she squirted some bacteria into her bloodstream from an intra-abdominal source."

"It's possible. I think we need to run her bowel, maybe get a CT."

Ruby was suggesting a series of radiologic procedures that might turn up some sort of intra-abdominal pathology like a tumor or an abscess. The pelvis was another potential source of infection.

"Were you able to do a pelvic?"

"Not as good as I'd like," Ruby said. "I examined her as best I could when she was in the ER. When I told her I'd like to do another exam up here, she sort of declined."

"I got the impression there'd been some friction between you two."

Ruby shrugged. "She'll be off our hands by morning and out on one of the general medicine wards. I'll suggest that the team that picks her up send her to the Ob-Gyn folks for a formal pelvic exam. It'll be their call."

Mac had a couple more hours of work, charting and looking in on his other patients, before he could call it a night. It was after nine o'clock before he was finally able to leave the ICU. As he walked out through the waiting area, he noticed a little girl sitting all by herself in the corner, staring out a window into the dark of night. Little Tiffany Bailey. Tears streamed down her cheeks.

"Hi, sweetheart. Are you all alone?"

She made a fist and swiped at her tears. "Jill went to get some coffee. She'll be right back." She hardly took her eyes off the window.

"Do you want to talk?"

"I'm not supposed to."

"Well, I'm helping your mommy, and I'd like to help you too if you want."

Tiffany looked up into Mac's eyes, and a new

flood of tears began. "Is my mommy going to die?"

Mac put his arm around her. "She's *much* better now. Can't you tell? What made you think she was going to die?"

The little girl turned back to the window and spoke so softly that Mac wasn't even certain he heard her correctly.

"Mommy has cancer," Tiffany said, "but we're not supposed to tell anybody."

SIX

When Mac arrived back at the ICU the next morning, he found that Sharon Bailey had been transferred out during the night. ICU beds were always at a premium, and a daily pecking order had to be established. There were twelve ICU beds, and they were occupied by the twelve patients in the hospital who were judged most likely to benefit from being in the ICU. If a new admission or a patient already in the hospital was very ill—and the ICU was full—a decision had to be made whether a patient now in the ICU should be "bumped" so that a bed could be made available for the newer, sicker patient. Sometimes this created very difficult choices. In the case of Sharon Bailey, it seemed evident that she was no longer in need of intensive care.

So for the next couple of days, Mac's communication with Sharon Bailey was exclusively by rumor. He had heard that she remained a diagnostic enigma. No one seemed to have any idea how little Tiffany had come up with the notion that her mother had cancer, but Sharon had decided that it would be better if Tiffany didn't visit for a while.

When the disciplinary committee met to determine the fate of Diego Valenzuela, he wasn't there to defend himself.

"I regret to inform you," Dr. Law told the committee, "that Mr. Valenzuela declines to participate further in this investigation. He has stated that he does not recognize the authority of this committee to determine his future.

"Also, I have had a letter from Mr. Valenzuela's attorney. He wishes to inform the committee that there is an extreme likelihood that his client will choose to press suit regardless of the outcome of our deliberations. He alleges violation of federal antidiscrimination statutes."

The members of the committee heard Dr. Law's recitation in silence and without discernible reaction. None of them was surprised by anything that was said. Gone were the days when an autocratic dean could whimsically admit and dismiss students from the school. Indeed, the disciplinary committee existed explicitly to provide the due process that the times required. Still, in this litigious society, whenever the committee acted, lawsuits resulted. Like night follows day.

"Since Mr. Valenzuela has declined further participation," Law continued, "I believe that we will be able to bring this matter to a final vote today. I would like to recall Turner Frost to answer any questions that the committee might choose to pose, and Mr. George Williams has asked to give a brief statement in behalf of Mr. Valenzuela. Does this meet with the committee's approval?"

There were nods around the table. In general, the committee members were quite content to go wherever Law led them so long as he was open and fair in the performance of his duties—which he unfailingly was.

Mac was not surprised to hear that George Williams wanted to speak to the committee. George was utterly committed to increasing the minority enrollment at the medical school. He worked closely with the admissions committee and participated actively in the recruitment of minority students. Mac knew that George had been particularly proud of his own role in bringing Diego Valenzuela to the school and of Diego's accomplishments over the past year and a half.

Turner Frost entered the room, confident and elegant as ever. He smiled at various faculty members and at Austin Delacroix, then abruptly shifted to a more solemn demeanor in keeping with the seriousness of the occasion. He focused his earnest expression intently on Professor Law.

"I have only one question," Dr. Law said, "then perhaps others will want to pose questions as well." He paused momentarily, perhaps to gather his thoughts, perhaps for emphasis. "We have heard your description, Mr. Frost, of what you heard. We have also heard Mr. Valenzuela's explanation of what happened. My question is simply this, did anything you heard or saw conflict with Mr. Valenzuela's statement? In short, do you know of any reason why the committee should not conclude that both of you are telling the truth as you know it?"

Law had thus quickly distilled the matter to its very essence. The carpeted, paneled conference room was suddenly plunged into absolute silence. You could have heard a feather hit the pile.

Turner Frost weighed the question thoughtfully. Twice he looked as though he was about to speak, then reconsidered. Finally he said simply, "There is nothing in what I heard or saw which contradicts Diego Valenzuela's testimony."

The pressure which had been building in the room instantly dissipated. Frost was excused, and George Williams was ushered in.

Mac had never been more aware of George's enormous size. Perhaps it was the smallness of the conference room. But, too, George was wearing his white clinic coat, a little too short in the sleeves, a bit too tight around his chest. Mac was reminded of the first time he had seen George in the newborn nursery—holding a tiny, premature baby. This giant of a man gently cradling that frail little life in his arms.

"Mr. Williams wants the committee to understand," said Dr. Law, "that he has come forward on his own without the request of—or even the knowledge of—Mr. Valenzuela. He does not have knowledge which bears directly on the facts of the incident in question, but rather wishes to make a statement regarding the character of Mr. Valenzuela. You may proceed, Mr. Williams."

"Thank you, Dr. Law, members of the committee. I just want to underscore what you have just heard. My being here is totally unsolicited. To the best of my knowledge, Diego does not even know that I have asked to speak to you. I am here because I know that it is not in Diego Valenzuela to do what has been suggested.

"I know for a fact that Diego has a child who has suffered from frequent ear and throat infections. Diego has missed class because of this child's repeated illnesses—staying home with the baby so his wife can go to work. There is no reason not to believe what he has told you. But more importantly, Diego's character would not permit him to cheat on an exam. The two things which he holds most dearly are his family and his good name. He would never do anything to jeopardize either.

"Nothing illustrates this more clearly than an episode which occurred when Diego was an undergraduate. The story was related to me by the professor involved in the incident. I was trying to recruit Diego to enter this medical school, and the professor thought it was relevant.

"Diego's father passed away several years ago, and while Diego was an undergraduate, his mother became quite ill. She subsequently died. During her illness Diego was often preoccupied with her care. This often interfered with his classes and studying. The class in question was a math class. The professor had given a pop quiz on a day when Diego had not been able to come to class.

"Soon after the test was given, a friend told Diego he had missed it, and Diego went to see the professor about a make-up exam. The professor said he would have to take the test on the spot. Diego said he wasn't ready, hadn't had time to study for over a week, hadn't been able to come to class. The professor was sympathetic but said that since it was a pop quiz, it wouldn't be fair to the other students to give Diego additional time to prepare. Diego saw that this was true and decided to try to take the test—nothing could be worse than the zero he would receive if he did not at least attempt the exam.

"The professor had a previous commitment and left Diego to take the test entirely on his own. Diego was to watch the clock and permit himself only one hour. He was on his honor not to receive any assistance of any kind during the exam. When he was done, he was to leave his paper on the professor's desk.

"When the professor returned to the classroom, he found Diego's exam paper on his desk, but also discovered that he—the professor—had inadvertently left the textbook on his desk, in plain view. The book was unopened and in exactly the spot he had left it. Since the exam came straight out of the text, Diego could easily have cheated if he had been so inclined, but he didn't."

Austin Delacroix could no longer remain silent. "This means absolutely nothing. All Valenzuela had to do was put the book back exactly as he had found it. Besides, there are a dozen other ways he could have cheated. Someone could have told him the questions on the exam before he ever went to see the professor. He could have had his own copy of the text available. From what you've told us, he could have even had someone else take the exam for him while the professor was out of the room. So how can you come in here with this apocryphal story and claim that Valenzuela didn't cheat?"

Despite the tirade, George Williams remained quite calm. "How do I know he didn't cheat?"

George asked. "I know he didn't cheat because he failed the exam cold. The professor said he hardly got any answers right at all."

After that, there was very little discussion. George Williams was excused. The committee generally agreed that Diego Valenzuela had made his case. The only strong dissension expressed was by Austin Delacroix.

Delacroix was livid. "The man was caught in flagrante delicto. After he's heard the charges, he simply concocts a story to fit them. Then a friend of his comes up with a story which is, at the very least, irrelevant—and probably untrue. There is absolutely nothing before this committee which verifies a single word of what either Diego Valenzuela or George Williams has said. If the honor code is going to have any value at all, we must have the courage to convict those who violate it. And what about Turner Frost or the next student who catches a student cheating? If we don't support them, no one is going to come forward—"

"Thank you for your thoughts, Mr. Delacroix." It was Professor Law who finally cut Delacroix off. "I think that, unless I hear an objection"—at this point he gave Austin Delacroix a look which indicated quite clearly that he didn't want to hear anything more from Austin—"unless I hear an objection, I feel that a formal vote is probably unnecessary. Mr. Valenzuela has provided a satisfactory explanation of the incident, and Mr. Frost does not contradict it." Professor Law's eyes searched the room for evidence of dissent. "Hearing no objection, this meeting is adjourned."

Outside in the hallway, George Williams awaited the decision. Mac threw him a smile which told the whole story, and then he gave George a high-five. Actually, it was a higher five for Mac than it was for George. Not really a *low* five, more like a *middle* five for George.

Turner Frost was waiting for Austin Delacroix. Their encounter was somewhat less jubilant. When Delacroix spoke, he made certain that George could overhear his words. "The two quota boys stuck together."

Mac heard the words too and immediately looked up at George, hoping that he wouldn't allow himself to be baited. What Mac saw in George Williams' eyes was stone-cold fury.

It was only much later that Mac would ask himself if, in that moment, the first seed of murder had been planted.

SEVEN

"Got a new patient for you, Mac—really a great case." There was more than a little sarcasm in Ruby's tone.

Mac cast a surreptitious glance at a nearby clock. It was still a few minutes before five. Just a couple minutes more and the new patient would have been someone else's responsibility.

"What's the story, Ruby?"

"A guy named Benny 'Beano' Smith. Prefers to be called Beano—if you can believe that."

Mac grimaced. The nickname had a familiar ring. "Is he a shooter?"

"Shooter, pusher, pimp—all-around nice guy. Thirty-three-year-old white male. Multiple previous admissions, mostly for drug overdoses. Usually leaves against medical advice as soon as his acute problem eases up."

"Tell me he doesn't have a fever, Ruby."

"Let's see . . ." Ruby began to scan the papers

that had come up from the ER with the patient. Mac could tell she was enjoying this.

"Ruby?" A fever work-up would keep Mac in the hospital a couple of extra hours at least. He and Jennifer had plans that evening. Mac would be late. Jennifer would not be a happy camper.

"Looks like he was dropped off at the front door of the hospital," Ruby said, "by some 'friends' who immediately disappeared. Beano was completely zonked out. Pinpoint pupils. Needle tracks all over both arms. The folks in the ER, being their usual cynical selves, surmised that Beano had once again partaken of a bit too much of his favorite recreational narcotic and gave him a dose of Narcan—after which Beano began to once again participate in normal human activities like breathing and opening his eyes."

"Ruby," Mac asked, "did anyone bother to take the guy's temperature?"

"Oh, yeah, here it is. 102.4."

"You're a peach, Ruby."

Mac looked through Benny Smith's chart and found four admissions in the last ten months when he'd come into the hospital under similar conditions. Each time he'd signed himself out of the hospital after a couple of days.

Mac tried his best not to be judgmental, to approach each patient with an open mind, to make certain that each of his patients received the same quality of care. Even patients who made their living selling illegal drugs to children. He took a deep breath as he approached Benny Smith's bedside.

"Mr. Smith?"

Smith cracked his eyelids slightly to give Mac a quick, appraising once-over. "Beano," he said, then shut his eyes.

"I'm Mac McCall. I'm a fourth-year medical student, and I'll be helping take care of you while you're here."

Smith had no apparent interest in this information. His eyes remained closed, his arms folded tightly across his chest. Huge forearms, Mac noticed. Muscular biceps. And a massive neck. Beano was apparently a bodybuilder. Probably abused steroids as well as narcotics.

"I'll need to ask you a few questions and then examine you," Mac said.

This got Smith's attention. "I've been examined enough. Everything you need to know is in my chart."

"You've got a fever. That could represent something serious. I need to look for the source. We'll need to do some more blood work."

"No more needles." Beano turned away for emphasis, showing Mac the back of his head, where his dirty blond hair was gathered in a long ponytail.

It was a paradox which Mac had seen many

times before. A big, muscular guy like Beano, an intravenous drug abuser who injected himself with dirty needles every day of his life suddenly developed a strong aversion to needles once he was in the hospital.

What the hell, Mac thought, might as well go for the whole ball of wax. "You were unresponsive when they brought you to the ER. With the combination of fever and an altered state of consciousness, we like to do a spinal tap to make certain there's nothing going on in the central nervous system."

"No way," Beano said. Mac's fever work-up was getting shorter and shorter.

"Let me just have a listen to your heart, then," Mac said. Experience had taught him that he could usually do a fairly good physical exam by going at it one organ at a time, as though that was all he was going to do. Beano let him do a cursory exam but still wasn't very forthcoming regarding his medical history.

But as Mac was finishing his exam, Beano became increasingly agitated. His heart rate had increased, and he was beginning to perspire. Goose bumps developed on his skin, and he had noticeable muscle twitching.

"It's the damn Narcan," Smith said. "They gave me too much. I need some Demerol to take the edge off."

Mac shook his head. "You're getting the maximum effect of the Narcan now, but it will wear off quickly. When that happens, the heroin or whatever you're on may kick in again. You may go back into coma and we'll have to give you more Narcan. It's a delicate balance. That's why you're in the ICU. So we can watch you carefully."

"Look," Beano said, "just give me some Demerol and then you can draw whatever blood you want. Hell, you can even do the spinal tap."

"No bargaining, Beano. If you don't want your fever evaluated, that's up to you, but for now you get no narcotics."

Smith raised himself up on his elbows. "If you know what's good for you," he told Mac, "you'll give me the Demerol."

Mac looked him straight in the eye. "If you threaten me again, you'll finish your hospital stay in the jail ward. Just try me."

EIGHT

Mac knew when he opened the apartment door what was coming, and he wasn't disappointed. He was late, and there would be a price to pay.

"You're late." Jennifer sat in a chair, legs crossed, arms folded, glowering. The chair had been turned to face the door so that she could greet him the moment he arrived. "Why do you always do this to me?"

"I'm sorry." It wasn't Mac's fault, but he *was* sorry. "Attending rounds went longer than usual, and I had a new patient to work up."

"This party is important, Mac."

Mac shrugged noncommittally. For the life of him, he couldn't understand why anyone would consider this party, *any* party, important. Besides, if it wasn't for Mac, Jennifer wouldn't even be going to the party. Of course, if it wasn't for Jennifer, Mac wouldn't be going either.

The invitation from Dr. Law had been addressed to Mac McCall and guest. Mac's first thought had been, How could he get out of going? It was easy enough to find a conflicting obligation. But Jennifer had been ecstatic at the thought of going to a big shindig at the Law estate. She went out and bought new stationery just to write an acceptance note—and nearly went through the entire box before she had finally crafted one she was satisfied with.

"Did you hear about Sharon Bailey's blood cultures?" Mac tried to move the conversation to neutral ground.

Jennifer didn't respond. Her expression didn't change. Not a muscle in her body moved.

"It looks like there's an anaerobe and maybe one other bug—probably a slow-growing streptococcus." When Sharon Bailey was in the ER, they'd taken blood for culture. Now, three days later, bacteria were growing from the blood. This confirmed that she had been "septic" at the time of admission. The types of bacteria recovered provided a clue as to which part of her body was diseased.

Jennifer was unimpressed. "How nice for her," she said.

"I think she's probably hiding something in her abdomen. Maybe she has a subacute appendicitis."

"It's not getting any earlier," Jennifer said. "I've been ready for over an hour."

So, in spite of himself, Mac said what he wasn't going to say, what he'd told himself the moment he walked into the room he wasn't going to ask, "Is that a new dress?"

"Don't start, Mac. This isn't about me."

Probably no point in mentioning the new shoes and earrings.

"I'll go take a shower and get ready." A thought occurred to him on his way to the bedroom. "We'll have to stop and get gas on the way. I'm running on empty."

"We can't arrive at Dr. Law's house in *your* car. We'll take mine. The gas tank's full."

Of course she couldn't be seen in his car. What was he thinking of?

Mac showered and dressed as quickly as he could. The only decent dress shirt he had was one which required cuff links—a gift from Jennifer. What the hell had he done with the cuff links?

"Jen? Have you seen my cuff links?"

No answer. It was going to be a long evening.

Mac turned the bedroom upside down. The cuff links were nowhere to be found. He could try safety pins, but Jennifer would be furious—probably refuse even to go to the party. Mac was pretty certain that would end their relationship once and for all. Maybe that wouldn't be such a bad thing.

Wait a minute! There they were, in the back of a desk drawer. Now he remembered throwing them back there. They'd had a bit of an argument.

But there was something else in the back of the drawer. An envelope. From the phone company. Last month's bill. Unpaid.

NINE

They rode in silence to Law's house, and by the time they arrived, the long, winding driveway was already clogged with parked cars. Unless they parked on the street, they would either have to block another car or put at least two wheels onto Professor Law's golf green-like lawn—neither of which Mac was willing to do.

It was only because Mac had been late, Jennifer was quick to point out, that they were now forced to leave their car on the street. Like the hired help, Jennifer said. She was furious.

But Jennifer was able to check her fury on the front steps. When the door was opened by Professor Law himself, Jennifer became instantly gregarious. She was effusive. She was fawning. Mac was embarrassed.

"This is the biggest house I've ever *seen*, Dr. Law!"

Mac thought so too, but it would never have entered his mind to mention it.

"Good evening, Dr. Law," Mac said. "Thank you for inviting us."

"It's a pleasure to have you here, Mac, Jennifer. Please let Mary take your coats . . ." But no sooner had he started to lead them in than the doorbell rang. More late arrivals. "I'm afraid I'll have to let you find your own way into the living room," Dr. Law apologized. "To your left."

Mac helped Jennifer off with her coat, then handed it to Mary, a middle-aged woman dressed in a black and white uniform. Mac had never before encountered a servant in a private home. He felt acutely uncomfortable. Jennifer giggled as he took her coat, then was off like a shot.

"Thank you, sir," was all Mary said, her voice devoid of emotion. She and the coats quickly headed for the wide, circular staircase which dominated the entry hall. About halfway up she passed an especially sullen-appearing Austin Delacroix, who was on his way down. Neither acknowledged the other's presence.

To Mac's eyes, the "living room" looked more like a hotel ballroom. But despite its size, the room was packed with people. Mac recognized many faculty members and a smattering of well-known physicians from the community. There were only a few medical students sprinkled here and there, all juniors and seniors, the top few students in each class.

There were at least two bars set up. Servers wandered among the guests with trays of hors d'oeuvres and napkin-wrapped bottles of champagne. At the far end was an entryway to a paneled library or study. The smokers appeared to have congregated there, and it looked as though the air-circulation pattern of the house had been designed to prevent smoke from wafting back into the living room.

Just at the entry to the study Mac could make out Turner Frost and Peter VanSlyke, smoking long cigars and sipping at snifters of brandy. Mac had heard of Professor Law's affection for cigars. The family fortune reportedly had its origins in tobacco. Still, it had always seemed incongruous, the man of medicine's fondness for a well-made cigar.

And as he watched, Jennifer entered the picture, cozying up to Delacroix and Frost. She hadn't wasted any time getting there. Mac wondered whether it was their wealth or simply their generic maleness which attracted her. Perhaps he wasn't being fair. Jennifer would know only a few of the people here, and she would naturally feel more comfortable with medical students than with faculty.

Things could be worse, Mac thought. He and Jennifer could be married. But Jennifer hadn't mentioned marriage in quite a while. That was probably a plot clue.

"Want some company, sailor?"

Mac turned and found Karen Anderson looking up at him from an overstuffed chair. He smiled. "I think I've been abandoned."

"She went that-a-way," said Karen, gesturing toward the study with her glass. She started to get up, carefully balancing her drink, and Mac offered her his hand in assistance. "This chair is like a giant pillow," she said. "If you hadn't come along, I might never have been able to get up."

"You're sure it's not the alcohol?" he teased.

"Naah." She shook her head. "The drink's just a prop. I've hardly touched it. Let's get you something, though."

"Not yet. I haven't had anything to eat in about twelve hours. If I have a drink, I'm likely to do something memorable."

"Go for it, Mac. A little table dancing is just what this party needs. Too many people taking themselves too seriously around here."

"That would pretty much cinch my internship in Tierra del Fuego, wouldn't it?" Mac laughed. "But I'd be happy to help you up onto a table."

Mac looked down toward the study once again just in time to see Peter VanSlyke teaching Jennifer how to cut the end off a cigar she was obviously just about to smoke.

"Karen, how are you?" The voice belonged to a slightly built man about fifty years of age. He was balding but had a neatly kempt salt-and-pepper beard, proof that he could in fact still grow hair.

"Hello, Dr. Carver. I'm fine, thank you." Karen introduced Mac and explained that Dr. Carver was an infectious-disease specialist she had met while doing a clerkship at another hospital.

They made some comments back and forth about the weather, then Mac said, "We've had an interesting infectious-disease case recently. A young woman came in septic and had positive blood cultures, but she got well very quickly and we still don't know the source of her sepsis."

Carver nodded. "I heard about the case. She had some anaerobic bacteria in her blood?"

"Yes, and streptococci. The lab was still trying to sort it all out, the last I heard. Meanwhile, the patient's about ready to go home."

Carver looked perplexed. "How long has she been in the hospital?"

"Just a few days."

"Oh," Carver said, "I obviously was thinking about a different case. I don't remember exactly, but it was probably a month or six weeks ago that somebody asked me about this other patient. It's funny how these cases come in bunches. I remember one week when I was asked to see three patients with brain abscesses. That's more than I usually see in a year."

"What did the source of bacteremia turn out to be, Dr. Carver, in the patient you heard about?"

Carver laughed. "I never got any follow-up. That's one of the big problems with doing the kind of consultative practice I do. People stop you in the hallway and ask you about various therapeutic and diagnostic problems, and you give the best advice you can—but no one ever tells you how things turned out."

Carver and Karen Anderson began talking about various characters they knew from the other hospital, and Mac excused himself and began to wander about among the other guests. As the evening wore on, he began to worry about how he was going to extract Jennifer from the smoking salon. Every time he looked in that direction, there she was, having a high old time with the same group of medical students. To her credit, it did appear that she'd abandoned the cigar after just a few puffs.

Mac knew that, left to her own devices, Jennifer would be the last guest to leave. He decided he would just retrieve their coats and present her with the fact that it was time to go. He'd hear about it later, of course, but it was the only way he could think of to get her out of the house before they turned out the lights.

Mac had seen Mary head up the stairway with their coats. There was no way he could bring himself to send her back up to fetch them. He figured he was pretty capable of doing that on his own. But once he had climbed the stairs, he was no longer quite so sure of himself. The reality that the second floor of the Law house was just as big as the first floor suddenly registered. He was confronted by a maze of long corridors and closed doors.

Mac decided he might as well try a few of the doors. He found a couple of closets, a bathroom, a gigantic sitting room, two rooms that were dark as pitch and therefore, he assumed, not what he was looking for. He was expecting to find a bedroom with a couple of beds piled high with coats. Finally, at the back of the house, he found a sitting room that led onto a bedroom. The bed itself was in an alcove of the huge bedroom, and Mac was well into the second room before he realized that he was not alone.

Mac started at the sight of the woman, but she didn't seem to notice. "I'm so sorry," he said. "I was only looking for my coat."

She said nothing. She remained motionless—except for a fluttering of her eyelids—just lying there on the bed. Her bedclothes were smoothed perfectly over her. Her hair was carefully combed. Her makeup had been artfully applied.

She was every bit as young and beautiful as everyone said.

Had it not been for the subtle eyelid motion, Mac would have been unable to shake off the macabre impression that this was a body laid out for viewing.

"Did you wish to speak with Mrs. Law?"

Mac was startled once again, this time by the sound of a woman's voice just behind him. He turned to find a slightly graying but sturdily built middle-aged woman in a nurse's uniform.

"You can speak with Mrs. Law if you like. I'll show you how." She seemed eager to render any assistance she could.

"I'm sorry. I just wandered in here by mistake, looking for my date's coat." Mac turned his head first toward the nurse, then back toward Mrs. Law, uncertain just whom he should be addressing and how. "Mrs. Law doesn't know me. We've never met. I'm sorry to have intruded."

It was an incredibly awkward situation. Mac didn't want to appear unwilling to speak with Mrs. Law. On the other hand, there was no reason for him to believe that she considered his presence anything more than a totally unwarranted invasion of her privacy.

"If you could just tell me where I might find the coat," he said to the nurse.

"The cloak room is at the far end of the hall

on the right. It's the room with the door split in two so the upper half can be opened separately."

Of course, Mac thought, the *cloak* room. He should have known.

Before he left, Mac once again apologized to Mrs. Law. "I'm so sorry to have disturbed you." She remained motionless except for another slight fluttering of her eyelids. He had no idea if she had even heard him.

TEN

Mac had heard rumors that Professor Law's wife had recently become "incapacitated" in some way. It had never been completely clear whether this reported incapacity was mental or physical—or both. Someone said she had had a stroke. Someone else had suggested that she had developed some sort of catatonic schizophrenia. Either way, it had been a terrible tragedy.

Professor Law had been a confirmed bachelor until well into his forties—so the story went—when he met the soon-to-be Mrs. Law. She was much younger than he but already establishing her own reputation in the university's philosophy department. There had been a whirlwind courtship and a marriage which many members of the Law family had reportedly regarded as precipitous, but that was some years ago now. The two shared an interest in ethics, and until relatively recently Mrs. Law had participated in her husband's medical-ethics seminar as a sort of ad hoc consultant in philosophy.

As he plunged back into the perpetual drama of the ICU, the encounter of the evening before was quickly relegated to the hinterlands of Mac's consciousness. He had to assume that, sadly, Mrs. Law's once brilliant future was now forever gone. But for the moment, Mac had more immediate concerns.

Annie Williams, George's estranged wife, had been transferred to the ICU sometime during the night. Her heart continued to fail, due to the damage done to it by repeated infections of its valves. The heart is, after all, no more than a sophisticated pump, and without competent valves a pump cannot be expected to function properly. When a pump fails, the fluid which the pump is designed to move backs up behind it. In Annie's case, the fluid backed up into her lungs. She became severely short of breath. Without very aggressive intervention in the ICU, she would not have survived the night.

But Annie's heart, though severely damaged, was still young and possessed remarkable recuperative powers. By midday, after liters of fluid had been removed from her body through the use of diuretics, she was much improved. By late afternoon her condition had returned to baseline: comfortable at rest, but with severely limited exercise tolerance. She was just fine—so long as she restricted her activity to lying in bed or sitting in a chair.

There had been an ugly incident earlier in the afternoon when Mac discovered Beano Smith in Annie's room. Beano was recovering quickly from his drug overdose. He had been released from the ICU that morning and sent to a general medical ward. He no longer had any business in the ICU. That was all Annie needed, to have Beano deliver narcotics directly to her room.

Mac sent a nurse in to ask Beano to leave so Annie could get a sponge bath. Then Mac cornered Beano in a hallway outside the ICU.

"Stay out of Annie Williams' room, Beano. I mean it."

"I've got a right to visit, same as anybody." Criminals were always such experts on *their* rights.

Mac took a step closer so he could really get right in Beano's face. "Look, you jerk, Annie Williams is a very sick lady. She needs surgery. If she starts using narcotics now, the surgeons won't want to have anything to do with her. Simply put, she'll die."

Beano put on his hard, squinty-eyed look. "I ain't sellin' her nothin'. The bitch owes me money. I'm just collectin'." Then he sidestepped around Mac and sauntered off down the hallway, giving Mac his broad shoulders and ponytail to admire.

"Stay away from her," Mac yelled after him. There was no response.

George Williams waited patiently for Mac to get off the phone. He had been very attentive to his wife during her period of extreme distress earlier in the day, but now that Annie had stabilized, George was maintaining a careful distance. He hadn't said it in so many words, but Mac understood that George wanted company when he went into his wife's room to collect his son.

"Thought we could go shoot some hoops," George had said. "You and George Jr. against me."

"No harm, no foul?"

George nodded. *No harm, no foul*, the way they played it, meant that Mac was allowed to tackle George, giving George Jr. a clear line to the basket. And when George Sr. drove for the hoop, Mac was allowed to hack his arms while George Jr. put a bear hug on one of his legs. The guy was six ten, after all.

When Mac finally got off the phone, he was done for the day—unless some emergency came up with one of his patients before he managed to get out of there. And as he and George walked into Annie's room, Mac had every confidence that, for once, he was actually going to leave the ICU at a decent hour. But such was not to be the case.

"Yo, Mac!" George Jr. greeted Mac with a high-five. Mac made him work for it, raising his right hand high above his head so that little George had to give it a pretty good jump.

"I see somebody's got some new clothes," was all his father said.

George Jr. hung his head a little and didn't say anything. He was dressed in a shiny black warm-up suit and unlaced, high-top basketball shoes. He wore a black baseball cap turned around so that the bill pointed backward.

"Come here, baby," his mother said.

The boy moved next to the head of her bed, and she put a protective arm around him.

Annie Williams looked thin and frail as she lay there in her hospital gown, propped up on three pillows. She looked maybe ten years older than her husband. In fact, she was two years younger. She wore large red plastic earrings. Her nail polish was the same color, but it was chipped and old.

"The boy wants to look like his homies," she said, "not like some *white* boy. Don't you, Shooter?"

George Jr. let his head hang lower.

"Shooter?" The father's anger so great his voice shook.

"Li'l Shooter," his son said without looking up. " 'Cause I play basketball."

The room was silent. Annie Williams stared defiantly at her husband. George's jaw muscles tightened and relaxed, tightened and relaxed. He made a fist, first with one hand and then the other. Mac couldn't tell if he was just trying to relieve tension or was about to hit somebody.

"This your new boyfriend's idea, get my son some new friends, ruin his life?"

"Anything's better than letting him turn into a piece of white bread like you."

"Mac, take George Jr. to the waiting room. I'll be along in a minute."

Mac didn't know if he was more relieved at the prospect of removing the boy from the middle of his parents' fight or at getting himself out of the room. But his relief was short-lived. As he moved forward, Annie spoke with more venom than Mac thought he'd ever had hurled in his direction.

"Don't you dare touch my baby." Her voice had become a barely audible hiss.

Mac stopped in mid-step.

George's voice was fierce but even. "This is *not* going to happen. You are *not* going to take my son down with you. I've told you before, I will do *anything* to keep that from happening. *Anything*." George stopped, breathing heavily, trying to compose himself. "You know I would have no problem getting a court to turn him completely over to me. You wouldn't even be allowed to see him." George looked over at his son almost apologetically.

"You are his mother. He loves you. But so help me, I won't let you do this to him. I won't let you do to him what you did to yourself."

With that, George snatched up his son and left the room, leaving Mac standing there alone with Annie. For Mac it was an excruciatingly uncomfortable moment—which Annie was able to remedy quite quickly.

"Get out," she said. And when Mac hesitated, trying to think of something conciliatory to say, she screamed in a voice that could be heard throughout the ICU, "Get out!"

ELEVEN

Mac emerged from Annie Williams' room with his ears ringing and every eye in the ICU turned toward him.

"With your bedside charm," Laura Rubenstein told him, "you might do well to consider a career in pathology or pure research." Then she added, "I hate to tell you this, what with your day already going so well and all, but Five North just called. Sharon Bailey is on her way back down. Looks like she's gone back into septic shock."

And with that Mac was forced to set aside, at least for the time being, his concerns for the Williams family. Gone too was any hope he'd ever had of leaving the ICU at a decent hour.

The scene that followed was one which occurred at least daily in the intensive care unit. To an outsider, it looked like something between controlled bedlam and total chaos.

Sharon Bailey arrived on a gurney, pushed by

one nurse and pulled by another. A metal IV pole extended about three and a half feet above the gurney, and several plastic bags filled with various intravenous fluids flapped and bounced every time the gurney was jostled. In the gurney's wake came the array of residents, medical students, and various hospital personnel who had been caring for her on Five North. A respiratory therapist trotted alongside the gurney. His job every few seconds, was to squeeze the black rubber bag that forced oxygen through the tube in Sharon's throat which now connected her lungs to the outside world.

As soon as Sharon arrived in the ICU, she was descended on by yet another avalanche of health-care providers, the team that would assume her care now that she was back in the Unit.

Her heart rate was 140; her blood pressure was not detectable; her temperature was 96 degrees. Without respiratory assistance she took only shallow, agonal breaths which did not adequately ventilate her lungs and thus could not provide the necessary, life-sustaining oxygen her body demanded. She was placed on a respirator.

While Ruby attended to Sharon Bailey's immediate survival needs—adequate oxygenation, blood-pressure support, and broad-spectrum antibiotics—Mac attempted to find out what had so suddenly gone so very wrong.

"She was going to be discharged *tomorrow!*" Tom Shoemaker, the resident supervising her care on Five North, didn't have any idea why she had deteriorated so quickly. "I talked to her a couple of hours ago. She seemed fine—maybe a little uncertain about going home since we hadn't found out what had made her so sick to begin with, but she was fine. Her little girl was with her, thrilled that Mommy would be coming home."

"What about her lab data?" Mac asked.

"All back to normal. Absolutely nothing out of whack. And we'd run her upper and lower bowel, did an abdominal CT—all normal. Follow-up blood cultures were negative. Her physical exam was essentially normal. She still had this vague abdominal pain, but there was absolutely nothing on exam.

"Then, about a half hour ago, her nurse found her unresponsive in bed. Since then she's just gone further and further downhill." Tom paused briefly, then asked, "You on call tonight?"

Mac shook his head.

"Sorry about that," Tom said.

Sharon Bailey was what was known as a "bounce-back." Mac's ICU team had taken care of her before when she was in the ICU, and would assume her care once again now that she had bounced back. It made sense in terms of continuity of care, but Mac's team was at the end of a shift that had started at eight a.m. yesterday. They always called it a twenty-four-hour shift, but they'd already been at it for nearly thirty-six. It would be several more hours before Sharon Bailey was squared away—assuming that was even possible.

But by nine o'clock they were able to convince themselves that she was beginning to turn the corner. Her blood pressure was up to ninety-five, systolic. Her temperature had risen to ninety-nine. There was reason to hope she would rally once again.

Mac and Ruby were standing at Sharon Bailey's bedside, feeling cautiously optimistic, when a nurse came into the room. "There's a little girl in the waiting room," the nurse said, "who wants to know how her mommy's doing."

"She's alone?" Mac couldn't believe it.

"Near as I can tell."

Mac found her as he had before, staring out the window, and not, he imagined, actually seeing anything out there.

"Hi, Tiffany. Remember me?"

She nodded. There were tears running down her cheeks.

"Your mommy is doing better."

"Can I see her?"

"I don't think so. Not quite yet. Perhaps in a little while." The improvement Sharon Bailey had registered so far was the kind you determined by understanding lab values and vital signs. Mac was pretty certain little Tiffany would not be very encouraged by the sight of her mother unresponsive and on a respirator.

"It's not my fault," she said.

It made Mac's heart ache even more. "Of course it's not your fault. How could it possibly be your fault?"

"Mommy said"—she was starting to cry now—"Mommy said, if I was a good girl, maybe God wouldn't take my mommy away." Between sobs she managed to add, "I've been trying *so* hard."

Mac picked her up out of her chair and held her to him as she cried. She was such a tiny little thing in his arms. So thin. She felt almost weightless.

It had been a very long time since Mac McCall had broken into tears, but he could feel himself on the brink now, with this sobbing little girl in his arms. And perhaps he would have if it hadn't been for a stronger, countervailing emotion, a sense of anger and outrage at the woman barely clinging to life in the next room. How could a mother say such a cruel thing to her child? How could *anyone* be so evil?

Mac needed to get back to helping care for Tiffany's mother, but first he had to make certain that Tiffany herself was properly looked after. For the time being he was able to get members of the ICU staff to rotate responsibility for the little girl as they took their breaks. At least she wouldn't be alone. Meanwhile, they were busily trying to find a relative or family friend to come get her.

Sharon Bailey now appeared to be stable. She would stay on the respirator, at least overnight, but she continued to make rapid improvement in all major parameters.

"I would bet a lot of money," Ruby said, "that by this time tomorrow she'll be back to baseline, and we still won't have a clue where the source of her infection is."

Mac walked over to the corner of the room and picked up the brown paper bag that had come with Sharon Bailey from Five North.

"One thing I've been thinking about," Mac said, "is that we ought to ask the nurses to inventory her belongings very carefully—just to make certain nothing gets lost." He paused momentarily and then added, "And of course we wouldn't want any hospital supplies to get lost in the shuffle."

Laura Rubenstein's first thought was that they had more important things to worry about. Then she understood.

"Suddenly it all makes sense, doesn't it, Mac? You just may pass your ICU clerkship after all."

But the search turned up nothing.

"Still," Ruby said, "it wasn't a bad idea."

"I've got one more idea," Mac said.

"What's that?"

"Five North."

"I'm looking for Sharon Bailey's room," Mac told the ward clerk.

"Gone to the Unit," the clerk answered. She didn't even look up.

"What room was she in before she was transferred?"

This time she looked up from her desk. "You the new janitor?"

"I'm her attorney," Mac answered.

"That would be Room 542," the clerk said with a polite smile.

The room was bare. The mattress had been stripped. Nothing under it. Nothing hidden in the springs. Both the mattress and the pillow were sealed. Nothing could be hidden inside them.

There was a small closet and a few drawers. All appeared empty. Mac took the drawers out and turned them over. Nothing. He inspected the back of the cabinet behind the drawers. Nothing.

Then he looked under the sink.

Bingo.

TWELVE

Mac had worried that, when his turn came around, he wouldn't be able to come up with a suitable case to present at the ethics seminar. Sharon Bailey had certainly solved that problem for him.

As she continued to recover from her most recent episode, and as all the evidence which Mac had painstakingly collected was presented to her, she finally acknowledged her own role in her illness. Her admission was a very important first step toward the possibility of recovery, but, unfortunately, her ultimate prognosis remained quite grave.

And Mac couldn't help but worry greatly about the prognosis for Sharon Bailey's abused daughter. Regardless of her mother's future clinical course, little Tiffany's psychological scars were likely to be deep and long-lasting.

Standing on the floor of the amphitheater to present a case was a very different thing from lounging comfortably someplace up there in the darkness. Mac knew that Dr. Law was up there somewhere. Also lying in wait were the Unholy Trinity: Frost, Delacroix, and VanSlyke. Mac could only imagine what abuse they might choose to rain down on him.

But as Mac began his presentation, he felt the tension leave his body. He was prepared. He knew his topic. He understood his patient—at least to the extent that understanding was possible.

"The patient is a thirty-four-year-old female who presented to the emergency room in septic shock . . ."

Mac went on to describe her hospital course, the fact that her blood cultures had grown several different species of bacteria, and the suspicion among Sharon Bailey's physicians that her infection must have originated from some site in her abdomen. The work-up, however, was negative.

"By this time the patient's condition appeared to have returned to normal, and it was decided that it would be reasonable to continue her follow-up as an outpatient. The patient herself expressed an eagerness to return home so that she could resume care of her daughter.

"However, on the evening prior to her scheduled discharge from the hospital, the patient once again went into shock—this episode much more severe than the first. As before, the patient responded to aggressive blood-pressure support and broad-spectrum antibiotic therapy. Once again her laboratory and physical examinations gave no clue as to the source of her recurrent sepsis.

"Because of this history of recurrent, unexplained sepsis, Munchausen's syndrome was suspected. A search of the patient's belongings and room was conducted, and a syringe was found taped beneath the sink in her room on Five North. Culture of material from the syringe revealed essentially the same organisms which were previously—and subsequently—recovered from her blood.

"When the patient improved sufficiently, she was confronted with the evidence. At first she became angry and demanded to leave the hospital. She threatened legal action against the hospital and all her physicians. She was told that a psychiatric evaluation would be required to determine whether or not she was mentally competent, and how much of a risk she represented to herself and others.

"During the psychiatric evaluation she eventually admitted injecting saliva into her veins to cause her sepsis syndrome. It was subsequently discovered that she has had six admissions to other hospitals over the last two years, each for the treatment of self-induced sepsis. She told her daughter and friends that her infections were related to ovarian cancer. She had told her daughter that God was going to take her mother from her because the daughter had been a bad little girl. The daughter is not quite five years old."

Mac went on to describe what was known about the disorder from which Sharon Bailey suffered. Munchausen's syndrome derives its name, he told them, from the eighteenth-century German nobleman Baron von Munchausen, who had a remarkable talent for fabricating stories. Patients with Munchausen's syndrome are not hypochondriacs. That is, they are not patients who believe themselves to be ill but who are in fact well. On the contrary, persons with this disorder do things to themselves which either cause illness or make it appear that they are ill.

Self-induced infections are among the more common manifestations of Munchausen's syndrome. Patients inject material directly into a vein—as Sharon Bailey did—or they inject into some body tissue causing local infection. Patients have also been reported to inject substances such as corn starch into veins, causing a syndrome which simulates pneumonia or pulmonary embolus.

Other patients have injected themselves with insulin, causing dangerously low blood-sugar levels. This leads physicians to suspect an insulin-secreting tumor.

Perhaps the most horrific manifestation of the disorder is the so-called Munchausen's by proxy syndrome. In this condition the patient causes illness in another person—usually a very young child. Children, often infants, have been injected with all manner of infectious agents, including HIV.

The cause of the syndrome is not well understood. Some have theorized that these patients suffer from a personal feeling of early abandonment, usually by parents, and are seeking to substitute a relationship with a physician for the one they feel they have lost. These patients often seem very eager to cooperate with medical personnel, until the true nature of their illness is suspected.

Treatment of Munchausen's syndrome has not been very successful. These patients *want* to be ill, and the psychological root of their problem is very deep. The disorder tends to be chronic, and may eventually be fatal.

"I've chosen to present this case here," Mac said, "because of all the obvious ethical issues raised, both in diagnosis and treatment. We are confronted by a patient who is at significant risk to cause herself great personal harm. In addition, the cost of her care is enormous, far in excess of one hundred thousand dollars over the last two years—a cost similar to performing bone marrow transplantation. In addition, it is difficult to calculate the emotional damage which she has inflicted on her daughter."

And with that the floor was opened for discussion.

"What gave you the right," a third-year student wanted to know, "to search her belongings?"

It was perhaps the most difficult question to be answered. Probably just as well it came first.

Mac considered the issue momentarily, then said, "I frankly don't know what a lawyer would say. I believe that, morally, we did the right thing. Our only motive was to help the patient. In fact, we turned out to be correct in our assumption, and by acting as we did, we made a diagnosis that we otherwise could not have made. This helped us better manage the patient's most recent episode of sepsis. It allowed us to avoid costly, useless, and perhaps even potentially dangerous diagnostic tests that the patient might otherwise have undergone. And finally, now that we have a diagnosis, we can attempt to treat her underlying disease."

"What about your current treatment plan?" another student asked. "What are you planning to do for her?"

"She is now completely recovered from a medical point of view and has been transferred to a closed ward on the psychiatry service. Their plan is for long-term, supportive group therapy, but they're pretty pessimistic about her future."

"Then what happens? Does she just get discharged and then come back here—or some other hospital—and do this all over again?"

"That's the dilemma, isn't it?" Mac said. "These patients typically go from hospital to hospital, sometimes traveling to different cities and even different states. If their underlying psychiatric problem does not resolve, they continue to be a threat to themselves and run up astronomical medical bills. The only answer would seem to be involuntary commitment to a psychiatric institution, but even in that type of setting these patients can still manage to injure themselves."

Another student wanted to know if anything had been discovered in Sharon Bailey's background which explained her behavior.

Peter VanSlyke decided to field that one. "Far too much time is wasted trying to come up with some convoluted explanation for why a crazy person acts crazy. What difference does it make whether she got dropped on her head when she was a baby or her parents got divorced when she was six? She's a totally dysfunctional human being. All the psychobabble in the world isn't going to make one whit of difference in her clinical outcome. The only thing that's going to keep her from harming herself is a straightjacket."

Mac said to Peter, "I guess you've pretty much given up on that psychiatry residency." That brought a round of laughter.

It was a cardinal rule of Dr. Law's seminar that nothing said would be repeated outside the group. The idea was that this would make students more comfortable taking positions, especially ones that weren't popular or politically correct. Mac thought that the rule provided cover for some fairly irresponsible statements.

The seminar ended with Dr. Law calling on various students to give follow-up information on patients previously presented.

"Dr. Williams, would you please tell us what has happened with your patient with endocarditis? I believe there was a question as to whether surgery should be performed."

"Her congestive heart failure worsened over the last week, but has now once again stabilized. Surgery has been scheduled for later this week."

"Dr. Delacroix," Professor Law asked, "do you have the final autopsy findings on your patient?" There was no response. "Dr. Delacroix?"

It was Turner Frost who finally answered. "I guess Austin wasn't able to make it today. My understanding is that the final microscopic results were negative."

"So the diagnosis of Alzheimer's disease was not confirmed?"

"No. I believe that the feeling now is that the patient was suffering from a bout of severe sub-acute depression. This can be very difficult to distinguish from Alzheimer's based on initial clinical presentation alone."

Delacroix had presented the Havlicek case at the seminar as an example of out-of-control medical costs. Here was a man with obvious Alzheimer's disease undergoing an enormously expensive diagnostic evaluation. For what? How were we ever to get a hold on health-care costs, Delacroix had complained, when so much money is wasted on cases like this? But as it had turned out, Delacroix could not have been more wrong. Havlicek, had he lived, might have benefited greatly from a proper diagnosis. Depression is often quite treatable. Sometimes it is transient, and patients recover with no specific therapy whatsoever. No wonder Austin Delacroix decided not to show up for today's seminar.

But about an hour later, when Mac opened his apartment door and discovered Austin Delacroix sitting on the couch with Jennifer, he quickly developed a very different idea of why Delacroix might have passed up the seminar.

THIRTEEN

In flagrante delicto. The term Austin Delacroix had himself used to describe the charges against Diego Valenzuela. *Caught in the act.*

The legal phrase actually flashed through Mac's mind when he opened his apartment door. So pathetically apt.

Delacroix was instantly on his feet. Flushed. Agitated.

"Hi, Mac." He sounded nervous. "I've been waiting to talk to you."

Right.

"You're home earlier than I expected," Jennifer said.

Mac was pretty certain that truer words had never been spoken.

Mac stood at the door, still in his winter coat, saying nothing. Jennifer remained seated on the couch, looking uncertain, as though she couldn't imagine what Mac was having a problem with. And Austin Delacroix just stood there in his preppy blue blazer and brightly shined penny loafers, shaking. Shaking! Visibly.

"So, Austin," Mac said, "how's tricks?"

Delacroix just kind of shrugged and looked down at Jennifer for help. Mac couldn't help but wonder if Delacroix was as surprised by Jennifer's next words as he was.

"I've got some shopping to do," she said. "I'll leave you two guys to talk."

Mac fixed an incredulous gaze on her.

"Austin has something he wants to talk over with you," Jennifer explained.

She picked up her coat and started for the door. As she passed him, Mac could smell alcohol on her breath. He glanced toward the kitchen and saw two empty wineglasses standing, unrepentant, beside the sink.

"Would you like another drink, Austin?" Mac couldn't be certain whether Jennifer had heard his words before the door closed behind her.

Austin shook his head.

But a drink sounded pretty good to Mac about now. He poured some bourbon into a glass and tossed in an ice cube as an afterthought. He took a good pull, then went over and sat in a chair opposite the couch, still in his coat, his drink resting on his knee.

"So what was it you wanted to talk about?" Mac was thinking, Did Delacroix want his permission to court Jennifer? Maybe he wanted to fight a duel.

Delacroix tried to make himself sit down on the sofa, but he popped right back up. He wandered around the room, stared out the window, plunged his hands into his pockets, then jerked them back out like there was something in there he was afraid to touch.

Austin Delacroix was slender and wore glasses with tortoise-shell rims. He always managed to look somehow professorial. A *wealthy* professor. Right now he looked like a frightened professor.

"Maybe this wasn't such a good idea," Delacroix said finally.

"Probably not," Mac answered.

"I really don't know you all that well."

Maybe he wants to court *me*, Mac thought. He noticed his glass was already empty and decided to get a refill. Delacroix seemed grateful for the interruption. Mac replenished his glass, sat back down, and Delacroix *still* hadn't said anything.

"What's on your mind, Austin?" Gone was the anger which had previously tinged Mac's words. Only boredom remained.

"I don't know if I know you well enough to discuss this with you."

Mac's suspicious thoughts toward Jennifer began to dissipate. This was beginning to feel like something else. Homosexual panic maybe. Austin Delacroix was about to jump out of the closet right before Mac's eyes.

"Whatever it is, you can tell me, Austin. It won't leave this room."

The look on Delacroix's face indicated that he still wasn't convinced. Finally he said, "Everybody thinks I'm rich, but really I'm quite poor."

Could have fooled me, Mac thought.

"Like you," Delacroix added.

Nice to be included, Mac thought.

"Oh, sure, my wife's got millions. I'm not gonna starve, but without her I'd be living just like this." He made a gesture with his hand to indicate Mac and Jennifer's apartment.

Ouch.

"Just so you understand," Mac said, "I wouldn't be living anywhere near this grandly if it wasn't for Jennifer's salary."

Delacroix could only stare blankly, unable to comprehend a lower level of subsistence.

"Your parents still alive?" Delacroix asked.

Mac nodded.

"Mine aren't. Murder-suicide, the police said. I think it was probably murder-murder, but what difference does it make? All they left behind was a pile of debt. My father had inherited millions and squandered it all.

"Luckily, I was already engaged. My wife's parents wanted their precious daughter to call the whole thing off, but she wouldn't. I think maybe she thought that calling it off would be more embarrassing than marrying into the scandal in the first place. So anyway, she now supports me, in the manner, as they say, to which I have become accustomed.

"Without her . . ." Delacroix's eyes swept the room, indicating the depth to which he might have sunk were it not for his wife's support. The mere contemplation of his narrow escape from the throes of poverty seemed to plunge him into even deeper despair.

"I think maybe you could use another drink, Austin." Mac got up to see if there was any wine left. He heard the door open behind his back. Good. Maybe Jennifer could help sort this out.

"Jennifer?" No response.

Then Mac heard the door shut.

"Austin?" Nothing.

When Jennifer finally came home, she acted as though nothing unusual had happened.

"What was that all about?" Mac asked her.

"What was *what* all about?"

"Delacroix."

"Didn't he tell you?"

"The first time I turned my back he ran out the door."

"All he told me was that he wanted to talk to you."

Why was Mac having such a hard time believing her?

"Didn't he tell you anything?" Mac asked.

"Not a thing."

"What did you talk about?"

Jennifer shrugged. "Mostly about when you'd be getting home."

Jennifer headed into the bedroom, finished with their conversation.

"Jennifer?"

Apparently she didn't hear him. Mac heard the bathroom door close.

Mac tried to worry the pieces together. He wanted to believe Jennifer. After all, he hadn't *seen* anything going on. Mac had come home and found Jennifer and Delacroix on the couch together. That was all. They weren't kissing or anything. They were fully clothed. Neither looked particularly rumpled. Delacroix was agitated. Jennifer was cool. But then, Jennifer was a pretty cool customer most of the time anyway.

So why didn't Mac believe Jennifer?

Simple. The most obvious explanation for what he had seen was that there was something going on between the two of them.

It bothered Mac a lot that he was so easily suspicious of Jennifer. What kind of a relationship was that?

It hadn't always been this way. When their relationship began, Mac thought that Jennifer might actually be the one—the woman he'd spend the rest of his life with. They seemed to have so much in common, so much to share with each other. And Mac was so impressed with what an intelligent, caring nurse she was.

Now Jennifer seemed like an entirely different person. They didn't seem to have a thing in common anymore. They never seemed to be able to find the time to do things together. And Jennifer didn't seem to care about anything— except money.

Was this a new Jennifer, or was the old Jennifer merely an illusion, a figment of Mac's imagination?

And what kind of a relationship did they have if Mac had to worry about coming home and finding Jennifer on the couch with Austin Delacroix?

FOURTEEN

The cardiology team was meeting in a conference room on Ten West, the oncology floor, because their regular meeting place had been usurped by the cardiac surgeons. By the time Mac finally found them, the cardiologists had already finished discussing the case he wanted to hear about—one of his former ICU patients—so Mac just turned around and headed back to the ICU. His mind was a million miles away, and the scene he saw out of the corner of his eye did not immediately register. So he went back for a second look.

What he saw was Beano Smith sitting in a chair at the bedside of an elderly cancer patient. Both the patient and Beano had their eyes closed, as though in prayer or meditation. Mac kept thinking, What's wrong with this picture?

Mac had no idea what ward Beano had been sent to when he was discharged from the ICU. Ordinarily it would not have been the oncology ward, but if the general medical wards were short of beds, they could farm out their patients anywhere in the hospital. But even if Beano was a patient on Ten West, it was difficult to imagine his paying social visits to spiritually enrich the lives of terminal cancer patients.

Mac walked back to the nursing station to look for Smith's chart, but couldn't find one.

"Could I see Beano Smith's chart?" he asked the ward secretary.

"Nobody here by that name."

"How about Benny Smith?"

She shook her head.

Mac pulled the chart on the patient in 1032. As he had surmised, she was suffering the terminal ravages of widely metastatic cancer. It was hard to believe that even Beano could stoop this low.

When the charge nurse returned to the nursing station, Mac had just one question for her. "Is Mrs. Sorenson, the patient in 1032, on PCA?"

The nurse nodded.

PCA, patient-controlled analgesia, is increasingly used in hospitals to allow patients to adjust the amount of pain medication they receive. They merely push a button, and a bedside machine dispenses a predetermined amount of drug into an intravenous line. The machine limits how frequently the medication is given, and studies have demonstrated that, overall, patients tend to use less narcotic medication with the machine than if they have to summon a nurse for an injection. Patient satisfaction is also higher—since there's no waiting for the nurse. The system is foolproof. Almost.

"If you have a minute," Mac said to the charge nurse, "there's something going on in Mrs. Sorenson's room I think you should see."

When they arrived at the door, all was as before. Mrs. Sorenson and Beano both had their eyes closed. Both could well have been asleep. The nurse shrugged at Mac. What was the problem?

"I bet Mrs. Sorenson has never seen that guy before in her life. She may not even know he's in her room," Mac said. Then the clincher: "He's a drug addict."

It took only a second for the nurse to understand the implications of all this; then she gasped. She started to walk into the room, but Mac motioned for her to stay put. "Let me do the honors," he said.

Mac slipped quietly into the room to get a closer look. Beano had simply clamped off the IV tubing as it went into Mrs. Sorenson's arm, then used another needle to shunt the medication into his own arm. Mac figured there might be some activity more base than stealing pain medication from an elderly cancer patient, but for the time being he couldn't come up with one.

In one motion Mac yanked the needle out and pulled Beano's arm around behind his back in a hammerlock. Mac lifted with all his might, and Beano came right out of the chair. There was a single sharp cry of pain, but nothing else.

Because it seemed like a good idea, Mac grabbed Beano's ponytail with his other hand and then, without a word of explanation, marched him out of the room and down the hallway—to the amazement of a number of patients and staff who happened to witness the action. Beano's face showed only surprise and bewilderment.

At the end of the hall there was a fire door which opened onto a stairwell. Mac threw Beano against the door, forcing it open, deposited Beano on the landing, then closed the door behind him. All of the fire doors were locked on the stairwell side. The only unlocked door was in the lobby. Maybe after walking down the ten floors, Beano would just decide to leave the hospital altogether.

"I'll call security," the charge nurse assured Mac.

"Suit yourself, but I think that throwing Beano off the floor is probably as much satisfaction as we're going to get out of this deal. I don't know what the hospital would charge him with, but whatever they come up with, he won't pay much of a penalty. The best we can hope for is that they'll make him persona non grata around here—keep him from pulling a stunt like this again. With any luck at all he's probably about to sign out of the hospital pretty soon anyway."

Mac rolled his shoulders and neck a little to ease the tension. Then he started to smile. "You know what?" he said. "That felt pretty good."

FIFTEEN

The night Annie Williams died was a typical ICU thrash. Too many patients, all trying to die at the same time.

Mac knew something significant was going on in Annie Williams' cubicle, but he hardly had time to think about it. Mac's efforts were focused on yet another critically ill patient, and besides that, Mac was knee-deep in surgeons. Hell, he was up to his eyebrows in surgeons.

"Are you gonna just stand there, or are you gonna get a new central line going?" The sound of the attending surgeon encouraging the surgical chief resident to do his best work.

"If you'd hurry up and put in that arterial line, I wouldn't have to try to guess the patient's blood gases." The chief surgical resident, instructing his intern as to the finer points of surgical technique.

"Where the hell's the lab data I asked you for

ten minutes ago?'' The surgical intern, patiently educating his students.

"Mac, get the lab data.'' The two surgical students, Peter VanSlyke and Turner Frost, assuming the mantle of surgeons.

"Eat my shorts.'' Mac, doing his best to contribute to the esprit de corps.

The patient's name was Ivar Bergstrom. He had come into the ER complaining of leg pain and had gone steadily downhill from there. He was a man of about sixty years of age with a history of heart disease. The discoloration in his leg had suggested a vascular problem, some type of occlusion.

By the time Mr. Bergstrom arrived in the ICU, the other leg was clearly involved. People began talking about an occlusion at the level of the abdominal aorta.

"But his temperature is 104, and his white count is thirty thousand,'' Mac had pointed out. This had earned him a patronizing smile from Peter VanSlyke. Mac was surprised that Peter didn't pat him on the top of the head.

When Mr. Bergstrom's left arm became involved with the same process, Mac facetiously told Peter that the occlusion must have moved to Bergstrom's heart. By that time everyone understood that they were dealing with rapidly spreading gangrene—some variety of what the popular press referred to as "flesh-eating bacteria."

"I think maybe we should call the infectious-disease team," Mac suggested.

"That's all we need, a few more fleas hopping around the patient," the chief surgical resident replied.

Mac had never completely understood why surgeons referred to internists as fleas. Perhaps it was their perception that internists tended to order too many blood tests (*phle*botomy—surgeons weren't necessarily the world's greatest spellers). Or maybe surgeons just regarded internists as too numerous, or simply irritating. At any rate, the term was in general use and did not imply either affection or a spirit of camaraderie.

"This man needs to go to the OR, *now!*" The chief resident had spoken.

Wheels began to turn. The OR was called and an operating room was scheduled. Antibiotics were begun. All the appropriate intravenous and intra-arterial lines were placed. Ivar Bergstrom was all but out the door when the attending surgeon returned from talking with the Bergstrom family.

"I discussed with them the likelihood that we would have to amputate multiple limbs, and that even then the prognosis was very, very poor. They feel that if Mr. Bergstrom was able to make the decision for himself, he wouldn't choose to undergo that kind of surgery. Even if he survived, he wouldn't want the kind of life he'd be left with. I can't say I disagree."

The likelihood of survival without surgery was essentially zero. Despite all the advances of modern medicine, despite the awesome power of current antibiotic therapy, surgery remains the cornerstone of the treatment of gangrene. Infected tissue needs to be excised. But the amount of surgery which Mr. Bergstrom would now require was too horrendous to contemplate.

The patient had long since lapsed into unconsciousness. Narcotics would be administered to make certain there was no pain as the infection traveled its inevitable course. It was now only a matter of time.

Silence engulfed the cubicle, broken only by the rhythmic keening of the bedside cardiac monitor and the occasional shuffling of mourner's feet. The faint but distinctive aroma of penicillin lingered in the air, mute testimony to the frequent futility of modern medicine.

For the first time in more than two hours Mac allowed his thoughts to wander away from Ivar Bergstrom. His gaze drifted to Annie Williams' bed and then abruptly stopped. Her cubicle was no longer a scene of frenetic activity. It was still as death.

* * *

"What happened?" Mac asked.

Jennifer shook her head. She had been Annie Williams' nurse all evening. "We found her unresponsive in bed, pupils constricted—pretty clearly she'd somehow managed to get hold of some kind of narcotic. We gave her Narcan, and she seemed to respond. Then, all of a sudden, she started to crater again.

"She developed this whole smorgasbord of arrhythmias. We thought she had some kind of supraventricular tachycardia—maybe she'd thrown an embolus. Then she developed a conduction block; then she clearly had ventricular tachycardia and finally V-fib. She didn't respond to anything."

"Was George here when she died?"

"He just now left. Said he was going to go tell his son and the rest of the family."

Mac had hardly known Annie Williams, so naturally his thoughts were more of George and George Jr. Despite all their family problems, her death would be felt as a significant loss.

Still, Annie Williams had endured a long and serious illness. Her death was not an entirely unanticipated event. And it was probably because of that fact that, in those first few hours and days following her death, Mac had not yet begun to worry that she had been murdered.

SIXTEEN

First thing the following morning Mac was in the microbiology laboratory, checking the cultures that had been set up on Ivar Bergstrom. Also, he wanted to take a look at the microscopic slides that had been made. Ordinarily, Mac would have gone down to the lab in the middle of the night to examine the slides, but when his patient died, review of the laboratory data became less urgent.

"So, what do you see?" Jake asked.

"Nothing yet," Mac answered.

"Keep looking."

Jake, the head tech in the micro lab, was used to Mac's coming in to review slides.

Mac must have looked at thirty fields before he finally found something. "Bingo."

"What?"

"Boxcars."

"Good work, Mac. The tech who was on last night missed them. When the blood cultures looked positive this morning, I reviewed the slide myself."

The organisms were very few and far between on the slide, but they were there. Blue, rectangular bacteria. Under the microscope they looked like railroad boxcars. Given the clinical setting, there wasn't much doubt that they would be some species of clostridia, the classic cause of gas gangrene.

"What did the blood cultures show?"

"The slides were negative," Jake said, "but there was definite growth detected. I'd be willing to bet the ranch that the blood cultures will grow clostridia."

"So would I."

The laboratory findings were no real surprise. They were almost a relief. Given the rapid progression of Mr. Bergstrom's infection, the only possible effective therapy would have been mutilating surgery—at a minimum, the amputation of an arm and two legs—and even that would probably not have saved his life. The only remaining question was the source of the infection. If they were ever going to get a handle on that, it would have to be at autopsy.

It was a remarkably quiet day in the ICU— the proverbial calm following the storm. No new admissions. Half the beds empty now with Bergstrom and Annie Williams dead and several other patients transferred out to general medical wards. Mac thought he might even have time to sneak off to the library and catch up on his reading of medical journals—a rare treat during daylight hours.

He was sitting at the nursing station, perusing sheets of laboratory data that the computer had spewed onto the desk, when suddenly his heart sank.

Annie Williams hadn't even been Mac's patient. Ordinarily, he wouldn't be looking at her lab data. It wasn't any of his business—but it was mixed in with all the other data, and this one value was flagged because it was far outside the normal therapeutic range. Anyone would have noticed.

And Mac's thoughts, which had already been with George Williams and his son, turned gloomier than ever. What would George do when he heard—how in the world could he ever tell his son—that Annie Williams had died as a result of medical malpractice? At the very least, gross negligence. What was the lawyer's term? *Res ipso loquitur*. The thing speaks for itself.

Mac thumbed through her other lab data, trying to see if he could find some explanation, some excuse that might possibly mitigate such a horrendous error. The only other thing he found was that Annie Williams had tested positive for opiates—indicating that she had managed somehow to get her hands on some narcotics. Actually, it wasn't too hard to guess where the drugs might have come from—Beano Smith.

"What's the matter?" It was Kathy Blake, the charge nurse. Mac's expression must have betrayed what was going on in his mind.

"Not much doubt why Annie Williams died," he said. "Digoxin toxicity."

Digoxin is one of the oldest and most useful drugs for the treatment of heart failure, but the dose needs to be carefully monitored. Too high a digoxin level in the blood can lead to a variety of problems, including serious irregularities of the heart rhythm—and death.

"No way she died of dig toxicity, Mac." Everyone referred to digoxin as dig—rhymes with Midge.

He handed Kathy the lab printout which reported a digoxin level of ten—an amount almost certain to cause death.

"It's a mistake," Kathy said.

"What makes you so sure?"

She was actually smiling. "Annie Williams wasn't on digoxin. She was on a new experimental drug, and the administration protocol specifically prohibited using digoxin."

"So how do you explain the lab report?"

"Probably just an error. Happens all the time—as you well know."

"Is her chart still around?"

Kathy pointed at a large stack of charts at a nearby table. "Help yourself."

When he put his mind to it, Mac was able to come up with a perfectly logical explanation for the episode. When Annie Williams' condition deteriorated, it was decided she should receive digoxin—either to help her heart muscle work more effectively or to treat an abnormal heart rhythm. In an emergency they would have ignored the experimental drug protocol which prohibited the use of digoxin.

That explained why she was on the digoxin, and why Kathy hadn't heard about it. But why was the digoxin level so high? Easy. It had been given through an IV line, and the blood level had been drawn from the same line or a nearby "downstream" line or vein. This could give an erroneously high result. Case closed.

The only problem was, as Mac worked his way through the data charted the night before, he could find no record of digoxin being given or of an order to obtain a digoxin level. Still, that wasn't terribly unusual. With all that had been going on with Annie Williams and in the ICU in general the night before, it wasn't too surprising that some things, even important things, didn't get charted. In an emergency patient care took priority over charting. It was only much later, when the lawyers took over, that people discovered that certain details hadn't been recorded.

Fortunately, Mac had an ace in the hole. He had intimate access to Annie Williams' primary nurse of the night before.

"Jennifer?"

"Who's this?"

"Mac."

"Mac who?"

Jennifer sounded more than a little sleepy.

"Wake up, Jennifer. This is important."

She finally rallied, but Mac still wasn't certain she was fully comprehending the import of his questions.

"You drew the digoxin level, Jennifer?"

"Yes."

"And Austin Delacroix was the one who asked you to draw it."

"By George, I think you've got it!"

"But Austin wasn't involved in taking care of Annie Williams."

"She arrested *three* times, Mac. Half the hospital was there at one time or another. Doctors and medical students were giving orders like there was a fire sale going on. It's always like that."

"But, to the best of your knowledge, Annie Williams wasn't on digoxin?"

"No. She was on the experimental drug. I thought maybe they just wanted the digoxin level, you know, to show that she *wasn't* on dig. To show that the protocol hadn't been violated."

As he hung up the phone, Mac wasn't sure he was much closer to understanding what had gone on. At least he now knew that a digoxin level had been deliberately drawn on Annie Williams. It wasn't clear why. But was the reported level accurate, or had an error been made, either in the laboratory or somewhere else along the way?

The next logical step was to contact Austin Delacroix—which turned out to be a lot more difficult than it sounded. In fact, it turned out to be impossible.

It was just after five o'clock, early for Mac to be leaving the hospital even after being on call. A cold rain was falling. Mac drove his car with one hand and tried to keep the windshield unfogged with the other. His defroster was on the fritz again. With the windows rolled down, the wind-chill factor made it colder in his car than on the sidewalk. If it wasn't so far, he would have been better off walking. Mac couldn't believe the neighborhood he was driving through.

No one seemed to know where Delacroix was. He hadn't shown up at the hospital today. He hadn't called to say why. Mac had telephoned Delacroix's home a dozen times—the line was always busy. So now Mac was on his way to find Delacroix, figuring he wouldn't be able to relax until he had sorted out just exactly what had happened to Annie Williams. It turned out that Delacroix's address was in a part of town most *faculty* couldn't afford to live in, let alone medical students.

Mac finally found it, an old brick town house that reeked of wealth. It was three, maybe four stories high, with tall, white-trimmed windows and dark green shutters. The front door was painted in the same dark green and adorned with elaborate brass hardware. Huge lantern-like lights hung on either side of the door.

Mac decided against using the heavy brass knocker. Letting it fall would send a violent tremor through the entire neighborhood. He pressed the bell and heard nothing. He waited. He pressed again.

He was about to risk the knocker when he heard a bolt slide. The door opened slightly. Before him stood a petite blond woman of about his own age. She had fine features and a dainty nose. There were tears in her eyes and she was trembling. Mac instantly regretted his intrusion.

"I'm sorry to bother you," he said. "I'm Mac McCall. I'm a classmate of Austin's. He didn't show up today at the hospital, and I was worried. I tried to call, but there was no answer." Okay, Mac had altered the truth a little to suit the circumstances. It seemed the appropriate course.

She seemed at first not to hear him. Just stood there, staring. Then the trembling became worse. She began to sob.

"Austin's dead," she said. "He's killed himself."

And with that, she shut the door, leaving Mac alone in the freezing drizzle.

SEVENTEEN

Mac shook his head. "I don't understand any of this."

"Like what?" Jennifer asked.

"Like *any* of it."

They were sitting in their apartment, Mac trying to put together everything he'd learned over the last twenty-four hours.

"Okay," he said, "why did Delacroix order a digoxin level on a patient he wasn't following— a patient who wasn't even supposed to be on digoxin?"

"It's not all that difficult to explain, Mac. A code had been called. Doctors and medical students from all over the hospital showed up. And I think you could say that Annie Williams' cardiac rhythm was certainly consistent with digoxin toxicity. Delacroix's a smart guy. He probably noticed the rhythm and assumed, since she'd been in heart failure, that she was on digoxin."

"Was."

"What?"

"Delacroix *was* a smart guy."

That stopped the conversation for a while.

Then, "But if drawing the digoxin level was such a big mistake, why did it turn out to be positive?" It still didn't add up for Mac. "Who gave her the digoxin?"

"Could have been a lab error. Might have been some other patient."

"But like you said, Jennifer, Annie Williams' heart rhythm was totally consistent with dig toxicity."

"Maybe someone ordered digoxin and it was just never charted."

"Maybe."

"What are you thinking, Mac?"

"*I* don't even want to know what I'm thinking."

"Come on, what?"

"That Annie Williams might have been murdered."

"Murdered? There could have been negligence, sure, but murder? I don't see that at all. Who'd want to murder Annie Williams?"

"Maybe the same guy who gave her the heroin."

A buzzer sounded, announcing someone at the apartment building's front door.

"Are you expecting someone?" As soon as he

said it, Mac realized that his tone sounded accusatory, not really for any good reason. "I'm sorry," he said.

Mac went to the intercom. "Yes?"

They were police officers, they said. They wanted to speak with Mac and Jennifer about the death of Austin Delacroix.

Mac buzzed them in, then waited outside the apartment door so that he could get a good look at the men before they got too near the apartment. Anyone could *say* they were police officers. Mac wondered if he might be getting just a teeny bit paranoid.

As it turned out, these two looked like the genuine article.

They showed their badges. "I'm Detective Mallory," the tall, slender one said, "and this is Sergeant Polanski."

They were two very different types. Mallory had his long hair swept back in sort of a Gordon Gecko-Wall Street kind of thing. He wore a suit which Mac would have described as Armani-esque, and had soft, slender hands with manicured nails. He reeked of cologne. Polanski, on the other hand, shopped at Kmart. He was blue-collar—and proud of it.

Mallory seemed to be the one in charge.

"Sorry to bother you," he said, "but we're investigating the death of a medical student named

Austin Delacroix. We understand that you were friends of his."

"Not really," Mac said. "He was a classmate of mine. I knew him, but we weren't close."

"His wife said you came by the house today."

"Austin didn't show up at the hospital today. I tried to call his home, but the line was always busy, so I just dropped by."

Polanski looked up from his notebook. "You weren't close, but when he didn't show up at the hospital, you called his number several times, then went clear across town to check on him?"

Polanski's tone was accusatory. Mac was beginning to feel guilty. "I had a question about a patient's medication, and no one else seemed to know the answer." Mac didn't want to get into too much detail about Annie Williams. He wasn't about to open that can of worms with these guys.

Jennifer didn't understand Polanski's attitude either. "Austin's wife told Mac that he had killed himself."

"That's our working assumption," Mallory answered. "Do you have any reason to believe that he was depressed or especially worried about anything?"

For Mac it was hard to believe that Austin Delacroix could *find* anything to worry about. "As far as I know, he had a lot fewer concerns than most senior medical students. He was rich, top of his class."

"Was he worried about his internship?" Mallory wanted to know.

Mac and Jennifer exchanged glances. Jennifer shrugged her shoulders as Mac shook his head.

"I don't know why he'd have any problem getting an internship," Mac said.

"When did you last talk to Austin Delacroix, Mr. McCall?" Polanski asked.

"He came by the apartment a couple of days ago. Said he wanted to talk to me about something."

"What was that?"

"I guess I never really found out. He seemed very nervous, then he said that he might have made a mistake in coming to see me."

"Why would he want to confide in you? You said you two weren't close." Polanski seemed to be trying to make some kind of federal case out of the fact that Delacroix and Mac weren't good friends.

"Again, I have no idea why he wanted to see me," Mac said. "He'd never even come to my apartment before. He'd never been invited, wasn't invited this time."

The officers considered this for a moment, then Mallory opened a manila envelope he'd been holding. He pulled out a piece of paper enclosed in plastic.

"This was found over at the medical school." He handed the plastic-enclosed paper to Mac.

On the paper was a brief, typewritten note:

```
I can't even get the internship I want.

I am a total failure.

                          Austin Delacroix
```

There was no signature. The name was typewritten.

"First off," Mac said, "I can't imagine that Austin Delacroix couldn't get any internship he wanted. Second, who the hell *types* a suicide note?"

Mallory shrugged. "His wife says he typed everything. Said she has typed love letters he's sent her."

Knowing what a cold fish Delacroix was, Mac could almost believe that was true. Still, he asked, "Did you check it out? *Was* this note typed on Austin's typewriter?"

Polanski shook his head. "The typeface doesn't match. We figure he just found a handy typewriter over at the medical school. We're still checking it out."

Mac handed the note to Jennifer. She looked at it and gave an audible gasp. All eyes were suddenly on her.

She looked embarrassed. "I'm sorry. It's just that medical students are so unbelievable. Why in the world would anyone kill himself over an internship?"

The policemen seemed to believe they'd gotten all they were going to get.

"If you think of anything else," Mallory said, "give me a call." He handed Mac his card.

When they were once again alone, Mac said to Jennifer, "I should have asked how Delacroix is supposed to have killed himself."

"What do you mean, 'supposed to have killed himself'?"

He didn't answer her right away.

"Mac?"

"I was wondering if maybe Austin Delacroix was murdered."

Instantly, Jennifer became very angry. "Don't talk crazy, Mac."

EIGHTEEN

Every time Mac thought about it, he came up with a different theory. There was only one thing he could really be certain of. Annie Williams had somehow gotten too much digoxin in her bloodstream, and that had killed her. At least that much was definite.

Well, at any rate, at least that much was *probable*.

Okay, *maybe* it happened that way.

Unless, of course, the whole thing was a lab error.

Annie Williams had narcotics in her blood when she died, but that seemed incidental. She was an IV drug abuser. In the past, at least, she had taken narcotics of her own free will. And there was no evidence whatsoever that any acute drug abuse had caused her death.

Suicide seemed unlikely, but there was always the possibility that Annie had died by her own hand—accidentally. It was possible that she had grabbed a syringe thinking it had something else in it—morphine, Demerol—and she had mistakenly injected herself with a fatal does of digoxin.

Another possibility was the malpractice theory. Someone—it didn't have to be a doctor, could be a nurse, a medical student—someone had accidentally given too large a dose of digoxin and then covered up by not reporting it. No record in the chart. Nothing to incriminate the wrongdoer. That person could have been Austin Delacroix.

But if Delacroix had made the mistake, why did he then turn around and order a digoxin level?

One thing Mac *could* understand, making an error like that—a mistake that cost the life of a patient—Mac could see where that could make you suicidal. In Delacroix's case, the suicidal thoughts wouldn't be due to any empathy for the patient, but rather the social stigma and personal disgrace associated with making such a horrendous error.

First thing next morning, Mac was once again in the basement of the hospital, this time in the chemistry lab.

"Yo, Harv!"

"Yo, Mac!"

Harvey Jessup was one of the regulars Mac played basketball with. Harvey had been a star in high school, then went off to college on a basketball scholarship. Somehow, things hadn't worked out in college, and Harv had never gotten his degree, but he did get his medical technology certificate and ended up loving his work in the lab.

"Up for a little round ball tonight, Mac?"

"Sorry, can't. If I get out of the ICU at a decent hour, I've got to put in some serious library time." No sooner were the words out of his mouth than Mac felt himself wavering. After all, he did need the exercise. But he stopped himself. If he didn't get some studying in, he'd have the rest of his life free to get all the exercise he wanted. "I think there may have been a screw-up on the lab data on a patient, Harv. Maybe the samples were mixed up or something."

"Somebody messed up down here?"

"I don't know. I doubt it, though. If I could take a look at the original request slip, I might be able to sort things out."

Even in this day of computerization, when a lab test is requested, a handwritten request slip must still be filled out. Without the slip no work could be done in the lab. Pam Wang, the doctor who ran the lab, liked to explain it this way, "No tickee, no washee." She always put her hands together and did a little bow as she said it. And smiled.

"If it was in the last three days, the original

should still be in that file over there." Harvey nodded toward a cabinet not far from the lab bench where he was working.

Mac quickly found the request slip, right where it was supposed to be. He instantly recognized the handwriting—Jennifer's. In the space which asked for the requesting physician, Jennifer had written "Delacroix."

"Find what you need?" Jessup asked.

"Yeah, but I'm not certain it's going to be much help."

"What's the deal?"

Mac was hesitant about telling Harvey very much. No reason to get him caught up in Mac's paranoia. He kept the details to a minimum.

"You know Austin Delacroix?"

Harvey nodded.

"Well, he ordered a dig level of this patient. Wasn't his patient. She wasn't even supposed to be on dig. Anyway, the level comes back astronomically high. None of it makes sense."

"What's the story on Delacroix and digoxin levels?"

"What do you mean?"

"He was in here a week or so ago trying to get us to run a digoxin level on some patient who had died. I told him we didn't have any serum left over to run the test, and he got real huffy. I told him to go talk to Dr. Wang if he had a problem with that. What a jerk."

"You remember the patient's name?"

Harvey shook his head. Then he said, "I remember it was a famous name, though."

"Havlicek?"

"That's it."

Now, *that* was an interesting bit of information.

"It might not be such a bad idea," Mac said, "to see if there's any extra serum around on *this* patient to recheck her digoxin level."

"What's the name?"

"Annie Williams."

"The shooter?"

Mac nodded his head.

"Forget about it. Every time they sent blood down on her, we had to call up for more. They always wanted more tests than they had blood—'cause she was real short on veins. I assure you, any blood we ever had on her we've long since used."

It was a common problem. Intravenous drug abuse was very hard on veins. For the narcotic addict, this meant it was increasingly difficult to find a site to inject drugs. Sometimes they would literally run out of veins they could use. In the hospital, difficulty finding veins could limit the number of lab tests which could be ordered.

So there was no way they'd ever be able to double-check to see if Annie Williams ever really had a digoxin blood level of ten. It could have been a lab error. It could have been blood from another patient. No one would ever know for sure.

So Mac decided to follow up his new lead. Havlicek.

Mac tried very hard not to regard the people in medical records as The Enemy. Keeping up with the hospital paper chase was nearly impossible, and overall they did a pretty good job, everything considered.

"I'd like to see the chart on John Havlicek, please."

"Is he a patient at this hospital?"

Mac took a deep breath. If Havlicek hadn't been a patient, why in hell would Mac be down here asking to see his chart? And Mac wasn't going to let himself fall into the old trap of telling her that the patient was deceased. You did that, and she'd send you straight down to pathology. In Mac's experience, charts were almost never in pathology.

Mac smiled and answered simply, "Yes."

"Hospital number," she said.

Mac theatrically sorted through a stack of three-by-five cards. "I'm afraid I must have misplaced it."

That earned him a chilling glare as the woman moved over to her computer. She would now have to enter the name Havlicek.

Mac anticipated the next problem. "H-A-V-L-I-C-E-K," he spelled.

The woman studied her computer screen. "First name."

"J-O-H-N or J-A-N."

"Which?"

"Either." It was akin to pulling teeth.

"It's signed out."

"Who has it?"

"Delacroix."

Probably not anymore, Mac surmised. "Thank you," he said.

With any luck, Mac would quickly be able to find the chart. When charts were signed out to physicians, unless otherwise specified, they were supposed to be left on a shelf in the medical records department. Areas of the shelves were alphabetized, and charts were filed under the physician's last name. Medical students were relegated to a lower status. There was a single, all-purpose slot marked MEDICAL STUDENTS.

John Havlicek's chart was, remarkably, right where it was supposed to be.

"When you're done, put that chart right back where you found it!" The woman at the counter had been carefully watching him.

"Yes," Mac said, "thank you for reminding me." He admired his self-restraint. You're a saint, Mac. Your reward awaits in heaven.

Mac quickly found what he was looking for,

Havlicek's EKG's and rhythm strips, the recordings of his heart's rhythm. The EKG done on Mr. Havlicek's admission to the hospital was essentially normal for his age. But the ones done in the ICU were anything but normal. The tracings were entirely consistent with digoxin poisoning. On the other hand, the rhythm changes were quite nonspecific. You could see the same changes in someone who wasn't on digoxin.

Still, Mac was suspicious.

But his beeper went off, and Mac knew he'd have to put his suspicions on hold for a while. He called up to the ICU and talked to Laura Rubenstein.

"Where the hell are you, Mac?"

"I'm in the dean's office. He wants me to bypass my internship next year and join the faculty right away. He says there's nothing more they can teach me."

"I need you, McCall."

"Nice to hear you finally admit it."

"Sharon Bailey's on her way back down to the ICU. It looks like she's septic again."

NINETEEN

"You've really done it this time, Sharon Bailey," Mac said.

She didn't hear him. She was beyond that. The various technicians, doctors, and nurses crammed in around her bedside nodded agreement. This time they might just be too late.

She was unconscious, unresponsive to painful stimuli. Her breathing was shallow, agonal. They were about to put her on a respirator. Her kidneys had quit. And of course she had no detectable blood pressure.

This time she'd really done it.

And there was a new twist. Mac was the first to spot it. Initially, it had seemed insignificant. Just a small red mark on her left hand. But it increased in diameter, became more angry-looking, and then there was a new skin lesion on the right foot. Again, quite innocuous at first, but slowly progressing, then more rapidly.

As they watched over the ensuing hours, the

small red lesions progressed to large purple blotches, then blisters. It became apparent that deeper, underlying tissues were involved in the process. It was, as Yogi said, déjà vu—all over again. She was beginning to look for all the world like Ivar Bergstrom, the patient who had died of gangrene.

The infection was overwhelming. Nothing they did seemed to have any effect whatsoever. The surgeons were called but had nothing to offer. Six hours after she was transferred back to the ICU, Sharon Bailey was dead.

The psychiatry ward which had housed Sharon Bailey was a so-called locked ward. Either entering or leaving the ward required the approval of the attendant who carried the key. It always made Mac feel uncomfortable, hearing the lock turn behind him.

"Hi, Lois. I was hoping I'd find you here."

Lois Brown, the psychiatric social worker, was sitting behind the main desk tending to her charting. She smiled back at Mac. "How's Sharon doing?"

Mac shook his head. "She finally got what she wanted."

"Oh, no. She died?"

Mac nodded. "Nothing we did seemed to help."

"You know that wasn't what she wanted at

all," Lois said. "She didn't *want* to die. All she wanted was attention."

"Of course. But what a dangerous way to ask for attention." Mac sighed. "Now the one who's really going to need attention is Tiffany."

The first thing Mac thought of, after Sharon Bailey died, was her little daughter and how very difficult this would be for her. Not only a terrible sense of loss, but, more than that even, the intense feeling of guilt her mother had instilled in her.

Mac had first checked the waiting area just outside the entrance to the ICU to make certain the little girl wasn't sitting there all alone. She wasn't. Then he headed up to the psychiatry ward, hoping he'd run into Lois Brown, knowing that little Tiffany would require a great deal of support for a very long time.

"Has Tiffany been around at all today?"

"No," Lois said, "I assume she's in school." She thought a minute. "I'll look into who's going to be caring for her now and start planning how we're going to break the news to Tiffany. It's not going to be easy."

"One other thing," Mac said, "I wonder if I could have a look at Sharon Bailey's room?"

Lois had to find the key. Not only was the main entrance to the ward locked, but many individual patient rooms were locked as well. In the case of Sharon Bailey, this was done for her own protection.

The inspection of the small room didn't take long. The first place Mac looked was under the sink. Just as before, he found a syringe.

"How do you suppose this got here?" he asked.

Lois shrugged. "She seemed to be doing so well. We let her go out on pass. She was supposed to be watched by her friends, but, in the end, if someone's bent on hurting themselves, there's not too much you can do—unless you strap them to a bed and post a guard. That's not the way we do things anymore."

Mac thanked her for her help, then left Lois to the difficult job of trying to guide Tiffany Bailey through her impending emotional crisis. Mac, syringe in hand, headed for the microbiology laboratory.

Jake, the head microbiology tech, looked like he was about to leave.

"Might have an interesting gram stain for you, Jake." Mac brought him up to date on Sharon Bailey's history.

"You're looking for clostridia again?"

Mac nodded.

"Lightning's not going to strike twice in the same week, Mac."

But Jake was hooked. He made a gram stain for examination under the microscope and set up the appropriate cultures to see what bacteria might grow.

Jake had spent only a few seconds looking through the microscope before saying, "You sure called this one, Mac." He stepped back to let Mac have a look.

The microscope field was filled with small blue rectangles. You never knew for certain until the culture was evaluated, but the bacteria certainly looked like clostridia.

"The intriguing thing is," Jake said, "this looks like a pure culture. How would she have gotten hold of that?"

Mac didn't have a clue. "Any break-ins down here? Any strangers walking around?"

"Not that I know of."

It was all very peculiar—and worrisome. "Did you get the final ID on Bergstrom's clostridium?"

"Just what we figured. It was a *C. septicum.*"

At autopsy, Mr. Bergstrom had been found to have a carcinoma of the large bowel. As soon as they'd heard that, Mac and Jake had been able to guess which species of clostridium had caused his death—*Clostridium septicum*—an organism with a peculiar propensity to cause severe infection in patients with underlying tumors.

"You ever hear of a Munchausen's patient developing clostridial sepsis?" Mac asked.

"Not my area," Jake answered.

"It's all very strange," Mac said.

He thanked Jake for his help and then headed back up to the ICU. At the time it didn't occur to Mac that it might have been a good idea to check the syringe for fingerprints.

TWENTY

He was driving Jennifer's car, of course. There was no way she would have let them show up at a high-society affair in his car. Not even a funeral.

"I hadn't realized that you and Austin were such close friends," he told her. She'd started crying the moment they entered the church and hadn't stopped until long after the casket disappeared into the hearse.

"What's that supposed to mean?"

Mac knew that if he didn't back off in a hurry, it would be a very long drive home. "I just hate to see you so upset."

"It's a pretty sad thing, a twenty-five-year-old guy kills himself." There was a pause before she added, "Not that you could tell it by looking at any of his so-called friends. Or his wife's family either, for that matter."

Maybe that's what made Jennifer's crying seem so out of place. Everyone else was so stoic.

Jennifer wasn't done yet. "You should have been a pallbearer."

"Let's not get into that again. Austin and I were not close at all."

"Half your class were pallbearers."

"They were all guys who'd gone to prep school with Austin—or knew him growing up."

When it became clear that only the immediate family would be attending the graveside service, Jennifer had a fit. For her it wasn't a question of kinship, but rather of class. She felt insulted, dismissed like one of the help, she had said. It had not escaped Jennifer's notice that the wives and dates of the pallbearers had all been ushered into limousines and taken to the cemetery.

Mac wasn't even certain it was appropriate for them to attend the funeral in the first place, but Jennifer didn't have any doubts. She had missed a day of work so that they could make the drive.

"What did you think of the bash back at the house?" he asked.

"It wasn't a 'bash.' It was quite tasteful. And you don't call a twenty-five-room mansion a 'house.' " Like she was never going to be able to teach Mac how to behave in polite society.

"Whatever. But I mean, how could you put on a spread like that on the day you were burying your son-in-law?"

"They have people to do all those things for

them. Besides, I thought it was nice. They knew a lot of us would be driving out from the city. It was like a responsibility they had. You wouldn't understand."

Mac chewed on that in silence. The last thing he wanted was another fight with Jennifer. Why had he let her talk him into going to the funeral in the first place? No one would have missed him if he hadn't shown up. No one would have said, *Where the hell is Mac? He should have been here.*

But the truth was, Mac had wanted to come. He thought he might learn something.

"I want you to walk through this with me one more time, Jen."

"Don't start, Mac."

"Come on. We don't have anything else to do."

Mac thought hard, trying to begin at the beginning. "The first thing we know that happened was Delacroix's trying to get a digoxin level on Havlicek. Why did he do that?"

"You said yourself, Mac. Havlicek's EKG looked like a textbook case of digoxin toxicity."

"But he wasn't on dig, and Delacroix knew he wasn't. He was Delacroix's patient." Mac thought through the whole thing once again in his mind, trying to get it right. "So why did he try to get the dig level?"

"I don't know, Mac. You tell me." With this

really bored tone in her voice that Mac tried his best to ignore.

"Next thing we know, Delacroix orders a dig level on Annie Williams. She's not even his patient. She's not supposed to be on digoxin. And what happens? Bingo. Her dig level's off the chart. Astronomically high. And of course her EKG is entirely consistent with a toxic digoxin level."

"It might have just been a lab error, Mac. Or maybe Annie just grabbed the wrong syringe. She thought she was shooting up some kind of narcotic and she got digoxin by mistake."

"Or maybe," Mac said, "somebody gave her the wrong dose of digoxin and tried to cover it up. Delacroix saw what was happening and ordered a level."

"So why did Delacroix kill himself?" Jennifer asked. "You think maybe he was the one who gave the digoxin in the first place? But if he gave the digoxin, why order a level? And why, when the level comes back high—which he knew it would—why commit suicide?"

"Maybe he didn't."

"We've been all through this, Mac. This is the whole *Beano Smith killed Austin because Austin saw Beano kill Annie Williams* thing. We both agree that digoxin is a little out of Beano's line. If he was going to kill Annie Williams, there's no way he'd do it with digoxin. And even though Annie somehow got hold of some heroin at the end, there's nothing to suggest that it caused her death."

Mac had to agree, at least to himself, that Jennifer was right about that.

"Look, Mac, Austin Delacroix is dead, and there's nothing you can do to bring him back. The police have called it a suicide and closed the case. No one's found a shred of evidence that he was murdered. Annie Williams is dead too. If somebody made a mistake and gave her a dose of digoxin she shouldn't have gotten, then that's too bad, but there's not a thing you can do about that now either—nothing that'll help Annie anyway."

Mac didn't say anything, just kept on driving. No point in getting into all the Sharon Bailey mess with Jennifer. They were almost home.

"Would you mind stopping for gas?" Jennifer asked. "It's your turn."

The way it worked, the only time they went anywhere together, they took Jennifer's car. So when they shared gas expenses, it was always for Jennifer's car.

But he found a station and started to fill the tank. Premium, unleaded. Mac started to have this sinking feeling and checked his wallet. One five-dollar bill. That was it. He stopped the pump just in time and paid the man. Jennifer wasn't too pleased.

"Five dollars worth?"

"Money's tight, Jen." She ought to understand that if anyone did.

They rode in silence till Jennifer asked, "You want to stop and get something to eat?"

Mac could feel the thinness of the empty wallet in his back pocket and was, in spite of himself, embarrassed by it.

"I have to study, Jen."

"Or," she said, "we could take a shower."

TWENTY-ONE

It was getting late, and there hadn't been much action in the ICU for several hours. Mac had the feeling he was there only to baby-sit the monitors. The patients were mostly asleep. So far as anyone knew, there were no new admissions on the way. The ICU was darkened except for the focused lighting around the central nursing station. Mac was just sitting there, watching the little blips on the screens, wondering if he dared try to slip off to the library. Then he noticed his watch. It was after midnight. The library was closed.

Sometimes, on slow nights like this, the medical students were allowed to go home. No need to hang around just for form, even if they were on call. The interns and residents had to stay, of course. That's why they got the big bucks (about three dollars an hour). But so far Ruby hadn't said anything about Mac taking off, and he wasn't going to raise the issue himself—a sign of weakness—give Ruby a chance to go on and on about how different things had been when *she* was a student.

"I think I'll go get something to eat," Mac told her. "You want anything?"

Ruby shook her head. "Don't go too far. I thought I heard a helicopter."

Ruby was always hearing helicopters.

"By actual count, Ruby, you've now heard nineteen of our last seven helicopter admissions."

"I had a sarcastic student on my service last year," Ruby replied. "Last I heard, he was trying to get into law school."

"I thought that was an old boyfriend. You've got this reputation, Ruby. Find 'em, flunk 'em, and forget 'em."

Mac gave her a little farewell smile and headed for the stairwell. The cafeteria was five floors below the ICU; Mac began climbing the stairs, floor after floor, upward.

He hadn't really lied to Ruby. If she'd wanted something from the cafeteria, he'd be headed in that direction at this very moment. But somewhere between the ICU and the stairwell the same old persisting, nagging uncertainties had once again gained the upper hand and were now pulling him relentlessly skyward.

Discussing his concerns with Ruby was not a possibility. Jennifer had taught him that. Jennifer said that Mac had become a certifiable nut case. She would no longer listen to any of his theorizing about the deaths of Austin Delacroix, Annie Williams, Jan Havlicek, and Sharon Bailey. Jennifer suggested that he call Oliver Stone, see if he could work out some kind of a movie deal.

Two doors opened onto the tenth-floor landing. One served as an exit from Ten West, the oncology ward. The door could not be opened from the stairwell side. The other door led into the old tower.

A century or so ago, the tower had been both landmark and tourist attraction. It was visible from all over the city, and people made the climb for the view. Now it was more likely to serve as the site of clandestine liaisons of a romantic nature. Most recently, Austin Delacroix had fallen from the tower to his death on the unyielding pavement below.

The hospital administration was all for sealing the door permanently, but the fire marshal would not hear of it. So in the end it had been decided to put an alarm on the door and a sign warning that it was to be used only in the event of conflagration and that—should the door be opened—the alarm would sound. Remarkably, however, persons unknown—but presumed to be medical students—were apparently quite knowledgeable in the arcane science of alarm disabling. It was well known that the alarm never functioned.

But that was then and this was now, and Mac had good reason to worry that recent events would have once again brought the tower door to the administration's attention. He stood there on the empty landing, in the middle of the night, and wondered what he was going to do if the alarm sounded. Then he reached out and grabbed the handle. And prepared himself for the inevitable blast.

And nearly jumped out of his skin.

The moment Mac touched the handle, the door opened before him. It was a toss-up who was more startled, Mac or Turner Frost.

Mac recovered first. "What's the matter, Turner? Couldn't sleep?"

"Just got out of six hours of surgery and needed a little peace and quiet. What're you up to?"

"It's a slow night in the Unit. I figured a little fresh air would wake me up." Mac wondered if he was the only one who was lying.

Mac stepped aside so Turner could get by, then went through the door himself.

"Be careful up there," Turner said. "There's—" and then the heavy metal door closed between them, and Mac was once again alone.

And it was not a pleasant feeling.

The interior of the tower was cold and dimly

lit. A rickety wooden stairway wound upward along the tower's ancient brick walls, leaving a central opening which grew ever deeper as Mac climbed higher. The staircase seemed far too narrow for comfort, and Mac found himself pressing against the outer brick wall for safety. When he looked down, it occurred to him that the tower's design allowed aficionados to think of suicide as either an indoor or an outdoor activity.

The last time Mac had made this climb, it was summer, and broad daylight. He had pledged that, should he survive, he would never again test fate with such a foolish act. It was difficult to imagine someone like Turner Frost coming up here just to relax. Mac tried not to think about what might have been going through Austin Delacroix's mind as he climbed the stairway for the last time. Dejection? Utter hopelessness? Or simply blind, helpless, psychotic depression?

At the top, the staircase became more like a ladder as it finally entered the small rectangular opening in the floor of the tower's observation level. Once you had pulled yourself onto the flooring, there was an aura of safety—that is, if you hadn't paid too much attention during your upward climb to the aging beams on which the flooring relied for support.

And it was at this highest level that Mac was

forced to confront his acrophobia face to face. The freezing wind whipped first in one direction and then the opposite, shrieking mournfully as it ripped through the tower. But what Mac feared most was not that a gust of wind might blow him out of the tower or that he would fall, through his own carelessness, through one of the gaping portals in the tower's walls. What Mac feared most, what was at the very heart of his acrophobia, was the very real possibility, the likelihood, that given the opportunity, he would succumb to the irrepressible urge to hurl himself out into the darkness.

Then, suddenly, illusion became reality, and Mac was falling.

Ice. That's what Turner Frost had been trying to warn him about. "Be careful up there," he had warned. "There's—" Ice!

But in the instant of his fall, it wasn't the drop to the street which Mac feared, it was the other thing. The ominous dark rectangle which had loomed above him as he ascended the stair was now a hole in the floor. The opening through which he had climbed was now an abyss into which he might fall.

He landed on his back, and then his head cracked against something hard. And then there was nothing.

He didn't know how long he was out. Probably not long. Probably just stunned for a few seconds. He was safely on the uppermost floor of the tower. He was okay, but he wasn't inclined to move any time soon.

And then his beeper went off.

That would be Ruby, he thought. But Ruby would keep for a couple of minutes. He had come this far. There would be no turning back until he had stared death directly in the eye.

Mac pulled himself to his feet. His back ached and was already stiffening, but it would be fine. His head throbbed violently with each beat of his heart. The headache was going to take longer to go away. He felt light-headed, and it was difficult to sort out whether that was due to his fall or the result of his recurrent, dizzying acrophobia. Mac's world was beginning to spin.

He walked carefully to one of the tower's giant portals, using the deliberate, broad-based gait of the alcoholic, then tried to steady himself against the edge of the wall. Nothing seemed willing to come into focus. There were only a few twinkling stars fifteen stories below.

What was it that allowed a man to leap into that darkness? Was it courage or despair? Insight or confusion?

Before making this climb, Mac had had the unshakable conviction that Delacroix had been killed elsewhere, perhaps hit on the head, then brought to the tower and thrown over the parapet. Now he was certain that hadn't happened.

Even for two people that would have been physically difficult, and the risk to the perpetrators would have been prohibitive.

Whatever had happened, Austin Delacroix had come to the tower voluntarily. The only remaining question, Had he been alone?

Mac's pager beeped once again. The libidinous Dr. Rubenstein was eager. She must be satisfied.

He turned and walked very cautiously, keeping a sharp eye out for lurking ice. Had Austin Delacroix himself fallen victim to the ice? Had his death been only a terrible accident?

The answer was in Mac's mind before the question was framed. People don't foreshadow accidents with suicide notes.

Typewritten notes at that.

TWENTY-TWO

"In summary," Peter VanSlyke was saying, "the patient is a fifty-two-year-old chronic alcoholic who, because of his alcohol abuse, is now suffering from end-stage liver disease. Because his shrunken, cirrhotic, nonfunctioning liver can no longer clear ammonia and various other toxic substances from his bloodstream, these substances accumulate in his brain, resulting in the condition of hepatic encephalopathy. The patient's mental condition alternates between various levels of confusion, drowsiness, and stupor. Without constant medical intervention he would long since have lapsed into coma.

"And now we are asked to give this man a second chance. We are asked to dip into the public coffers—to the tune of *at least* $100,000, and probably much more—to finance a liver transplant. It would be difficult to come up with a less appropriate use for precious public resources. Society must somehow learn to say *no*."

It had actually been Austin Delacroix's turn to present a case at the seminar, but of course that wasn't going to happen. On less than twenty-four hours' notice, Peter VanSlyke had agreed to present in Delacroix's place. Most students spent weeks preparing for such a presentation. Not Peter VanSlyke. The seminar had always provided an opportunity for people like VanSlyke and Turner Frost to showcase their brilliance. Today, Peter had a chance to demonstrate just how truly effortless it all was. His summary of the case seemed aimed more at stifling than stimulating discussion.

The room had fallen silent. There were occasional coughs and the sounds of listeners shifting their weight in their chairs in an effort to make themselves more comfortable. One or two students had already begun to gather together their belongings in anticipation of an early end to today's session.

Then, without warning, a lone voice came out of the darkness. "I believe," Mac said, "that there's a little more to the story than that."

"Oh, really?" To say that VanSlyke's tone was sarcastic would be a little like saying that Adolf Hitler was naughty.

The ensuing silence was filled with the subtle sound of all the students settling back as one into their seats. The battle had been joined.

"First off," Mac said, "there's the issue of the role played by hepatitis C."

Mac knew what VanSlyke was thinking. How the hell did Mac come to know so much about *his* patient? Mac gave Peter an encouraging smile.

"What *about* hepatitis C?" VanSlyke was stalling, clearly thrown off stride.

"The patient's blood tested positive for hepatitis C. Hep C is a cause of chronic liver disease which frequently progresses to cirrhosis and even carcinoma of the liver. It's not at all clear to me how much, if any, of this patient's liver disease is due to alcohol."

"Oh, it's not, is it?" Once again heavily laden with sarcasm. VanSlyke was stalling—probably mostly in an effort to gain some control over his brimming indignation and anger that anyone could have the audacity to challenge his carefully crafted presentation.

He received another encouraging smile from Mac.

"I didn't want to overcomplicate the history," VanSlyke was clearly on the defensive. He was groping. "The patient does have a history of intravenous drug abuse many years ago. Presumably, that's when he acquired the hepatitis C virus. The drug abuse is just one more reason why he shouldn't be transplanted."

"But," Mac argued, "if his liver disease is due

to hepatitis C, and he's no longer abusing alcohol or other drugs . . ."

"People with hep C shouldn't be transplanted anyway. There's too much likelihood that the virus will persist and destroy the new liver." VanSlyke was making up the rules as he went along.

"Do the transplant surgeons agree with that?" Mac asked.

"Asking a surgeon if someone is a candidate for surgery is like asking a barber if someone is a good candidate for a haircut. There's a big conflict of interest. My point is, *someone* has got to be able to say no."

"And that *someone* is you?" Mac couldn't resist giving the knife one last turn. VanSlyke had no business modifying the case history to meet his own needs. The whole point of the seminar was to look at all sides of complicated issues.

But VanSlyke continued as though he hadn't heard Mac's comment. "Besides, even if the patient has given up drinking—which I doubt—there's no support structure for him. When he leaves the hospital—*if* he leaves the hospital—there's no one out there for him. Just his old drinking buddies to return to. I would estimate his risk of recidivism at near one hundred percent."

Mac resisted the temptation to say, Oh *would* you? He figured he'd inflicted enough pain for the time being. People like Peter VanSlyke got so overinflated, you just had to stick a pin in them once in a while. You were actually doing them a favor.

From the look he was receiving, Mac was pretty certain that VanSlyke didn't share his point of view. There was no real sense of appreciation being conveyed at all.

"So, here we are once again." It was Dr. Law's voice which finally penetrated the silence. "How best to shepherd precious resources? This seminar has been revisiting this question for more than thirty years, and with each generation of students the facts change but the issue remains the same. Too little supply, too much demand.

"For the cost of a single organ transplant we could vaccinate ten thousand children. The politicians tell us we lack the funds to do both.

"Should we outlaw certain treatments for the sole reason that they are too expensive? Or should we decide that only certain people are worthy of that expense? Is the patient with an inherited disorder such as Wilson's disease more worthy of liver transplantation than an alcoholic or drug addict? And who is to make these decisions? Physicians? Politicians?"

Mac had been attending the seminar for less than a year now, and he already had a fatiguing sense of the perennial nature of these questions. He wondered how Law, after all these years, could possibly maintain his interest and enthusiasm for the chronically insoluble.

As the seminar broke up, Mac found that Peter VanSlyke's concerns were far more mundane and immediate. "From now on, McCall, keep the hell out of my cases."

"But they're so fascinating. And besides, if I hadn't read the chart, I wouldn't have had any appreciation for your creative talents. You've got a real future in the world of fiction."

VanSlyke's face reddened and his voice shook. "You've been warned, McCall. I'm the last guy in the world you want to have as an enemy." And with that he turned and started to walk away.

"Peter," Mac said.

VanSlyke stopped and looked back over his shoulder.

Mac threw him one last captivating smile. "Have a nice day."

VanSlyke's face reddened yet another shade. "Bullocks!" he screamed.

Bullocks?

TWENTY-THREE

If Mac had been ranked in, say, the middle third of his medical school class instead of at the top, he would likely have been one of those students the faculty never noticed. He was not the type who asked a lot of questions in class. He wasn't much of a joiner—which meant he didn't have a lot of extracurricular interactions with faculty. And he certainly wasn't one of those who solicited private conferences with faculty members as a means of self-promotion.

So when he entered the office of Professor Arthur Sterling Law that evening after the seminar, it was for the first time—and Mac was duly impressed.

Where other faculty offices tended toward metal cabinetry and laminates of wood by-products, Law's office conveyed the same elegance as his home: a luxuriant mix of thick pile, sumptuous leather, and exotic woods. The paneled walls were laden with plaques and certificates indicating that Law had been the recipient of nearly every conceivable honor which the medical profession had within its power to bestow.

The desk, though vast, was a perfect fit for the Great Man sitting behind it, as if he'd visited a tailor who specialized in mahogany. And the desktop was as fastidiously maintained as the man. The only book on its surface was one of the large leather-bound volumes in which, everyone knew, Law kept meticulous records of every patient ever presented at his ethics seminar. Companion volumes occupying a nearby shelf chronicled the seminar's history back through the decades of its existence. It would be fascinating, Mac thought, to thumb through those early records and see what ethical concerns had preoccupied students thirty years ago.

"Well, Mac, you're certainly not a frequent visitor to this office," Dr. Law said. "I trust that there is nothing seriously amiss."

"I guess I'm not sure, Dr. Law."

Professor Law sat across that vast expanse of polished wood, white-haired and dignified—a man whose very arrival could hush an auditorium full of colleagues—and waited patiently to hear the troubles of yet another student.

"It's about Austin Delacroix," Mac said.

"I thought it might be." Law awaited patiently, then added—by way of encouragement, "You're not the first to express concern."

Mac wasn't certain where to begin. "He was the last person in the world I thought would ever commit suicide."

"Appearances," Law said, "can be quite deceiving. Behind that brave facade which Austin displayed to the world lurked a very unhappy young man."

"But a *typewritten* note with a claim that he couldn't get the internship he wanted? I mean, that's a little difficult to swallow."

"If you're suggesting that his death was anything other than a suicide, that's simply not the case. The police have made a very thorough investigation. On the other hand, if you're saying that there was more to this than a concern about his internship, I'm very certain you are quite correct."

"Was it true, though? Was Austin Delacroix really not going to be allowed to stay here for his internship? He's, what, the number three student in the class?"

Law seemed to hesitate, as though uncertain how much he should divulge.

"Let me answer you this way. Sometimes we discourage even our very best students from staying here for internship and residency—especially if we feel that they may want to later return here and join the faculty. The experience away can be very enriching."

"It's just that I'm so sure there's more to his death than that."

"As I said, I am quite certain that you are correct on that point."

"Austin came to visit me just before his death. We weren't close. We were never together socially except by accident. He had never even been in my apartment before. But for some reason he sought me out. There was something he wanted to tell me."

Mac's mind drifted back to that day, trying to glean some insight into Austin Delacroix's actions.

It was the sound of Professor Law's voice which jerked him back to the present.

"What?"

"I'm sorry?" Mac's mind had strayed far away. He didn't have a clue what Law was after.

"What was it that Austin wanted to tell you?"

"Oh. I don't know. He suddenly just got up and left when my back was turned. He must have changed his mind. Or lost his nerve."

There was silence again. This time it was Mac who wasn't certain how much to divulge. Finally, he said simply, "There's something else."

Where to begin? "There was a patient, Annie Williams, who died of digoxin toxicity—and she wasn't even supposed to be on dig."

"I heard something about that," Law said. "The chief of medicine investigated the matter fully and concluded that the laboratory had made an error. Another patient in the hospital at the same time did in fact have an elevated level. It is believed that a test tube became mislabeled."

"I didn't know anyone had looked into it."

"We don't hide from our mistakes, Mac, but there's not much point in getting everyone upset before we know the facts. These kinds of issues come up from time to time. We try to investigate them in as quiet and unobtrusive a manner as possible." The issue was closed as far as Law was concerned.

"But why did Austin order a digoxin level in the first place?"

"My understanding is that the unfortunate young woman's cardiac rhythm was entirely consistent with an elevated digoxin blood level. I was told that she had not been Austin's patient, so he ordered the test without knowing that digoxin toxicity was not a possibility. Then the unfortunate lab mix-up occurred. A matter of coincidence, nothing more."

"There was another patient," Mac said, "That Austin Delacroix tried to get a digoxin level on."

"I would guess that there were several other such patients whom Austin encountered in the pursuit of his normal duties. Surely there is nothing sinister in that?"

"This was a patient who had died."

"If you are concerned, Mac, give me the patient's name and I'll see that it's looked into."

Mac could feel the ground he was standing on become shakier with each passing second.

"No, that's all right, Dr. Law. I've taken up far too much of your time already." Mac stood up, ready to leave. He desperately needed to gather his thoughts, a chance to fall back and regroup.

Professor Law stood as well. "Listen, Mac. A word of advice. Austin Delacroix's unfortunate death has taken a toll on many of your classmates as well. That's only to be expected. Sadly, he was a very weak young man. Brilliant but weak."

"You're in your final months of medical school. You have compiled a record to be envied, and you have a very bright future ahead of you. But it's very easy to become distracted. Life is full of unexpected twists and turns—and, yes, tragedies. You must not allow your career to become waylaid.

"The best thing in times like this is to throw yourself into your work. It's what I've always done, and I've never regretted it. Above all, don't allow these types of concerns to become an obsession. I've seen it happen to students before, and it always ends badly."

Law came out from behind his desk and offered his hand to Mac. With his other hand he gave Mac's shoulder an affectionate squeeze.

"And remember, Mac, my door is always open. And if you'd like for me to arrange for you to speak with someone else—professionally, I mean—I would be quite happy to work that out as well."

Mac assured him that wouldn't be necessary. All he needed now was for Dr. Law to think he needed psychiatric support.

Law's office door had one of those hinges that closed it automatically. As Mac left, he noticed that the door didn't quite close completely. There wasn't that satisfying click at the end.

Perhaps that was Law's way of letting you know, literally, that his door was always open. Or maybe it was a metaphor. The door was not yet closed on the Austin Delacroix suicide.

Or maybe, just maybe, what it meant was that the hinge needed to be repaired.

TWENTY-FOUR

Mac's first thought: This is not the same woman. Excuse me, I'm here to see the Widow Delacroix. I believe she's expecting me.

Then he decided that, despite calling ahead to arrange the meeting, he'd still managed to arrive at an inconvenient time. She was obviously dressed to go out. Someplace fancy.

"Hi, Mac!" she said with a great deal of enthusiasm. "I'm so glad you dropped by." Apparently there had been no mistake. He was expected.

She turned to lead him through the house, and he noted that her dress was cut even lower behind than in front. He followed her well-tanned back across the paneled entry hall and through a set of double doors into a cozy front room overlooking the small park across the street. A freshly laid fire was crackling away in the marble fireplace.

"I know how hard you guys work," Eleanor

Delacroix said. "You never have time to eat. So I had Cook make up some hors d'oeuvres.

"Oh, and I made a pitcher of martinis."

Uh-oh.

Mac took the seat she indicated on the couch and accepted the canapé she offered. When she bent over in her low-cut dress to present the tray of hors d'oeuvres, the accompanying visual effect was quite invigorating.

"Those little things on the bottom are really delicious," she said.

I'll bet, he thought.

"What an extraordinary house this is," Mac said. It looked like the kind of place Arthur Law might buy, if he was ever able to scrape together enough money.

"It feels so empty now. This place really needs a man to make it feel like a home."

Oh, my.

"I'm so sorry about Austin," Mac said. "I felt terrible that I bothered you that day. Of course, I didn't have any idea what had happened. Now I feel like I'm intruding once again."

"Don't be silly, Mac. I'm glad you called. I'm sure I didn't give you a very good impression, all that crying and slamming the door in your face. It's just that I felt so betrayed."

Betrayed?

"I wanted to ask you about Austin, Eleanor.

I hope you don't mind. I'm still trying to make some sense out of what happened."

She had gotten up to retrieve the pitcher of martinis and now bent over in front of him to pour.

"One olive or two?" she asked.

"Both," he said. Then, recovering, "I really shouldn't have anything to drink. I've got several hours of reading still ahead of me tonight."

"Nonsense. All work and no play—as they say."

Eleanor Delacroix poured herself a drink and began to sip thoughtfully. "About Austin, there's really not all that much to understand. He was weak, and he was unhappy. I think it was the lack of strength which was his greatest source of unhappiness."

"In what way 'weak'?"

"In every way. He refused to stand up to my family. He let Peter VanSlyke and Turner Frost order him around. I'm afraid he even let me walk all over him. No woman can respect that."

"But he had so much going for him. He was at the top of his class. A great future ahead of him. He had all this." Mac made a gesture which was meant to encompass the town house and everything in it.

Then, so she wouldn't think he had included her as Austin's chattel, he added, "And a beautiful wife." As soon as the words were out of his mouth, he knew they would be misconstrued.

"Not anymore," she said. "I mean, I'm not a wife anymore." With a bit of a smile just at the end.

"Was there something troubling Austin? Something in particular that was going on at the hospital?"

"Something was always troubling Austin. And he never did anything about it. He just whined, or sulked. At the end he was doing a lot of sulking."

"So there was nothing in particular going on?"

"I assume there was always something in particular. I told him to deal with it and quit whining about it."

"But nothing about a particular patient, or some accident which might have occurred, say, giving a patient too much of a heart medicine or something?"

"Not that he told me about."

Mac took a sip of his martini. It wasn't bad.

"Look, Mac, we're both adults. We don't have to play games. You're in a relationship that isn't going too well."

Mac started to protest, but she interrupted.

"I hear things, Mac. I understand that you need to be discreet. I'm recently widowed, so I need to be discreet as well. All I'm saying is, there's no reason why we couldn't be discreet together."

Mac tried to let her down gently. "I'm sorry,

Eleanor. I mean, I'm flattered and all, but I'm afraid I'd always feel Austin looming over us."

"That's nonsense. The two of you hardly knew each other. Besides, if it's any comfort, Austin never liked you much. He always resented your self-confidence, how easily everything came for you. Let me assure you, if the shoe were on the other foot, Austin wouldn't have had the slightest hesitation."

Reason number twenty-seven for Austin Delacroix to commit suicide: his wife's infidelity. Maybe this wasn't her first rodeo.

Mac took a last look at the martini he'd hardly touched and stood to go. "Like I said, Eleanor, I'm very flattered, but this just isn't the right time for me."

"It may be closer to the right time than you think." Her demeanor was more angry than hurt. Then rising to her feet, she gave him one last appraising glance. She brightened slightly as she said, "Perhaps in your case I'd consider issuing a rain check."

Mac took this upbeat note as his cue to exit. "Thank you again, Eleanor, for seeing me." Then he found his way out.

As he pulled the front door closed behind him, there was a resounding metallic click.

There was a note of finality in that sound. It might have meant that the door was closed on the Delacroix suicide. Or it might have meant that he had forever shut behind him the possibility of an intimate relationship with the Widow Delacroix.

Or maybe, just maybe, what that sound indicated was that a woman of Eleanor Delacroix's affluence could fit her front door with the best goddamn hardware money could buy.

Mac turned up his collar against the cold and rain, and started down the street in the general direction of his car. If his thoughts and attention had not been turned entirely inward, he would probably have noticed the other car, might even have realized that it had been waiting there for him—waiting for him to come out of Eleanor Delacroix's town house.

When Mac turned down the street, the car— more than half a block behind him—began to inch forward, keeping pace. It was a low-slung black coupe with darkly tinted windows. The high-powered engine throbbed softly as it pulled against the clutch, as the driver waited patiently for Mac to cross the street.

Mac stepped out from between two parked cars and angled his way across the street toward his own car—still a couple hundred feet away. He had subliminally noticed the black car as he looked back over his shoulder, but didn't see any movement and presumed it was double-parked, waiting. It never occurred to Mac that it was waiting for him.

The screech of tires and engine roar came just as Mac reached the center of the street. He lost valuable, potentially life-saving time when he turned in the direction of the sound. The car was screaming toward him, perhaps no more than fifty feet away—a distance it would travel in about a second.

There was no time to think. No time to understand.

Mac didn't run; he didn't jump; he didn't yell. In that split second he simply dove—like a base-ball player sliding head-first into second base—toward the line of cars parked across the street. The force of the landing was absorbed by his chest, pushing all of the air out of his lungs. His body cried out for oxygen. Mac ignored it. He allowed his momentum to turn him into a side-ways roll, and finally came to rest under a parked car. Only then did he permit his lungs to gasp for breath.

There had been a tremendous rush of air as the car passed, but there was no pain. Mac had heard another squealing of tires and then a crash, the sound of metal being torn and bent. Then silence.

He lay on the wet pavement, trying to catch his breath, content for the moment to savor the simple truth that he was still alive and in one piece. When he finally did pull himself out from under the car, Mac saw that he was all alone on the quiet street. He began to walk slowly in the direction the car had taken, toward the sound of the crash.

Tire marks on the street showed clearly that the driver had braked hard to make a turn at the next corner, then stomped the accelerator once again. Apparently he had started to swerve, then over-corrected. He had sideswiped a couple of cars on one side of the street and then run head-on into a parked car on the other side. A crowd had begun to gather around the wreckage.

Mac saw that the driver's-side door was standing open. When he looked into the car, he saw that the ignition switch had been popped out of the steering column. The car had been stolen.

"The kid ran off that way," he heard someone say.

"Didn't look like any kid to me," someone else commented.

Mac turned back toward his own car. The police would arrive soon, but he knew nothing that would be of any help to them. Fortunately, no one had been hurt. Some kid had stolen a car, and Mac had nearly become an innocent victim.

He glanced up at Eleanor Delacroix's house as he drove by. A wry smile crossed his face. Declining Eleanor's romantic overtures had very nearly cost him his life. Somehow that didn't seem fair.

TWENTY-FIVE

When they rolled Frank Hartman into the ICU, Mac didn't immediately realize who he was. It wasn't until he noticed Peter VanSlyke and the surgical team flitting around the bedside that it occurred to Mac that this was the same patient Peter had recently presented at the ethics seminar—the man they'd been considering for liver transplantation.

Even though Mr. Hartman had been admitted to the ICU, he wasn't Mac's responsibility. He was on the surgical service. But Mac figured he'd just mosey on over to the nursing station and cop a peek at the chart. Maybe Peter needed some guidance.

Reading the chart, Mac discovered that Frank Hartman had been relatively stable until sometime around midnight, when his condition had abruptly deteriorated. The first thing that happened—kind of a blessing, really—the patient had lapsed into coma. He became unarousable. Then they realized he was bleeding.

That's when they brought Frank Hartman to the ICU and the thrash really began.

There's probably nothing much more terrifying for a patient—or his family—than to start vomiting large amounts of blood. Fortunately, Frank Hartman was already in a coma, and his family had long since abandoned him. So the only people left to be terrified were his doctors.

"If you'd get the hell out of my way, I might just be able to get this patient endoscoped *today!*" The surgical attending physician, clarifying a technical point for his chief resident.

"Goddamnit, these are *packed cells.* I told you to order *whole blood!*" The chief surgical resident, demonstrating the surgical version of the Socratic method for an eager intern.

"Draw another tube for type and cross, and if you come back with another unit of red cells I'm going to feed them to you." The ever patient intern, taking time out of a busy day to educate his students.

"McCall! Get the hell away from that chart!" Peter VanSlyke, pretending to be a surgeon.

"You still think surgeons have the same clinical judgment as barbers, Pete?" Mac, trying to promote greater understanding between Peter VanSlyke and his superiors on the surgical service.

"I warned you, McCall."

Mac ignored him. "Have you taken a look at

his coagulation profile? I'm afraid a needle and thread aren't going to do much for him."

The surgical attending tossed the endoscope in the general direction of his chief resident and grabbed the lab reports out of Mac's hand. He spent about ten seconds reviewing them before he exploded.

"Where the hell's the fresh frozen plasma? Why didn't somebody tell me about these reports?"

"Peter," Mac said, "I'll be in the Unit all day. Just give a shout if you need any more help." He started back toward the nursing station, then turned back. "Oh, and Peter, I'll be keeping an eye on you."

VanSlyke was literally shaking with anger. Mac decided against wishing him a nice day.

The question of Frank Hartman's liver transplantation became quickly moot. He continued to hemorrhage from multiple sites. There was nothing anyone could do. Within two hours of his transfer to the intensive care unit, he had expired.

Long before that happened, Mac was once again completely immersed in the needs of his own patients. It was more than forty-eight hours later before he found time to review Frank Hartman's chart. When he did, Mac felt that once again his own involvement was too little, too late.

According to the chart, Hartman had been doing remarkably well on the day prior to his admission to the ICU. The surgeons had decided that he was doing well enough to be placed on the transplant list—meaning that if a donor liver became available, Mr. Hartman would be eligible to receive it. Then all hell had broken loose.

In retrospect, it was easy to explain why Mr. Hartman had slipped into coma. He had first bled into his gastrointestinal tract, which caused the production of ammonia and other substances that his defective liver couldn't get rid of. The accumulation of these substances in his blood caused the coma. This scenario was, unfortunately, quite common in patients with liver failure. But *why* had he bled?

Patients with liver disease are prone to hemorrhage from any one of a number of gastrointestinal sites. But when they were finally able to look into Hartman's esophagus and stomach with the endoscope, what they found was that he was oozing blood from *everywhere*. There was no discrete bleeding site which was amenable to surgical repair.

Frank Hartman's problem was not that he had a specific injury to his GI tract. His problem was that his blood wouldn't clot.

"So what, Mac?" Jennifer was totally unimpressed with his sleuthing. "People with liver disease have clotting problems. Everybody knows that."

"Sure, Jen, but look at this." Mac showed her the data he'd carefully copied from Hartman's hospital record. "His coagulation profile was essentially normal just a few hours before he started bleeding. Then all of a sudden his numbers are clear off the chart."

"So it was acute, Mac. What does that prove?"

"It was *too* acute. Somebody gave Frank Hartman a truckload of anticoagulant—probably heparin."

"Why would anyone want to do that?"

"I don't know, Jen. I'm still working on that part."

They were in the bedroom. Mac had gotten home late. Jennifer had long since been sound asleep. He hadn't intended to bother her with any of this, but then she woke up, sort of. Now she was wide awake. When she sat up and turned on the light, he noticed she was naked. It was the kind of thing a guy would notice. Still, he tried his best to keep his mind on the game.

"I'm really beginning to worry about you, Mac. This isn't like you. You usually have such good common sense."

"I can't help it. There's something going on, and I'm going to get to the bottom of it."

"You know what you're saying. You're essentially saying that this guy was murdered."

"I'm saying someone gave him a push, just like someone gave Austin Delacroix a push."

"That's crazy, Mac. Just listen to yourself!" There was real anger in her voice now. "What, there's some kind of conspiracy—someone going around killing patents and medical students? I'd appreciate it if you'd give me a heads up when they start killing nurses."

Mac shrugged. It was like one of those three-dimensional magic pictures that everyone was staring at these days. You either saw what was hidden there or you didn't. You couldn't really explain it to someone else. They had to see it for themselves. He opened the drawer of a bedside table.

"What are you doing?"

"Looking for the card the detectives left when they were here."

"Mac, don't." She was pleading now. "You're making a fool of yourself."

He found the card, started to dial the number, but Jennifer pressed the disconnect button.

"Come on, Mac. At least sleep on it. There's no hurry. The man's already dead. He's not going to get any more dead."

Mac hesitated. Jennifer kicked her covers off. "Come here," she said. "Let's talk about it."

Perhaps she had a point.

TWENTY-SIX

Lieutenant Mallory stood behind his desk, a mug of coffee in one hand and the phone receiver in the other. With the coffee hand he motioned Mac into an uncomfortable-looking plastic chair. As it turned out, the chair was nowhere near as comfortable as it appeared.

The whole precinct house looked like something right out of a television series. There was a harried desk sergeant downstairs who impatiently pointed Mac in the general direction of Mallory's office. The building was probably built in the thirties and not redecorated since. Mallory's "office" was a cubbyhole which, judging from the four ancient metal desks crammed into the space, he shared with three other detectives. The elegantly attired Mallory seemed completely out of place.

"Let me explain it to you one more time, Dwayne." Mallory pronounced it Dee-wayne, his tone hanging somewhere between exasperation and abject hopelessness. "You give us the information first, and *if* we can use it, *then* you get the money." Mallory shook his head at Mac and shrugged.

"Listen, Dwayne." Mallory had to wait. Apparently Dwayne wasn't ready to listen. "Dwayne, shut up. Dwayne . . . Dwayne . . ."

Mallory took the receiver away from his ear and banged it on the desk a few times. When he put it back to his ear, he apparently had Dwayne's attention.

"Look, Dwayne, if you get the information I can go a hundred. No more. And that's only if I really like what you've got. When you get what I need, call me. Until then, be a stranger."

Mallory hung up the phone and slumped into his chair.

"The problem with Dwayne," he said, "is that Dwayne doesn't know anything. If he did, he wouldn't be bothering me with these phone calls. But Dwayne needs a fix, and he'd like the city to pay for it. The city, you see, is Dwayne's only legal source of income. We buy information from snitches like Dwayne. Sometimes I feel like the city buys half the heroin and cocaine that's sold around here.

"But if we don't pay these guys, (a) we don't get the information, (b) they get their drugs anyway, and (c) they get the money they need through the type of socially unacceptable behavior which has already earned Dwayne two tours at the state penitentiary."

Mallory looked at his watch and frowned, a gesture clearly designed to indicate that time was at a premium. "Now," he said, "how can I help you? You said something about the Delacroix suicide?"

Mac was here. There was no turning back. "How certain are you that it was suicide?"

"Very." Mallory's tone was dismissive. There was nothing more to say.

"A typewritten suicide note?"

"It happens."

"Over an internship?"

"I've heard of stranger reasons."

Mac shook his head. "I just don't believe he committed suicide."

"Frankly, and I don't mean this to sound harsh, but what you *believe* doesn't really matter. You think he was murdered, right?"

"Well, if the guy is dead and someone has forged a suicide note, murder seems the most logical explanation."

"Do you have some evidence that he was murdered?"

Mac shook his head.

"Do you have some motive, some reason why someone would want to kill him?"

"No."

"So what we've got here, we've got a guy,

you—a guy who has already told me that he didn't know the deceased very well—a guy who has a *feeling* that maybe the deceased was murdered. Is that about it?"

"There's a little more."

"I'm all ears." But as he spoke, Mallory gave his watch another long look.

Mac took a deep breath. "Before he died, Austin was investigating some deaths at the hospital."

"Malpractice? That's not our area. That's civil unless the prosecutor decides there's criminal negligence."

"No. I think we're talking murder."

"*More* murders?" Mallory made no effort to disguise his incredulity. "How many?"

"I believe four—not counting Austin Delacroix."

Mac recounted what he knew while a weary Lieutenant Mallory alternated between reluctant note taking and studying his watch. He didn't interrupt, he just let Mac drone on. Finally, Mallory had had enough.

"Look," he said, "I really don't see very much here. The first patient, Havlicek, developed this funny heart rhythm and died. You tell me that his heart rhythm could have been caused by digoxin, but could have occurred spontaneously, and there's no evidence whatsoever the man was ever near the drug.

"The Bailey woman, by your own admission,

was injecting herself with all kinds of bacteria. This last bug she got, well, we don't know how she got it, but we know there was another patient who had it. You found the syringe in her room. There's just nothing to investigate.

"Hartman bled to death. You tell me this is common in patents with liver disease. There's no evidence at all that someone harmed him.

"The one confusing patient is this Annie Williams. I'll have to think about her. But still, you tell me the hospital has already made an investigation. I doubt I'm gonna find anything more."

Mallory raised himself out of his chair. "Did I miss anything?"

"No," Mac said. "And like I told you, everything you've said is one possible interpretation of what we know. But it doesn't explain Austin Delacroix's suicide, and it doesn't explain why Annie Williams had such a high digoxin level."

"But that might have been a lab error. You admitted that."

Mac shrugged.

Lieutenant Mallory came out from behind his desk. "Look, I appreciate your coming in. I'll look into this Williams case, and if I have any questions I'll give you a call. Meanwhile, the best thing you can do is just go back to school and hit the books. All this is over, and you're not going to do yourself any good getting all worked up about it." Then he added, "And I've got a bunch of *real* murders to solve."

And then he was gone.

Ladies and gentlemen, Detective Mallory has left the building.

TWENTY-SEVEN

Mac thought back to the Disciplinary Committee meeting when Diego Valenzuela had been accused of cheating on an exam. Mac had tried, at that time, to put himself in Diego's shoes, to try to understand how Diego might have felt.

But Mac had failed miserably. He realized that now. What he'd really done was put Diego in *his* shoes. He had thought about the humiliation, the terrible waste of all those years of study. Those would have been Mac's primary concerns. But Diego, Mac now understood, had more important worries.

They had all heard about Diego's sick child—more important than his microbiology exam. But of his wife, they had heard nothing. Except that she was a nurse. And that she had been home caring for their child. There had been no mention of her own illness—of her lifelong battle with cystic fibrosis.

It was a battle which might now end at any

moment. And if it did end soon, it would not have been a battle which she had won.

Maria Valenzuela was standing beside her bed in the ICU, hunched over her bedside table, gasping for air. She was so tiny, so desperately ill, and so very, very beautiful.

"Hi, I'm Mac McCall, one of the students on the ICU team."

Maria was far too breathless to speak, but she managed a heartrending smile.

"I'll be able to get your history from the chart and your doctors—and from Diego. So I'm not going to wear you out with a lot of questions you've already answered ten times for other people."

Once again that beautiful smile. And she managed to mouth the words *thank you.*

"You just stay right like you are, and I'll have a quick listen to your chest if that's okay."

Mac gave the diaphragm of his stethoscope a vigorous rub, warming it a little to reduce the shock of the cold metal against bare skin. This earned him another gratefully mouthed *thank you.*

What Mac heard, or, rather *didn't* hear, was at least as ominous as Maria's appearance had been when he first walked into the room. Despite her efforts to maximize her breathing— standing, leaning over the table, breathing through her mouth—she was hardly moving any air at all into her lungs. It was a wonder she was conscious.

Mac tried his best to hide his concern.

"We'll be talking everything over with your pulmonary doctors," he told her, "to see what we can do to make you more comfortable as quickly as possible."

Ordinarily, Mac's initial meeting with a patient might last well over an hour by the time he'd done a complete history and physical. But in Maria's case, everything he did, every question he asked, would only be an unwarranted distraction from her need to devote all her attention and energy to the act of breathing. She was just that fragile.

"I'll check back in a little while," he told her, "to see how you're doing and to discuss the game plan we've come up with."

She gave him a look which was meant to express gratitude and encouragement but which also conveyed a sense of resignation. As he left, Mac felt a lump in his throat.

Mac carefully reviewed her chart. What he found was a rather typical chronology of her relentless disease. Over the years Maria had experience increasingly frequent bouts of infection in her lungs. Now, infection was a chronic, continuous problem, the damage to her lungs irreparable. Periods of remission, during which she might enjoy some semblance of normal activity, were now rare.

Mac thought of the young woman struggling for air in the next room and how terribly unlucky she was to have cystic fibrosis. The size of the genetic alteration which led to the disease was truly mind-boggling in its smallness. If all of Maria's genetic material was thought of as filling two rather large sets of encyclopedias, a mistake the size of a single letter on a single page could lead to cystic fibrosis. This infinitesimal mistake in genetic coding caused a tiny change in an important protein. The altered protein caused cells throughout the body to malfunction, especially in the lungs. This in turn led to repetitive pulmonary infections and progressive, irreversible destruction of the lungs themselves.

Thirty years ago, the vast majority of patients with cystic fibrosis died during childhood. Now, with advances in antibiotics and other supportive measures, more and more were living to adulthood, but only one in ten survived past the age of thirty. Recently, a new hope had appeared on the horizon—lung transplantation.

During her years of treatment, Maria Valenzuela would have come to know many other patients with cystic fibrosis. Most of them would now be dead. Such a tragic childhood. Not only her own struggle but losing so many friends, seeing her own future reflected in her friends' short lives. And to handle all of that with such grace, dignity, and courage was truly remarkable.

"Pretty rough, huh?"

Mac turned to find Karen Anderson looking over his shoulder. He had seen her notes in the chart. As a student on the pulmonary service, she had been following Maria on the ward.

"She seems so brave and uncomplaining."

Karen nodded. "And that isn't the half of it."

Mac waited expectantly.

"Two pregnancies," Karen said.

"I hadn't even thought about that." Pregnancy could be a life-threatening condition for a patient with cystic fibrosis. "I hope you're not going to tell me that Diego insisted on having children."

"No," Karen said. "I've actually gotten to know them both pretty well. It was Maria who desperately wanted children. All Diego wanted was Maria. I think she kind of tricked him."

"Women," Mac said.

Karen smiled.

"Are the kids okay?" Maria carried two doses of the cystic fibrosis gene, which was why she manifested the disease. Her children would automatically get a single dose of the gene from her. That would not be enough to cause disease. As many as one in every 2,500 people had a single dose and were perfectly healthy. But if

Diego also carried a single dose of the gene, then it would be possible for their children to have the defect which caused cystic fibrosis.

"So far as we know, the kids are fine," Karen said. "The only one we have to worry about right now is Mom."

"What's the plan?"

"For now, maximize her antibiotics and her breathing treatments, try to keep from intubating her."

Intubating meant putting a tube in Maria's throat and attaching it to a ventilator, a machine used to force air into her lungs. The problem with putting a patient with cystic fibrosis on a ventilator was that you might never be able to get her off.

"She's going to get awfully tired, breathing like that."

Karen nodded. "So far the pulmonary docs say her oxygen and other blood gasses are adequate. They think she may still turn around. She's a fighter."

"How's Diego doing?"

Karen shrugged. "It's tough. Two babies at home. A wife in intensive care. And he's trying to make it through medical school. Most of us find that difficult enough all by itself.

"And, as you can imagine, the Valenzuelas aren't wealthy people. I don't know how they make ends meet."

"What about transplantation?" It was Maria's only hope for long-term survival.

"She's been on the list, but they took her off when her condition deteriorated. The pulmonary docs think she needs to be in better shape for surgery."

Mac heard himself stating the obvious out loud: "But without surgery she may never get in better shape."

Just then they were interrupted by Laura Rubenstein. "Got a call from Dr. Law's office, Mac. He'd like to speak with you."

Mac looked at his watch. It was after six o'clock. "I'll check in with him in the morning."

Ruby shook her head. "The word 'now' was used, McCall."

Uh-oh.

Karen and Ruby were both giving him worried looks.

"Is it my fault," Mac asked, "that the man cannot make the simplest decision in his life without consulting me?"

TWENTY-EIGHT

"Have a seat, please, Mac. I need you to help me understand something." Professor Law appeared calm, but he spoke in a troubled tone of voice.

"If I can," Mac said, taking a chair.

"I've had a call from a police detective named Mallory."

Uh-oh.

"We are both very concerned about you." Dr. Law let that hang out there in the air for a while, clearly hoping Mac would make a grab at it.

For his part, Mac figured it wouldn't be such a great time for him to launch into a long, voluntary exposition. Better to see what Law had on his mind first.

"I thought," Professor Law finally said, "that we had sorted out all your . . ." he paused here, groping for just the right word, ". . . uh, *concerns* regarding the Delacroix suicide."

"We did talk, Dr. Law, and I appreciate your

taking time to discuss everything. It's just that, in the end, I still had questions. Still do."

"So it would seem, Mac. So it would seem."

Arthur Sterling Law was his usual, deliberate self. He played his cards close to the vest—always difficult to guess just exactly what he was thinking. This was one of the reasons he was so good at moderating the ethics seminar. He was able to stimulate discussion without taking sides or promoting a position of his own. But Mac had the nagging suspicion that Professor Law was about to pick a side.

"I have to confess, Mac, when you first came to me with your concerns, I thought it all a bit wild, not at all well thought through. Perhaps simply a combination of your inexperience, medically speaking, and an overly vivid imagination. But I could understand why you might be disturbed by a classmate's suicide, and the other cases, well, I had my doubts, but I didn't want to make any hasty conclusions. You brought your concerns to me, and I investigated them. And the chief of medicine investigated them. And the police have investigated them.

"All of the issues that you have raised have perfectly sensible explanations, and those explanations have been provided to you. And yet you say you still have questions. Why is that, Mac?"

"I'm just not satisfied. There have simply been far too many coincidences."

"Is there something you haven't shared with Lieutenant Mallory or myself? Is there some piece of evidence known only to you?"

Mac shook his head. He was beginning to guess where this was all headed, starting to feel like a man taking a long walk on a short pier.

"So what I am trying to come to grips with, Mac, is why a sensible young man like yourself is unable to accept such logical explanations. Everyone has already spent far too much time with all this. The facts are plain as day."

Law's tone became suddenly much more severe. "Do you feel that you know more medicine than the chief of the department?"

"Of course not."

"Then, are you more expert in police matters than Lieutenant Mallory?"

Mac shook his head.

"I've been having a look at your file." Law indicated the manila folder lying in front of him. "Your undergraduate performance was outstanding. Your work at the medical school has been equally exceptional. Personally, I have always had a very high regard for your scholarship. That is why you were invited to participate in the seminar.

"So, I have to ask myself, when a student's performance suddenly shows such a dramatic change, what might be creating the problem?"

Mac stiffened in his chair. "I wasn't aware

that anyone had suggested that my performance had changed one bit."

"Well, perhaps I chose the wrong word. This is more of a *behavior* problem."

Behavior problem?

"Tell me, Mac, have you been under any unusual pressures of late? Has there been an emotional strain of some kind?"

"Absolutely not, Dr. Law."

"Because if we can't find some underlying factor, some stress or something, to lay this all onto, how are we going to deal with the problem?"

"I guess I'm not quite understanding this, Dr. Law. Just exactly what are you calling a 'problem'?"

"As I see it, we could approach this from either of two points of view. First, are we dealing with a psychiatric problem?"

"Psychiatric problem?" Mac tried, unsuccessfully, to keep the edge out of his voice.

"Mac, this matter appears to have become a driving obsession with you. The facts are evident to everyone else, yet you persist. One has to even wonder if there might be an element of delusion on your part."

"I'm not psychotic, Dr. Law." Mac even managed to summon a slight smile as he said, "And I'm no more neurotic than the average medical student—or doctor, for that matter."

"Which leaves us with the second possibility.

That what we are dealing with is strictly a disciplinary problem."

"In what way?" The edge was back in Mac's voice. There was very much a sense of déjà vu here. He was back in junior high school, in the principal's office. Someone had tried to clean out the building's plumbing with a cherry bomb, and he was the number one suspect.

"Surely you can see, Mac, that while you're running around like a chicken with its head cut off, you're violating all sorts of school rules. Not to mention professional ethics."

"For instance." The edge was becoming sharper.

"For instance, patient confidentiality. People are entitled to come to our hospital free of any fear that their personal histories will be blabbed to the public."

"I have not *blabbed* anything to anyone. I spoke, in private, with a police detective. I believed, I still believe, that very serious crimes have been committed."

"And then there is the matter," Professor Law continued, "of the confidentiality of the ethics seminar. All of the patients you are investigating came to your attention through your participation in the seminar."

"Not *all*."

"Don't quibble with me, Mac. This is quite serious. The first thing you were told when you came to the seminar was that nothing you hear there was ever to be repeated outside the room. Otherwise, there would be an unacceptable level of inhibition. No one would feel able to speak freely. It certainly appears to me that you have violated that rule. The specified penalty is immediate dismissal from the seminar."

Mac felt all the air go out of him. He'd just received a severe body blow.

"I'm afraid there might be quite a domino effect. If you were thrown out of the ethics seminar, I don't see how you could remain on the disciplinary committee. And, of course, all of this would go into your file. I don't see any way the school could withhold the information from the various internship-selection committees you've applied to. It would be very certain to have quite a negative effect. There would be no question of your becoming an intern here. I would even go so far as to worry that, should this kind of behavior continue, your very graduation might be in doubt.

"It's just that this is such an especially difficult time for a serious problem to develop—so late in your senior year. It would be very difficult to recover from."

It had never occurred to Mac to consider his actions in this light. He believed he'd acted honorably, courageously even. Law was describing his behavior a reprehensible, despicable. Mac's anger was now gone. He felt only humiliation and fear. Fear that all that he'd worked so hard to achieve in his life was suddenly so dangerously close to slipping forever from his grasp.

"As you know, Mac, the authority to dismiss from the ethics seminar resides entirely with me. I feel it incumbent upon me to inform you that I believe your dismissal from the seminar would be entirely appropriate. The only thing that prevents me from taking that action right now is the unhappy cascade of events which would necessarily follow. I feel, at this time, that those unavoidable aftereffects would impact your career in a way which would be disproportionately negative."

Mac felt his spirits lift. Law was holding out a ray of hope.

"What I would like from you today, Mac, is your assurance that you've put all this behind you, once and for all. That there will be no repetition of this behavior. I believe that I could then feel reassured that you have been acting in good faith. You had concerns. They were satisfied. We could write your previous actions off as a momentary lapse, a youthful indiscretion."

Mac thought about this, but not for long. He had a gun to his head, and he understood that Law had it well within his jurisdiction to pull the trigger.

"I understand how all this must look to you, Dr. Law. I *was* acting in good faith, in response to some very real concerns I had." Mac heard himself say "had" as though it were someone else's voice. "I appreciate your giving me a second chance. I'll do my best not to disappoint you."

Law came out from behind his desk and offered Mac his hand. He shook it warmly, then walked Mac to the door with a reassuring arm draped around Mac's shoulders. As far as Law was concerned, this was all behind them.

Mac left, emotions jumbled, not certain what to do. He listened, subconsciously, for the fateful click of Law's office door. He thought this time he just might have heard it.

TWENTY-NINE

Mac couldn't bring himself to go straight back to the ICU. He needed to get his head together first. So he headed in the general direction of his apartment. But he didn't hurry. He wasn't all that eager to hear Jennifer's comments. She'd pretty much already told him everything Law had said. They might as well have been reading from the same script.

Mac understood how lucky he'd been. Law had granted him a reprieve. All Mac had to do was keep his nose clean until he graduated. That shouldn't be too hard.

The most difficult hurdle was behind him. Mac now accepted that he had been wrong. Not that he shouldn't have raised the issues in the first place, but that he failed to maintain any semblance of objectivity in the face of irrefutable contradictory evidence. His was, as Professor Law had said, a mistake of inexperience. Of youth.

The brief anger he had felt toward Dr. Law had totally evaporated. Had it not been for Law's insight and compassion, Mac would now be in very serious trouble indeed. Law had handled the matter quite skillfully. Mac wondered how many other students over the years Professor Law had saved from self-destruction.

Now that he had gained some perspective on the issue, Mac wondered how he could possibly have gotten so helplessly adrift in the first place. Everyone, *everyone*, had told him he was wrong. Jennifer, Law, Detective Mallory. The chief of medicine had done his own investigation. But Mac had thought that he knew better. And he had nearly paid a very dear price.

But now Mac had his pardon. He would feel some residual embarrassment for a while, but that wouldn't kill him. And in a few short months he would receive his medical degree. He had come perilously close to losing that.

Mac opened his apartment door thinking what he really needed was a drink. And a good night's sleep. Unfortunately, both were out of the question. He was supposed to be back in the ICU. He could play hooky for only so long.

A light was on in the living room. The bedroom door was closed. Good. Mac could sit and regroup and still put off talking to Jennifer— perhaps even until tomorrow.

He slumped into a chair and closed his eyes. Just for a couple of minutes, he told himself. He reached up and turned off the lamp beside the chair. He was instantly asleep.

Mac had no idea how long he had dozed. Perhaps only a few minutes. It was quite dark out. Mac tried to clear the cobwebs from his brain. He very much had the sense that he hadn't awakened spontaneously from sleep, that something or someone had awakened him.

Then, suddenly Mac was aware that he was not alone in the room. And the other person was not Jennifer.

Mac held his breath, trying hard not to make the slightest sound. He was certain that the other man thought *he* was alone in the room. It was definitely another man. That huge, dark profile was most certainly not feminine.

Mac's first thought, Was Jennifer all right? There was no sound from the bedroom.

What had wakened him? Was it a scream? A cry of pain? Mac didn't think so.

Jennifer was probably okay—if she was even in the apartment.

What time was it anyway? Mac couldn't make out his watch in the dark.

The other man was rummaging around, looking for something. Probably a burglar. Probably the last thing in the world the intruder wanted was a confrontation.

Besides, there was hardly anything in the apartment of any real value. Nothing Mac could think of that was worth fighting over—except for Jennifer. He'd just sit tight for now. The element of surprise was on Mac's side. He would spring into action if need be.

Mac tried to think what potential weapon might be lying close at hand. Too bad they weren't smokers. A heavy ashtray might be useful. If the phone had been closer, he might have tried to dial 911.

But for the time being, the most important thing was not to do anything foolish. Don't do anything that might endanger Jennifer.

There was a noise as the man bumped into something, then a muffled profanity.

"Why the hell don't you just turn on a light?" The voice belonged to Jennifer.

"I can't find the switch." Another familiar voice.

"Then why don't you just come on back to bed?" In her most alluring voice.

"Be right there."

Mac waited until the dark form had disappeared into the bedroom, then quietly left via the front door.

As soon as he got back to the ICU, he called the apartment.

"When I get off my shift tomorrow night, I'll

come home and pack up my things," he told Jennifer. "I'd appreciate it if you weren't there."

"But, Mac. Why?"

"I'd also appreciate it if George Williams wasn't there."

He slowly hung up the receiver. There really wasn't anything to discuss.

THIRTY

"How'd it go?" Laura Rubenstein wanted to know.

Mac stared at her, wondering how she possibly could have known about Jennifer's infidelity. For several seconds it didn't even occur to him that she was asking about his meeting with Law.

"Oh, just fine," Mac finally replied. "He's got to give a speech before the National Academy of Sciences. He just wanted to get my opinion. Could have waited till morning."

Ruby gave him The Look.

"How's Maria doing?" Mac asked, seeing the crowd gathered near her room.

"Terrible. They're trying to decide whether or not to put her on a ventilator."

Mac eased past the gaggle of pulmonary specialists and surgeons who were gathered outside Maria's door, debating her future. He found her all alone in her room.

Maria was able to breathe more efficiently

when she was upright, but she no longer possessed the strength to stand or even to sit up. So they'd cranked the head of her bed up as high as it would go and put pillows behind her back. She was wearing a face mask to provide humidified, oxygen-rich air. Ruby was right. She looked terrible.

Her eyes were closed in concentration. Her hair and face were damp. Every ounce of strength her body possessed was being summoned to accomplish the task of breathing. Maria had long since enlisted her abdominal muscles to assist in the breathing process, and with each shallow respiration her entire torso undulated.

Maria's eyes opened just slightly. Mac had no idea if she could see him or, at this point, whether she was even at all aware of her surroundings. He gave her a supportive smile but saw no response. He didn't want to disturb her. All of her energy resources had to remain dedicated to satisfying the demands of respiration.

Mac turned and joined the ten or so physicians and staff who had assembled to make the difficult decision. There were two medical students in the group, Karen Anderson on the pulmonary team and Peter VanSlyke with the surgeons. The surgeons were involved because of the possibility of lung transplantation.

The question was straightforward; the answer

was not. Unless Maria was intubated and placed on a ventilator, she would not survive the night. There was no doubt that the ventilator would be life-saving—in the near term. But would it, in the end, only prolong her agony?

Maria's disease process was so far advanced that she might never improve enough to survive *without* the respirator. Allowing her to survive tonight only to spend a few additional days or weeks on a respirator might not be a true act of kindness. On the other hand, the respirator would give her a chance to rest and save her energy. The pulmonary therapists would be able to use the artificial airway to suction harmful secretions from her lungs. She just might improve and survive this crisis. Maria might get a few more weeks, or even months, of meaningful time to spend with her husband and babies.

And there was one more kicker. Maria Valenzuela was now on the transplant list. If a donor became available, a lung transplant could give her *years*. A suitable donor might become available this very night, or might never be found within Maria's lifetime. All that was necessary was for someone with healthy lungs—and a reasonably good tissue match—to die. Somebody had to die in order that Maria Valenzuela might live.

The discussion had obviously been going on

for some time. Mac didn't notice Diego Valenzuela until he spoke.

"Maria and I have discussed this over and over," he said. "Now that she's on the transplant list, she wants to be kept alive as long as it takes—until a suitable donor is found. She has two little children who need their mother to help them grow up. It's not just *her* life we need to consider." Diego was trying to remain unemotional and doing a pretty good job of it. His voice broke just slightly at the end.

It was an extremely stressful situation for everyone involved, but being handled with remarkable equanimity. Until Peter VanSlyke ventured an opinion.

"Intubating this woman at this time would be nothing short of a criminal act."

It was the kind of extreme posturing which might be acceptable at the ethics seminar. But not in the real world. Not in front of a family member. Mac briefly caught Karen Anderson's glance. She rolled her eyes in disbelief.

For his part, Diego Valenzuela was no longer in control of his emotions. He trembled as he spoke. His voice shook. "No one gives a damn what you think, VanSlyke. You're a medical student. I don't want you involved in any way in my wife's care. If I hear that you've been in her room, if you attempt to examine her, I'll file assault charges. You're not to go near her. If you do, I'll do everything in my power to prevent you from ever getting a medical license."

For the briefest instant it appeared as though VanSlyke was gathering himself for a response. Then he thought better of it. He turned and walked out of the ICU.

Art Smith, the pulmonary attending physician, said, "These difficult decisions put a great deal of pressure on everyone. Maybe we should take a break and meet again later to decide."

Valenzuela was tired of talking. "The decision has been made. I want my wife intubated. Now. If you're not going to do it, say so right now, so I can have my attorney go wake up a judge and get a court order. You just better hope she doesn't die waiting to be put on a ventilator!"

Art Smith hesitated but not for long. Mac could tell that Smith didn't like being threatened. On the other hand, he didn't really have much choice at this point.

"I think we all understand the issues," Smith said, "and a good case can be made for either intubating or deciding not to. Since Diego and Maria are firm in their decision to go forward with the ventilator, that's clearly what we should do." Speaking directly to Diego, he said, "If you and Maria had decided against intubation, I would have supported that decision as well."

Diego only nodded, unable to trust his voice.

He left the group and returned to his wife's bedside.

Mac became busier and busier as the night wore on. Two new admissions plus Maria to look after. It was just as well. The issue with Professor Law had been resolved. And as far as Jennifer and George Williams were concerned, there was really nothing to think about. That ship had sailed.

THIRTY-ONE

All Mac hoped for, as he opened his apartment door the next evening, was that Jennifer wouldn't be there. Mac didn't want a scene. It was over. He just waned to grab his things and leave.

Where he would go, he wasn't so sure. Probably just some motel tonight. Then try to find a more permanent place over the weekend. What he really needed was a roommate, preferably male. Otherwise, he had no idea how he would make ends meet between now and graduation.

Until yesterday he could have counted on George Williams for a place to stay in an emergency. At least a couch to sleep on and a place to take a shower. Now there was no one. Maybe the Widow Delacroix. She might be able to find a comfortable spot for him. But that wasn't Mac's style.

So he hoped that Jennifer would at least have the grace not to be there when he opened the door. But it wasn't to be.

There she was, sitting in a chair, waiting for him to get home. Mac noticed some filled boxes and a couple of suitcases ready to go.

Jennifer looked like she was dressed to go on a trip. She didn't exactly look like she'd been crying her eyes out for the last twenty-four hours.

"I thought it made more sense for me to leave than you," she said. Not exactly apologetic.

Mac shrugged. "Where will you go?"

"I've found a place. Across town. I've already taken a bunch of stuff over there."

Mac noticed one or two things missing. He wondered if she'd had help. But most of their furniture was rented with the apartment.

"I know I haven't been keeping up my share of the rent, Mac, so I saw the manager today and paid up through the end of May. We paid the first and last month when we took the lease, so that will get you through graduation."

"I hate to think of your getting deeper in debt, Jen." The reason Jennifer hadn't been paying any rent was that she was spending the money on other things. The only way she could have gotten this kind of money was to max out one of her credit cards with a cash advance.

Or maybe she'd saved some money on that new apartment she'd found. Maybe Jennifer would be the one staying with George Williams. And not on the couch.

"Don't worry about me," she said. "I'm learning to manage my money better. And I think I may have a line on a new job, outside of nursing. A lot better money."

"If I'm going to be staying here," Mac said, "I think I'll pour myself a drink." He offered Jennifer one, but she wasn't interested. Said she needed to be going.

Mac found the bourbon right where it was supposed to be, but noticed he was going to be a little short on glasses between now and graduation. He didn't say anything.

"Mac," Jennifer said, "we weren't going anywhere. It just wasn't going to work." Then she added, "You're years away from where I want to be."

He wasn't sure what that was supposed to mean. How was George Williams supposed to be any closer to anything than he was? Maybe she thought that, in a few years, he'd grow up to be George's height. Mac didn't say anything. Just sipped his bourbon.

"Look, Mac, I'm sorry. All right?" They locked eyes for the first time. Then she added, "It's not like you haven't had any outside interests."

"If you're saying that I've been fooling around, Jennifer, you're wrong. I haven't."

"Well, I'm sure you've thought about it plenty of times."

Mac started to reply, then decided that Jennifer's comment didn't deserve an answer. He sipped a little more bourbon, just trying to get through this without making some angry or hurtful remark. It was over. They should try to get through this with as much dignity as possible. Try to be civilized.

Then Jennifer suddenly shifted gears. "You've got to get over this obsession you have with Austin Delacroix's suicide and those other deaths. People are beginning to talk."

"Who?"

"Everybody. A lot of people think you're acting pretty nutty, Mac."

"I've promised to be a good boy in the future."

"Promised who?"

"Doesn't matter. I realize now that I overreacted. I was probably hit harder by Austin's suicide than I was willing to admit—even to myself. He was my age, a classmate. We were under a lot of the same stresses. I'm sure it hit closer to home than I thought."

"I'm glad to hear you've had a change of heart, Mac."

Jennifer rose from the chair and crossed the room. Mac just stood there, holding his glass. They were only inches apart. Mac knew from experience where this was headed.

"I'm sorry, Mac," she said, looking up into his eyes. "I really am."

"I'm sorry too, Jennifer, but this just isn't going happen."

She shrugged and gave him a weak smile. "You can't blame a girl for trying. For auld lang syne."

"Maybe I'd better help you with your things," he said.

They made a couple of trips to the car. She'd already gotten most of her stuff. Finally, he put her in the driver's seat and shut the door behind her. She rolled down the widow.

"Good-bye, Mac."

She looked like she wanted a kiss good-bye, at least on the cheek, but Mac couldn't let himself do it.

"Why don't you give me your new address and phone number," he said, "in case I need to get hold of you?"

"I don't have a phone number yet. I left the address upstairs." Then she added awkwardly, "Beside the bed."

"Good-bye, Jennifer."

And she drove off into the night.

Upstairs, Mac found the pad with her new address written on it. It was in a yuppie area of town. Trendy. Expensive. He could be pretty certain that George Williams wasn't going to be her new roommate—not unless he was going into hock with her.

Mac finished his bourbon, then poured himself another. He refused to feel sorry for himself. His problems were mostly of his own making. And besides, they looked pretty minuscule alongside the burdens which Maria and Diego Valenzuela were carrying.

THIRTY-TWO

For now at least, Maria Valenzuela was much better. Once the desperate work of breathing had been turned over to the ventilator, she'd finally been able to rest. This morning she was bright-eyed and very interested in everything that was going on around her. She communicated with hand signals and by writing notes. Mac thought that Maria was as beautiful as any woman could possibly be with a breathing tube stuck down her throat.

The lower end of the endotracheal tube was in her chest, in the upper portion of the airway. It extended up through her throat and out her mouth. At that point another piece of tubing connected the endotracheal tube to the ventilator. The ventilator made periodic soft, whooshing sounds as it forced oxygen-enriched air into her lungs.

Mac listened carefully to her chest and felt her pulse. It was much stronger this morning.

"You're doing a whole lot better, aren't you?" he asked.

She gave him a thumbs-up sign and tried her best to smile—a pretty difficult feat with that tube in her mouth.

Maria now had a new intravenous line which entered a central vein in her chest just below the clavicle. This would make it possible to increase her nutrition and give her antibiotics without having to constantly change IV lines in her arms. Also, there was now a catheter in the radial artery of her right wrist. This could be used to measure oxygen and other arterial blood gasses without having to do a new needle stick every time.

If all went well, in a few days Maria would be in maximum shape for a lung transplant. All she needed was a donor.

Maria gestured to Mac that she wanted to write a note. He handed her a notepad and pen, pretty certain in advance what she wanted—the same thing she'd been asking everyone. She quickly passed the note back to him.

"When can I see my babies?"

"I think we can probably work that out," he told her, "but we have to be very careful. Your babies could bring in a virus or something which could be bad for one of the other patients in the unit. We'll try to work something out."

She nodded and tried not to look too discouraged.

"I'll be back to check on you later," Mac promised as he left.

Coming out of the room, Mac saw that the code which had been going on for an hour or so on the other side of the ICU was finally over. He had offered to help out when it all started, but Ruby had waved him off. Too many helping hands already, she had said. From the look of things, it hadn't gone well.

Turner Frost had scrunched himself up at one end of the nursing station to review lab values and make a final note in the chart. Mac sat down beside him.

"Didn't make it, huh?" Mac asked.

Frost shook his head. "This guy'd been living on borrowed time for a couple of years. Been on the transplant list for more than a year."

"Heart?"

Frost nodded. "A couple of weeks ago he came to the end of the line as far as medication was concerned. He got admitted for a balloon pump. There's been nothing but trouble ever since."

The intra-aortic balloon is a device which is inserted into the aorta to reduce some of the workload of a failing heart. It is connected to a mechanical pumping device at the patient's bedside. As long as the balloon is in place, the patient must lie in bed with tubing entering an artery, usually in the groin, connecting the pump at his bedside to the balloon next to his heart. The system works remarkably well—for a short time.

But with time complications ensue. Ideally, the pump would be used only for a day or two. But more and more, intra-aortic balloons were being kept in place for weeks—usually while the patient waited for a donor heart to become available. The situation was in many ways analogous to Maria Valenzuela's. The balloon pump, like the respirator, bought some time but did nothing to alter the underlying disease process.

These days it was easy for an ICU to become a pre-op holding ward for transplant surgery, filled with patients waiting for life-sustaining organs to become available. Especially in the case of hearts, the demand far exceeds the supply. It is not unusual for patients to remain on the heart-transplant waiting list for a couple of years—*if* they are able to survive that long.

"What was the terminal event?" Mac asked.

Frost frowned. It was almost as if he didn't want to answer the question. "Arrhythmia," he said finally. "He's been going in and out of various tachyarrhythmias for a couple of days."

Mac began to absently sort through the pile of papers on the desk in front of him. Turner Frost kept casting wary glances in his direction. As he looked at the EKG, Mac started to feel that all too familiar hollow feeling in the pit of his stomach.

"Was he on digoxin?" Mac asked.

Frost sighed deeply. His voice turned angry. "Look, Mac, let's not get started on all that, okay?"

"This rhythm strip is certainly consistent with dig toxicity."

"And a lot of other things."

"Was the patient on digoxin, Turner?"

"Mac, I've always respected you," Turner said. It was the first Mac had heard of it. "I don't know what's gotten into you, all this craziness lately. But it's got to stop. The whole medical school is laughing at you. If you keep it up, I don't think they'll let you graduate." Frost had spun in his chair so that he faced Mac as he spoke. He had put on his most serious expression.

Mac looked him straight in the eye. "Turner, *was* the patient on digoxin?"

Frost sighed once more and turned back to the chart in front of him.

"If you don't tell me," Mac said, "I'll just look it up later."

"No, McCall," Frost said, "he wasn't on digoxin."

"Mac! Where the hell have you been?" Harvey Jessup was his usual exuberant self. "You give up basketball completely?"

"You know how it is," Harv. Mother Medicine."

"You're taking it far too seriously, Mac. Gotta live a little. Otherwise, you're not gonna be any good for your patients anyway."

"If only they'd make you dean, Harv." Mac took a deep breath. "I need a favor."

Harvey Jessup was instantly cautious. Not the old Harv at all. "What kind of favor?"

"I need a digoxin level on a patient."

"So order a digoxin level."

"It's not that easy."

"Why did I know you were going to say that?" Harvey said. "What's the problem?"

"Patient's dead."

"And?"

"He wasn't my patient."

"Do you have any authority at all to order the test?"

Mac shook his head. He said simply, "It's important, Harv."

"Mac, you know I'm your friend, but sometimes it's a friend's job to say no." Harvey wrinkled up his face. You could tell he was trying to decide whether or not to say something. Finally he said, "There's a lot of talk, Mac. About you. People are saying you've kind of lost your grip. Reality is kind of slipping away from you. There's talk that if there are any more problems, they'll hold up your graduation. Maybe you'll *never* get your M.D."

"*Who's* talking?"

"Everybody, Mac. Don't you know? You're like everyone's favorite topic. Everybody wants to know, what's the deal with Mac McCall?" Then he added, "I'm sorry about Jennifer," as though it were all part of the same problem.

How the hell did Harvey Jessup already know that Jennifer had moved out?

"We've been having problems," Mac explained, "for quite a while. It didn't have anything to do with—" he searched for the right phrase—"everything else."

From the look on Harv's face, Mac couldn't tell whether or not Harv believed him.

"I need your help, Harv,"

"It's not that simple, Mac. I'd be taking a big risk too. I can't afford to lose my job. Susan's pregnant."

"Hey, congratulations! When's she due?"

"Not for six months. But she'll have to quit work. We'd like for her to be able to spend a lot of time with the baby. If I lose my job, I don't know what we'd do."

"You know I'd never ask you to take that kind of risk," Mac said. "All I need is for you to tell me if there's some serum around here that you can use to run a dig level on Ralph Perkins, the guy who died. I'll do all the paperwork, take all the responsibility. You got a lab request, you ran the test. Just like you do all day every day. No one will ever know I talked to you."

Harvey shook his head as he considered all the ramifications of Mac's request. Finally he got up and shuffled off to one of the lab refrigerators. He was gone for only a couple of minutes.

When he returned he said, "There's plenty of serum that was drawn in the ICU just before he died."

"Thanks, Harv."

"You probably shouldn't be thanking me. A real friend probably would have told you to go to hell."

"Like I said, it's important." Mac wondered if he was trying to convince Harvey or himself. Harvey only shrugged. "And, Harv, be sure to congratulate Susan for me. That's great news."

"Sure, Mac." The trademark ebullience was now entirely gone from Harvey's voice. He had acquiesced without being convinced.

When he got back up to the ICU, Mac furtively filled out the necessary paperwork and tubed it down to the lab. Evening was approaching. There would be no answer until tomorrow. All he could do was wait. And worry. Perhaps, Mac thought, he should have worried a little more *before* he requested the digoxin level on Ralph Perkins.

As it turned out, Mac didn't end up having a lot of idle time to brood over his actions. The hospital operator paged him for an outside call.

"This is Eleanor Delacroix, Mac. I need to talk to you."

Mac told her he needed an hour or so to finish up in the ICU and agreed to drop by afterward.

THIRTY-THREE

If he hadn't known better, Mac would have once again thought that he had taken the Widow Delacroix by surprise. Perhaps this was the way the upper classes dressed when they entertained at home—an aspect of gracious living which Jennifer herself had picked up as she climbed the social ladder.

It occurred to Mac that he was not as well informed on the vernacular of women's fashion as he should be. The first label he applied to Eleanor's outfit was "nightgown."

"Mac! I'm so glad you could make it." Like she was throwing some kind of a party or something. Mac felt guilty that he hadn't brought a bottle of wine.

But he didn't dwell on the guilt. He had more important things on his mind. Underwear. He'd caught her in her underwear. A silky, slinky black slip of some kind. Designed to have something quite small worn over it. Well, she certainly wasn't wearing anything over it right now. And Mac was pretty confident that she wasn't wearing anything under it either.

"I know you're not on call, Mac. This time I'm not letting you get away without a good stiff drink. You deserve it. Bourbon, right?"

He was going to ask her how the hell she knew that, but decided not to bother.

"Rocks?"

"Fine."

They were in what Mac would have called a living room, but he was certain Eleanor would have some fancier name for it. The furnishings were far too ornate for his taste. On the other hand, the people at *Architectural Digest* hadn't asked for his opinion on anything recently. Everything was gilded. Probably French. The previous owners had most likely parted with the furniture at the same time they'd parted with their heads.

Eleanor handed him his drink and then placed the obligatory hot hors d'oeuvres in front of him. Cook had been busy. But Mac had more important things on his mind. He'd been right about one thing. There was certainly no underwear under her underwear.

"So, Mac, how's your investigation coming along?" Like, *Seen any good movies lately?* She took a seat beside him. *Right* beside him.

Mac tried to take a sip of bourbon. This unavoidably placed his elbow in contact with a portion of Eleanor's body which would normally be covered by a swimming suit. Even a very tiny swimming suit.

"I still don't have a good handle on why Austin committed suicide," he said. He decided not to ad, *if* he committed suicide.

"Oh, I wouldn't waste any more time worrying about that. The more I've thought about it, the more I think it was just about Austin's speed, committing suicide when the going got a little bit tough."

This was one cold woman.

"But how about all that other stuff you're looking into? All those patients dying and everything?"

"How'd you happen to hear about that?"

"*Everybody's* talking about it, Mac. People think you've really gone off the deep end over all of that stuff."

"There does seem to be a building consensus in that regard," Mac said.

"So tell me about it." With the exuberance of a high school cheerleader.

"There's not really anything to tell." Mac wasn't about to unburden his soul to Eleanor Delacroix. He certainly wasn't going to mention his latest concern, Ralph Perkins. "I think I did get a little carried away, but that's all behind me now."

"Well, I for one am glad to hear that," Eleanor said. "You have a lot of friends at the medical school who just want to see you do well." She eyed his half-empty glass. "Here, let me freshen that for you."

When she returned with his drink, she was suddenly more pensive. "I was sorry to hear that Jennifer moved out. I really was."

Mac was thinking he should have picked up this morning's newspaper. Jennifer's move must have made the front page. He shrugged. "It had been coming for a long time."

"Sometimes these things work out for the best," Eleanor said.

Was it his imagination, or had she edged closer as she spoke?

"You know, Mac"—her voice became suddenly smokey—"there's something I'm afraid I may not have made clear last time you were here. I think you probably thought I was pretty heartless, showing so much interest in you so soon after Austin's death. But you have to understand, our relationship had already been dead for a long time. I was sorry that Austin died and all, that he killed himself, but at that point we no longer had a personal relationship. He was just somebody I happened to know who happened to die. Does that sound cold?"

No colder than a brass toilet seat at the North Pole, Eleanor.

"Anyway, Mac, I'm a healthy woman with normal, healthy needs, and Austin hadn't been satisfying those needs for a very long time."

Eleanor was sort of pivoting to bring her face directly in front of his, and as she moved, Mac's peripheral vision told him that the front of her dress-slip-nightgown had opened up and things were beginning to fall out. He was like a guy standing at some terrible height, knowing that if he looked down he might be overcome by dizziness and fall headlong into the precipice.

The next movement in Eleanor's routine, Mac was pretty sure, would be a straddle mount. She probably thought of it as a required maneuver. Her lips were closing in on his. She'd probably use the lip lock for leverage.

Mac took her firmly by the shoulders.

"Eleanor, this isn't going to happen. Like I said before, I'm flattered. I'm sure you're a wonderful person, but I've just got too much going on right now to even think about a new relationship."

Eleanor looked hurt. There was no way she couldn't feel rejected—after he'd just rejected her like that.

"I'm sorry," he said. "I think I probably should just go."

"No, don't be silly." She forced herself to brighten. "Stay and finish your drink. Have something to eat. I promise I won't attack you again." She tugged here and there at her outfit, trying to get everything back in place, and threw Mac a slightly embarrassed little half smile as she completed the job. You can't blame a girl for trying.

Mac returned the half smile and shook his head as gently as possible. "Thanks," he said, "but I really do have some things I have to attend to. I'm afraid all this stuff at the hospital has really gotten me behind in my reading."

As he left, Mac wondered whether he'd given Eleanor the opportunity to convey whatever it was she'd called him about in the first place. "I need to talk to you," she'd said on the phone. Mac even thought about going back, just to ask if there was anything else.

Don't be stupid, he decided. There wasn't a minute of their little get-together that wasn't completely choreographed. Except maybe the end.

THIRTY-FOUR

Mac arrived in the ICU the next morning to find both Laura Rubenstein and Karen Anderson there ahead of him, both visibly upset. Mac was certain he knew why.

"Maria Valenzuela?" he asked.

But Ruby shook her head. "Maria's fine. Stable anyway."

The two young women exchanged glances.

Karen said, "I'll see you later, Mac. Call me if you want to talk." Her eyes looked watery.

"Okay, Ruby," Mac said, "what the hell's going on?"

"Law called again. He wants to see you right away."

"What about?"

"Oh, Mac, goddamnit. You know very well what it's about."

"Another National Academy of Sciences speech?"

"It's not funny, Mac. They're talking about

pulling you off the ICU rotation. If that happens, you won't graduate—not this spring anyway." Then she added, "And, of course, they're putting a lot of pressure on me. Saying that if I had been supervising your work properly, you wouldn't have messed up the way you have."

"I'm sorry, Laura. It's not fair for anyone to blame you."

"Your actions affect other people, Mac. They reflect on your colleagues, the hospital, the medical school. It's time you learned that. Actions have consequences."

"I *had* to do it. People are *dying*."

"It's a hospital, Mac. People are going to die."

There wasn't much point in going on and on about it. "Look, Laura, I had to do what I had to. I'm sorry you're involved. I'd better go deal with Law. I'll be back as soon as I can."

"They may not let you come back, Mac."

Mac wasn't sure what to expect from Professor Law. Most likely anger. What he got was worse. Disappointment.

"I thought we had an agreement, Mac. I trusted you." There was real emotion in his voice as he said, "I can't do that anymore."

"Dr. Law, I did resolve to put all of those concerns behind me, and I was quite sincere in that. But something new came up. Something I couldn't ignore."

"And just what was this 'something new'?" An unmistakable note of weariness had crept into Law's voice.

"Another patient has died. A man named Ralph Perkins. He's another in this long line of patients with complicated, costly medical problems who has died unexpectedly. His terminal rhythm on EKG was consistent with digoxin toxicity—and he wasn't supposed to be receiving digoxin."

Law frowned at that. "Tell me what you know, Mac."

Mac launched into what he knew of Ralph Perkins' history. When he finished, Law was shaking his head.

"You said this man died unexpectedly. It sounds to me like he's been cheating death for more than a year."

"They don't kill people who are healthy. That's the whole point." The thought had hardly been formulated in Mac's mind before it was on his tongue.

"Who is 'they,' Mac?"

Mac shrugged. He wasn't quite ready to begin pointing fingers publicly. "Someone who has access to all these patients. Some amoral sociopath. Or someone who's just plain psychotic."

Professor Law sighed deeply, a man whose patience was plainly at an end.

"The reason I called you into my office this

morning is because it was brought to my attention that you'd ordered a digoxin level on Mr. Perkins. Is that correct? Did you request a digoxin level on this man who was not your patient—on no one's authority but your own?"

Mac nodded.

"What did you hope to accomplish?"

"Like I said, he wasn't supposed to be receiving digoxin, but his terminal rhythm was consistent with dig toxicity. If he had a high level, it would be evidence of malpractice—at a minimum—and possibly murder."

"Tell me, Mac, what is a normal digoxin level?"

"It's a little difficult to be precise," Mac said. "Maybe between one and a little over two."

"Actually, that's not correct. What you've given me is the *therapeutic* digoxin level. The *normal* level is zero. Most people are, of course, not receiving digoxin."

Mac didn't say anything. It was very unlike Professor Law to be so pedantic. Finally, Law continued.

"I have received the result of Mr. Perkins' digoxin blood level test. Not surprisingly, it was normal—which is to say zero. Since he was not on digoxin, it was to be expected that none would be detected in his blood."

Mac felt like his legs had been kicked out from under him. Perkins had been his last chance to prove to the world that he wasn't crazy. What next? Dr. Law had the answer readily at hand.

"Perhaps," he said, "I am partially to blame for the fact that this has all gotten so far out of hand. I probably should have been less receptive to your concerns during our first conversation, a little less accommodating of your—what shall we call them—your idiosyncrasies. When we talked again, I should have made it clear that your behavior was quite beyond the pale.

"But that's all water over the dam. We have to move forward from here. Fist of all, there can be no question of your continuing in the ethics seminar. I am using my authority to dismiss you forthwith. Just as clearly you can no longer sit in judgment of your fellow students as part of the disciplinary committee. In fact, you can expect to receive a formal letter quite soon informing you of the intent of the disciplinary committee to investigate *your* behavior. Finally, a report of this episode will be placed in your file. None of this will be helpful to your internship aspirations."

Professor Law paused. Mac waited.

Then Law asked, "Do you have any questions?"

Mac held his breath. He knew he should be devastated by Law's decision, but all he could think of was, *Is that all?* Could he really continue with his ICU rotation? He didn't dare ask the question point-blank. There was still a chance he might graduate with his class. No point in giving Dr. Law any additional ideas.

"I'm sorry, Dr. Law. I know I've let you down. I truly believe that what I did was appropriate, necessary even. But it won't happen again."

Law said nothing. Mac knew that he had made promises to the professor before. There was no reason for Law to believe him now.

"I appreciate your time, Dr. Law. If there's nothing else, I'll just go on up to the ICU and get back to work."

Law nodded.

Mac could still breathe, but only just barely.

THIRTY-FIVE

Mac slipped back into the ICU by a side door and quietly took a seat at the nursing station, where Karen Anderson was poring over lab data.

"So, what's the verdict, Mac?"

"I'm grounded," Mac said, "but I still have to go to school."

Karen gave him a look.

Mac said, "No more ethics seminar, no more disciplinary committee—unless I'm the guest of honor. I can't go to pep rallies, after-school dances, or band practice."

"But no restrictions on your clinical activities?"

"No more autopsies on living patients. Law was quite clear about that."

Karen reached over and squeezed the back of Mac's hand. "Mac, you've got to start taking this seriously."

"I am, Karen. The thing is, it's a question of

which is more important, my career or all these patients dying like flies."

"Just try to be careful, Mac. They could still pull you off the ICU rotation, keep you from graduating. Law probably doesn't have the authority to do that on his own, but the disciplinary committee sure does. And they'll go wherever he wants them to go."

Mac nodded noncommittally, then changed the subject. "How's Maria doing?"

"She's still stable, the best she's been."

"Any chance of getting that tube out of her throat?"

"Not yet. And if we can't get her off the ventilator—and a donor lung doesn't materialize—pretty soon people are going to start asking whether or not we should do a tracheostomy."

A tracheostomy would allow them to attach the ventilator to a tube inserted directly into the trachea, the air passage in the neck. Minor surgery would be involved, creating a hole in the skin in the front of the neck. Then Maria wouldn't have to have a tube in her mouth anymore, but she'd have the hole in her neck—for the rest of her life if she couldn't get off the ventilator. No one wanted that.

"Has Diego been around?" Mac asked.

"He was here briefly, poor guy."

"Not doing too well?"

"He's had about all he can take. Wife in the

ICU. Two babies at home. End-of-quarter exams coming up. If I were Diego, I'd be ready for a padded room."

The remainder of Mac's day in the ICU had been agreeably busy. Three new admissions. Not much time to worry about his problems. Law had been right—immersing himself in work was a pretty good antidote for Mac's troubles, at least in the short term.

But when he got home, it all began to press down on him once again. The apartment felt empty. Emptier than if Jennifer had simply been not at home. Jennifer was gone. Forever.

And he'd been stripped of the signal accomplishment of his medical school career, his participation in Professor Law's seminar. And he was about to be called before the disciplinary committee. It had only been a few short weeks since he had sat on that committee and felt empathy for Diego Valenzuela's humiliation at the hands of Turner Frost and Austin Delacroix. Now it would be Mac's turn.

He threw the mail on the table without paying it much attention. Mostly bills, it looked like. Mac poured himself a bourbon, then wondered if he'd been a little heavy-handed. Was he drinking too much? No way. Good for the heart.

He took a drink and absently sorted through the mail. He'd been right. Bills. There was one letter, business-size envelope, typed address, no return. He'd seen these before. Jennifer owed somebody. They put it in a plain envelope so it would get opened. This one was addressed to Mac. What had she done now? It had been a little too convenient, Jennifer moving out with all the bills paid in full. Would this be the first in a long line of creditors pursuing Mac in an effort to collect on Jennifer's debts?

He stared at the letter, willing it to go away, but it simply refused. Nothing to be gained by ignoring it. Might as well see the rest of the bad news this day had brought him.

He ripped open the envelope and found a single typewritten page inside. Its message was brief and threatening.

Mac McCall,

    Quit investigating Austin Delacroix's

    death, or you will end up like he did.

Mac stared at the page, disbelieving, then smiling, and finally laughing out loud. He couldn't stop. Had anyone in history ever been so pleased to receive a death threat?

In your face, Arthur Sterling Law! Here's all the proof I need. I'm not nuts. I'm on the right track, and somebody is desperate to get me off the case. Desperate enough to threaten murder.

In his exultation Mac gave no thought whatsoever to any personal danger he might be in. All that mattered was that he had been exonerated.

He found Lieutenant Mallory's card and dialed the phone.

THIRTY-SIX

When Mac walked into the precinct house, it looked pretty much the same as last time. Same desk sergeant. Same types of people milling around. The sergeant had his head down, entering something into what appeared to be some kind of logbook. Mac figured, Why bother him?

He hurried up the stairs, half expecting to hear, "Hey, you! Where d'ya think you're goin'?" But no one said a word. Probably not much of a problem, people breaking into police stations.

The squad room upstairs was empty except for the sergeant who'd come to the apartment with Detective Mallory that day. Mac couldn't remember his name. The man had his nose in paperwork. Lots of scholarly guys around here.

"Excuse me," Mac said. "I'm supposed to meet Detective Mallory."

"Yeah, right," the sergeant said. "I'm Sergeant Polanski. I was at your place that time. Mallory asked me to take the message." And from his tone Polanski wasn't too pleased by the assignment.

"Did he tell you what it was about?"

"Something about the Delacroix suicide and patients that were supposed to be getting killed and you being in a hell of a lot of trouble over at the medical school."

This wasn't going to be easy.

"I got a death threat," Mac said.

"Who from?"

"I don't know."

Polanski gave him a look like, Then what am I supposed to do about it?

"It was anonymous. In writing." Mac offered the envelope to Polanski. He seemed reluctant to take it. Mac was beginning to understand that he had developed a bit of a credibility problem. "Maybe I should talk to Mallory," he said.

Polanski took the envelope and started to open it. Mac thought he was being pretty careless about it.

"There may be fingerprints on that," he warned.

"I never thought of that," Polanski said. "You been in police work long?"

Polanski studied the typed page, then stood. "Wait here a minute," he said. "I wanta check something."

Polanski started to leave the room, then returned to his desk and picked up the letter and envelope. He eyed Mac suspiciously as he walked by the second time. "I'll be back in a minute," he said. "Don't try to leave."

Don't try to leave? What the hell was going on here?

Mac cooled his heels for nearly twenty minutes before Polanski finally returned. He had Detective Mallory in tow.

"Hello, Dr. McCall," Mallory said. "How are you today?"

"I'm okay," Mac said, "you know, except for the death threat." It sounded like a bad joke. Other than that, Mrs. Lincoln, how was the play?

"Now, about this death threat, Doctor," Mallory said, "what would you like us to do about that?"

"Mac."

"Pardon?"

"You can call me Mac. I'm not a doctor."

"Sure thing, Mac. Now, what would you like us to do about this letter?"

Mac couldn't figure out what kind of game they were playing. "I don't know what you mean. I got this letter in the mail. It's threatening. It looks like it's related to Austin Delacroix's death. I presume you'll want to investigate."

Polanski said, "You don't seem too upset by all this. Someone said they were going to kill me, I might be just a little bit upset."

Mac was still trying to find his balance. "I

guess I've been so caught up in all these deaths, my first thought was that this might be a clue."

"You're gonna be a great doc," Polanski said. "You don't give a damn about yourself. All you care about is other people." There was more than a trace of sarcasm in Polanski's tone.

"Give me a break. You know the kind of pressure I've been under. No one wants to believe what's going on. Everybody wants to just sweep it under the carpet. This letter goes a long way toward proving that something really is going on."

Mallory said, "So this letter really gets you off the hook, doesn't it? All of a sudden you're right, everyone else is wrong?"

Suddenly. Mac knew where they were headed. "You think *I* typed this letter? You can't believe that!"

It was Polanski's turn. "Nobody said anything about you writing the letter. What made you think that?"

Mac was really getting irritated. These guys thought they were being so cute.

"Look," Mac said, "I've done my duty. I brought the letter to you. If you guys don't want to do anything about it, I can't make you. I think it's time for me to go." Mac got up out of his chair.

"No concern at all about your own safety?" Polanski asked.

"If you guys aren't going to do anything, obviously I'll have to look out for myself."

"Of course," Polanski said, "if you typed the note, then you *know* there's nothing to worry about."

"Look, I know no one else believes me about all the deaths. I've only tried to do what I thought was right. But if you guys start suggesting I've committed some kind of a crime, faking this note, I'm gonna find the best lawyer in the city and come after you. I've had it with all this crap."

"Might be a good idea," Polanski said, "getting a lawyer."

"Or, if you can't afford one," Mallory added, "an attorney will be provided for you."

Mac stared at Mallory. "What are you talking about?"

"You should understand," Polanski said, "that you have the right to remain silent. Anything you say can, and will, be used against you."

Mac was bewildered. "Are you arresting me?"

"Not yet," Mallory said.

"Really, come on. What's this all about? You guys can't believe I wrote this letter."

The policemen shrugged in well-rehearsed unison.

"Why would I do that?"

"We had a guy come in here a couple of years ago," Polanski said. "What was his name?"

"Jackson."

"That's right. Thanks, Lou. Jackson. Anyway, this guy Jackson kept coming in here, telling us his wife had been killed. We kept saying, don't worry, she's just run off. She'll be back, you know, or not. Nothing for us to do about it if the guy's wife has decided to take a powder. She'd been promising to leave him for years. All the neighbors knew that.

"Anyway, the guy kept getting madder and madder at us because we didn't believe him. So one day he comes in with this big butcher knife, says it's the murder weapon. We go, *What murder?* We don't have any evidence of a murder. Next day, he starts bringing in parts of the body."

"Great case," Mallory said.

"Other guys we've dealt with," Polanski said, "think they're smarter than us. They like to slip us a few clues, tease us a little. We think maybe you're kind of a tease, Doc."

Mac felt all the wind go out of him. He eased himself back down into his chair. "I just can't believe this is happening." He struggled to regain his composure, to regain control of his thoughts. Then instinct suddenly told him there was a piece missing. "There's something you guys aren't telling me, isn't there?"

Polanski and Mallory exchanged quick glances. Mallory shrugged his assent.

"You see this letter you brought in?" Polanski held it in front of Mac.

Mac reached for the paper.

"Don't touch it," Polanski said. "Just look at it."

Mac looked. He didn't see anything more than he'd seen before.

"See how the *e* looks?" Polanski said. "The typeface is broken. It's very distinctive."

So what? Mac thought. He stared at Polanski.

"The same typewriter," Polanski said, "was used to write the Delacroix suicide note."

THIRTY-SEVEN

Mac arrived back at his apartment to an increasing sense of overwhelming claustrophobia. It wasn't a feeling of walls closing in. Mac could have dealt with that. But not with this. Not with this sensation of being buried alive.

He was suffocating. Minute by minute, hour by hour, they were sucking the life out of him. It was reason number one not to have a gun in the house: the temptation, at a time like this, to point the barrel at your own head. Relief. Instant and permanent.

And no matter how far out onto the horizon he looked, there was no sign of reprieve. Mac could tell himself that this was the bottom, that he could sink no deeper. But that would be a lie. What he faced now was the *prospect* of a very bleak future. Actually living in that future would be far worse than simply imagining it.

He was certain to be called before the disciplinary committee. Polanski and Mallory seemed intent on drumming up something to charge him with. Mac could work himself into a deep funk without even thinking about the death threat. If somebody out there really wanted to kill him, they'd have to get in line.

Only a few short weeks ago, graduation from medical school had been a slam-dunk. Now it was a pipe dream.

The more Mac had dug, the deeper the hole he'd found himself in. There could be no question that the smart move now, the smart move from the very beginning, was to try to climb out of the crater he'd made for himself. The dumbest thing he could do would be to dig deeper. Mac needed a ladder, not a shovel.

So why was he sitting here, in the dark, with a shovel in his hand? Because something really was going on. The death threat had proved that. Beyond a shadow of a doubt.

He could have dismissed the letter as a hoax if it hadn't been written with the same typewriter. Someone had access to that typewriter and understood its significance. And it sure as hell wasn't Austin Delacroix. Dead men are notoriously bereft of syntax.

So the use of the same typewriter could not be dismissed as either hoax or coincidence. But why would anyone use the same typewriter? Sheer stupidity? Didn't whoever sent that note know that the typewriter could be traced? Surely no one was *that* stupid. Mac assumed that all typewriters left features that could be traced. Perhaps not as obvious as this one, but still . . .

Did the sender *want* Mac to know that it was the same typewriter? That made more sense. If Mac realized that the typeface was the same, then he'd know that the sender was serious. But that was quite a reach, assuming that Mac would recognize the typeface, having only glanced at it briefly once before.

Or was it simply an attempt to frame Mac? Did the person who typed the threat assume that Mac would take it to the police, and that the police would surely recognize the typeface? Now that made more sense.

But what would be the point?

Mac drew a blank. This was as far as his reasoning would take him. After that, it was a lot like those maps of the earth that they drew up before Magellan. You got to the edge of the known world, and beyond that it was all serpents and dragons. Who knew?

Mac reached up and turned on a light. It was late, nearly midnight. But there was no possibility of sleep. And he was too wired to study. Not that there was much point wasting a lot of time studying medicine at this juncture.

The apartment was a mess. Part of the blame belonged to Jennifer. She'd done a lot of rummaging, trying to find her things before she moved out. But Mac hadn't put too high a priority on housekeeping over the past few days. Entropy had taken over.

He started in the kitchen, which was easier than he thought it would be. Most of the dishes had belonged to Jennifer. Then he worked his way through the living room and into the bedroom. He was cleaning out a closet when he found it.

His first instinct was to throw it away—with everything else. It wasn't something which meant anything to him anymore, or ever would again. He sat there, cross-legged on the floor, holding it in his hand.

It was a note from Jennifer, sent to him just after they'd started dating. Kind of a joke, really. The kind of silly thing people do at the beginning of a relationship.

Mac, Meet me at the tower at midnight.

> Your Secret Admirer

He'd forgotten about their meeting up there. He'd never liked that tower. Never understood its appeal. The note itself was another long-forgotten memory.

But the note revealed a great deal. At long last the myriad far-flung pieces were beginning to converge to form a picture.

The note had been typed. On a very familiar typewriter.

THIRTY-EIGHT

He had to push the call button at the apartment building's front door three times before there was any response. It had been only a short walk from his own apartment. *How convenient*, Mac thought.

The walk in the cold night air had not cooled Mac's temper.

Finally, an angry voice spoke over the intercom. "What?"

"It's Mac. We need to talk."

"Do you have any idea what time it is?"

Mac didn't respond. He just pushed the button for the fourth time. He heard the buzzer releasing the lock on the door.

When he arrived at the apartment, George Williams was standing there, bare-chested, in his pajama bottoms. He looked very angry and about thirteen feet tall in his bare feet.

"Is George Jr. here?"

"He stays with my mother. So he can go to the new school."

"Good," Mac said. And without further exchange of pleasantries, he took his best shot. A sucker punch right in the solar plexus. It was about as high as Mac could reach.

George Williams went down like a ton of bricks. Make that two tons. Mac stepped over him and shut the door.

"We need to talk, George."

George Williams sat on the floor, trying to catch his breath. Finally, he was able to get out, "I guess I had that coming. I'm sorry about Jennifer. I thought you guys were quits. That's what she told me. Just living together for convenience now."

"That wasn't about Jennifer, George. Not directly, anyway. That was for Annie."

"What're you talkin' about?" George had bewilderment in his voice, but his eyes told a different story.

"Look, George, I already know everything."

"Everything about what? I don't have a clue what all this is about."

"Oh, I think you do," Mac said. He could see that this was going to be difficult. George wasn't going to admit the truth unless he saw it as his only way out. Mac's job was to convince him that he didn't have a choice, that the truth was his only salvation.

"Tell me, George."

"Tell you what?"

"Tell me you didn't kill Annie."

George was breathing easier now. He managed to get to his feet, then took a couple of steps to the couch and sat down heavily. He looked Mac squarely in the eyes.

"I did not kill Annie. Satisfied?"

"How about Austin Delacroix?"

"No, I didn't kill him either. Or John F. Kennedy. Or anybody else, for that matter."

"Why don't I believe you, George?"

" 'Cause you're stupid. Or maybe you're just bitter about Jennifer. Maybe some other part of your body's doin' the thinking. Some part other than your brain."

"I gotta hand it to you, George. It almost worked. If I hadn't realized it was Jennifer's typewriter, I would never have tumbled to your plan. Once I realized it was Jennifer's typewriter, all I had to ask myself was, *Who had access to it?* The answer was 'George Williams.' Then everything else fell into place."

"I still don't have the vaguest idea what you're talkin' about."

"Okay, George. Here's the way I put it together. You wanted to get rid of Annie, get her away from George Jr. But the more you tried, the deeper she sank her hooks into little George. You were afraid she would live long enough to drag him down into the same mess she'd gotten herself into.

"So you killed her. But somehow Austin Dela-croix figured out what you were up to. He was trying to prove that you did it. That's why he ordered the dig level on Annie. That's why you killed him.

"Then I thought, what about all those others? Havlicek and the rest. Why did they have to die? That was just cover, wasn't it, George? If there were a bunch of murders, Annie's death wouldn't stand out.

"Obviously, Austin knew that Havlicek had been murdered. That's why he tried to get the digoxin level after Havlicek died.

"How about it, George. How close am I?"

George looked him squarely in the eye. "You don't know squat, Mac."

Once again George pulled himself to his feet. He walked across the room to the counter which separated the living area from the kitchen and stood with his back to Mac, deep in thought. Then, without turning around, he asked, "You want a drink, Mac?"

"Sure, why not?"

"I got beer, and I got scotch."

"Beer makes you fat," Mac said.

Mac could hear George futzing around in the kitchen. Cabinet doors opening and closing, ice cubes knocking against glass. Then George came back, handed Mac his drink, and took a seat on the couch. Mac sat across from him in the only chair in the room. He had the very distinct impression that George was about to come clean.

George took a long drink of scotch, reflected a few moments longer, then said, "It's Delacroix, VanSlyke, and Frost. They've been killin' patients ever since they started their clinical rotations in their junior year."

Mac nodded encouragingly. "How do you know that?"

"I just *know* it, man. All you gotta do is just watch those guys. A patient gets presented at the ethics seminar, they think too much money is being wasted, next thing you know, the patient's dead—their idea of managed care."

"If you knew this was going on, why didn't you say something?"

"I said I *know* it. I didn't say I could *prove* it. I don't need to tell you what can happen if you go around making accusations you can't prove. Don't think I didn't want to. Those guys think they're gods or something. Think they have the right to decide who lives and who dies. Three medical students."

"How about you, George? You think you're God?" Mac could tell, just looking at George's face, that George knew what Mac meant, but he said it anyway, just to get it out in the open. "When you presented Annie at the ethics seminar, you knew what those guys were up to. You thought they'd kill her, didn't you?"

"I'm not proud of that, Mac, but I'd do it again. Annie had ruined her life. There was no saving her. But she was determined to drag little George down with her. There was no way I could let that happen, no matter what the consequences—for Annie or for me."

Mac tried to sort through all the facts in his mind. It was still pretty muddy. The scotch probably wasn't helping. So far George had confirmed only what Mac had already suspected. There were still a lot of pretty significant loose ends.

"What about Delacroix?" Mac asked. "Why was he checking digoxin levels?"

George shook his head. "Who knows? Maybe he developed a conscience. Maybe he was doing some kind of experimenting, like some kind of Nazi or something. The guy was pretty weird. We'll probably never understand what was really going on inside his head."

"What about the typewriter, George? How do you explain that?"

"How do I explain what? I don't know what you're talking about. What typewriter?"

"I got a letter saying that if I didn't stop looking into what happened to Austin Delacroix, I'd be next. It was typed on the same typewriter that Delacroix's so-called suicide note was typed on. Turns out, it was Jennifer's typewriter."

"I see. So you're saying, I had access to Jennifer, so to speak, so I had access to the typewriter?"

Mac nodded.

"I hate to be the one to tell you this, Mac, but if you're thinkin' along those lines, there's going to be a pretty long list of men who had access to that typewriter."

It was a conclusion Mac had come to on his own, even before he left his own apartment. He couldn't make a very convincing case for George's involvement in any death other than Annie's, and it occurred to Mac almost immediately that George's access to Jennifer's typewriter was unlikely to have been unique. Mac could see he was going to have to get used to the fact that there were a lot of things about Jennifer that he didn't know.

"Look, Mac, I'm sorry. That sounded cold. But it is true. I wouldn't have had anything to do with her if she hadn't made it clear that there had been others. She said you knew about it. The two of you had an arrangement. She said you had had an outside interest for some time."

"Who else was Jennifer involved with?"

George shrugged. "I don't know any names."

"Just for the record, who was my outside interest supposed to have been?"

"Karen Anderson," George said. Like everybody in town knew about it.

Mac almost managed a smile. "Well, at least my taste in women appears to be improving."

Mac couldn't think of any more questions to ask. He'd probably think of a hundred as soon as he walked out the door. He felt like a cop. He ought to tell George, *Don't leave town without checking with me. I may have some more questions I want to ask you.*

But he didn't. He just got up and left.

THIRTY-NINE

Mac was well aware that he had no business sneaking into the ethics seminar. He had been told, in no uncertain terms, that he would no longer be participating. Mac wasn't even certain *why* he was there. At any rate, no one seemed to notice him.

The whole atmosphere of the seminar had changed dramatically. There were more students than ever before, and they were boisterous, almost rowdy. Mac had trouble finding a seat in the crowd, and he was jostled more than once as he tried to make his way to the top of the amphitheater.

Law had instituted a new policy of actually bringing the patient to be presented into the room. This had been particularly difficult with Maria Valenzuela because of all the paraphernalia required to keep her alive. But there she was, lying in her bed, her respirator beside her. There were a couple of poles alongside the bed as well, used to hang bags of intravenous solutions. Mac was struck by the contrast between Maria's serenity and the carnival atmosphere in the room.

Diego Valenzuela stood at the head of his wife's bed, applying cold compresses to her forehead. He stared defiantly at the unruly mob looking down on him and his wife.

Then suddenly all was quiet. The lights of the amphitheater dimmed, leaving the patient spotlighted on the stage below.

Turner Frost, dressed especially elegantly for the occasion, began the presentation of the case.

"Today's patient is a twenty-four-year-old Hispanic female with end-stage cystic fibrosis." Mac winced at the use of the term "end-stage" in the presence of the patient and her husband. It seemed gratuitously heartless. But Frost was only beginning.

"The patient and her husband now come before you demanding lung transplantation. This is a demand which we must summon the courage to deny."

"But she has babies!" Diego Valenzuela called out. "Who's going to take care of her babies?"

"She should have thought of that *before* she had them," Frost replied.

Someone from the audience yelled, "Yes, she should have thought about that *before*." A loud murmur of agreement rose from the audience.

The whole thing was getting completely out

of hand. Where was Dr. Law? It was a terrible mistake to have the patient in the amphitheater. Didn't these people have any feelings at all?

Then, in another corner of the room, a familiar voice began to chant. Mac strained to hear what was being said, struggled to recognize the voice. Very familiar but strangely out of place.

"Pull . . ." something. The voice was chanting. Austin Delacroix! The voice was Delacroix's, no doubt about it.

Louder now. "Pull the plug. Pull the plug."

Others in the amphitheater began to pick up the chant. "Pull the plug! Pull the plug!" Louder and louder. The walls were literally shaking.

Everywhere around him, Mac could see students standing—fists beating the air like in one of those late-night television shows—screaming at the top of their lungs, "Pull the plug! Pull the plug!"

Mac noticed for the first time that many of the students were strangely garbed. Mac himself seemed to be partially reclining rather than sitting. Karen Anderson hovered over him, wearing some kind of tunic. She offered grapes and wine. As she bent forward, her tunic fell open.

Then, abruptly, there was silence.

All eyes were suddenly cast upward to the very top of the amphitheater. There, wearing a toga, a wreath in his hair, reclined Arthur Sterling Law. His left hand, extended skyward, commanded silence. Then the hand lowered, the palm turned upward. The gesture clearly asking, *What am I to do?*

Attention turned to Turner Frost on the floor of the amphitheater. He raised his hand into the air and dramatically turned the thumb down. Austin Delacroix and Peter VanSlyke gave the same sign. Others followed. The chant rose again, "Pull the plug. Pull the plug."

Arthur Sterling Law pulled himself to his feet and gazed down on his subjects. Everywhere he looked, thumbs were pointed downward. Turner Frost stood ready with the electric cord. He needed only to give a slight yank. Crescendoing cries came from everywhere: "Pull the plug! Pull the plug!"

Law raised his hand one last time, instantaneously hushing the crowd. What could he do? He wasn't really a participant. He only followed the dictates of his subjects. He gave his shoulders a tired shrug and turned his thumb toward the floor.

A single loud gasp came out of the silence. Mac saw Jennifer, standing in a corner, her mouth gaping open.

Then all eyes became riveted on the floor of the amphitheater. There was no sound.

Diego Valenzuela stood, still defiant. His wife lay quietly in her bed, at peace with herself and the world.

Then Turner Frost tugged on the electrical cord and all became darkness.

Mac became suddenly awake in that darkness, cold sweat pouring off his body and soaking his bed. His only waking thought, the grave danger Maria Valenzuela was in.

FORTY

Throughout the following day Mac constantly monitored Maria's room. No one went in without Mac's noticing. But he could not, by himself, maintain a twenty-four-hour-a-day watch. And he didn't want to alarm Maria in any way. She had enough to worry about. And Mac had no idea whether he had any credibility with Diego Valenzuela. He certainly didn't with anyone else.

So when Mac finally got out of the ICU that evening, the first stop he made was the last stop he'd made the night before. George wasn't exactly delighted to see him.

"Come on," Mac said. "Open the door."

"You know I'm not gonna let you sucker-punch me tonight, don't you?"

"I've got a different plan for tonight," Mac said.

He heard the buzzer releasing the door.

George Williams stood, filling the doorway,

fully dressed this time. Mac wasn't sure he was going to let him in.

"It's about Maria Valenzuela," Mac said. George instantly relented.

"You want a drink?" he asked.

"No, I've got some more stops to make."

"Well, I don't," George said.

George headed for the kitchen, and Mac heard a repeat of the bartending sounds of the night before. George emerged with a glass of scotch and took a seat.

"You know they're going to try to kill her, don't you? Just as sure as we're sitting here."

"Maria?"

Mac nodded. "She fits the formula, doesn't she? Expensive, ultimately fatal illness. The only way to keep her alive is with even more expensive treatment—a lung transplant."

"I guess I hadn't thought about it. You're right, of course. Sounds like the kind of patient they're after. So what do you suggest? Police?"

Mac tried not to laugh. "I've gone a couple of rounds with them already. I don't think they're gonna be much help right now."

"So what do we do?"

"The only thing I can think of right now is to keep a close eye on Maria. I can watch her pretty well while I'm in the unit, but I can't be there all the time. I need help."

"Okay," George said, "I'm in." He took a sip of scotch. "What about Diego?"

"I'll leave that up to you. We could use his help, but I can't imagine piling any more worry on his shoulders right now. It's hard to understand how that guy can even get out of bed in the morning. He makes Job look like a crybaby."

"How about your girlfriend?" George asked.

"Jennifer?" Mac couldn't see her playing much of a role.

"Karen."

This time Mac did laugh. "I hate to disillusion you, George, but there's nothing going on between Karen and me. There's nothing going on between me and anyone."

"I'll try to think of somebody else," George said. He set his glass down. "Guess I shouldn't be drinking this. Not if I'm going to be hanging out in the ICU all night."

"I'm sure neither of us got much sleep last night," Mac said. "How's the stomach?"

"I've been hit harder," George said, "but not much sneakier." He picked up his glass and headed for the kitchen to pour it out.

Mac got up to leave.

"What's on your schedule tonight, Mac?"

"*Chercher la femme,*" Mac said. "*Chercher la femme.*"

FORTY-ONE

Mac went back to his apartment first, just to change clothes. When he opened the door, he found two envelopes lying in ambush. Happily, neither contained a death threat.

One was a copy of a search warrant. A quick glance at his apartment told him that the warrant had already been executed. According to the warrant, they were looking for a typewriter. *Happy hunting*, Mac thought.

The second was from the apartment manager. Essentially, what he wanted to know was, *What the hell is going on?*

Mac stared at the mess the police had left behind. Polanski had left his card on the table. It sat there taunting Mac from across the room. Mac tore the card in half and tossed the pieces into a wastebasket. He probably wouldn't be inviting Polanski over for a drink any time very soon.

*   *   *

Judging from the look of her new apartment building, Jennifer had really come up in the world. She either had a new roommate or a sugar daddy—or both.

Mac did notice that there was only one name next to her apartment number at the front door. He pushed the button.

A familiar voice came over the intercom. "Yes?"

"It's Mac."

Silence.

"Remember me?"

Then, "Come on up, Mac." With quite a bit less enthusiasm than in the old days.

The building was, if anything, even more impressive on the inside. All glass and marble. Mac rode a mirrored elevator to the top floor and knocked on the paneled door that led into Jennifer's apartment.

"Mac, this is quite a surprise," Jennifer said when she opened the door.

I'll bet.

"Come on in. Can I get you something to drink?"

"No thanks, Jen."

She was wearing something soft and feminine. And new. Once again Mac's knowledge of the fashion world let him down. He had heard the term loungewear somewhere. This could be it.

"I see you're not missing the old furniture, Jen."

Everywhere he looked there were fancy new furnishings.

"I thought, since I'm starting a new life, I should start out with new things," she said. "Have a seat." Jennifer indicated a couch near the floor-to-ceiling window which dominated an entire wall of the interior. "I'm going to pour myself a glass of champagne. Sure you don't want any?"

Champagne? "No thanks."

Jennifer disappeared, then returned a couple of minutes later with a champagne flute in her hand. It looked like crystal. She settled herself on the far end of the couch.

"I'm glad you came by, Mac. I wanted a chance to tell you, you know, I'm sorry. I didn't mean for things to turn out this way. It's all my fault. You shouldn't blame George."

"That's what George said too."

Jennifer gave him kind of a half smile. She wasn't sure whether or not he was kidding. "So what can I do for you, Mac?"

"I just wanted to see how you were. Wanted to make certain you were all right."

In case he had any ideas, Jennifer headed him off at the pass. "I appreciate that, Mac. But, you know, it's over between us. There's no going back."

Mac shrugged. "Can't blame a guy for try-ing." No harm in letting Jennifer think he had come to reconcile. Maybe ease her guard down a little.

"I'm flattered, Mac. I truly am."

"How's your new job working out?"

Her expression became briefly quizzical. Then she said, "Oh, fine."

"Just exactly what are you doing?"

"It's kind of hard to explain. Research mostly."

"For who?"

"It's for a number of private individuals. I sort of have my own business."

"It obviously pays well."

"For the first time, Mac, I've got a future to look forward to." There was real emotion in her voice.

"By the way," Mac said, "I've got some letters to write, internships and so forth. I was wondering if I might borrow that old typewriter of yours."

Jennifer hesitated just long enough to incriminate herself. Then she said, "Oh, that old thing. I gave it away."

"When was that, Jen?"

"I don't know. Sometime before I moved out."

"Who'd you give it to? Maybe I could still borrow it."

"Oh, the Goodwill, or one of those." It came quickly. A prepared answer.

It was the kind of answer Mac was waiting for. A certifiable lie. There was no way she gave the typewriter to some randomly selected charity, then someone just happened to pick it up and write a threatening letter to Mac. That would simply be too big a coincidence for anyone to swallow.

"I received a threatening letter, Jen."

"Oh?"

"It warned me to quit investigating Austin Delacroix's death—or I'd be next."

"How awful!"

"Yeah, Jen, really icky. But there's more. It was written on your typewriter."

"I told you, Mac. I gave the typewriter away. I don't know where it is."

"Quite a coincidence, Jennifer. Some stranger threatens me using your typewriter."

She gulped the last of her champagne. "Stranger things have happened," she said.

Mac stared at her. He knew she was lying. She knew that he knew she was lying.

"You wrote that note, didn't you?"

She held his gaze for a few seconds, then nodded. "Why?"

"I did it for you, Mac, to try to keep you from ruining your life. You're important to me. I already felt bad enough about what happened. There you were, getting into all kinds of trouble. I figured the threat might pound some sense into your head."

"The police are looking for that typewriter, Jen. They've already searched the apartment."

She didn't seem bowled over by the news. "Did you tell them it was mine?"

"Not yet."

"Don't. Okay? There's no point."

"As you know, the alleged suicide note was also written on your typewriter. The police are interested in that. *I* am interested in that."

"I'm going to have another glass of champagne. You?"

Mac shook his head. He waited patiently to see what kind of a story she managed to come up with.

When she returned, he asked, "Who wrote the Delacroix suicide note, Jen?"

"Austin did."

"How did he come to write it on your typewriter?"

"I don't know why he wrote it on my typewriter, okay?"

"*How*, Jennifer? *How* did he come to have access to your typewriter?"

She took a gulp of champagne, then another. It wasn't a question she wanted very much to answer.

"Jen?"

"He had a key to the apartment, all right? He could come and go whenever he wanted. As long as you weren't around, which, as you well know, was most of the time."

"How long had this been going on?"

"A while."

"You were having an affair?"

"Yes, Mac, I was having an affair. Do you want me to draw you a picture?"

"And what about George Williams?"

"That just happened. Just one of those things."

"Just one of those crazy things, huh?"

"Mac, we're over. There's no point in going into all that now. I think you'd better leave."

Mac didn't argue the point. There was a lot he still had to figure out, though.

"There's a lot of interest in that typewriter, Jen. The police think I sent the death threat to myself. If there were murders committed, they think I might be involved."

"You're innocent, Mac. If they get specific about anything, you'll have alibis."

"Got everything figured out, haven't you?"

"Yes, Mac. Just about everything." Jennifer, on top of the world.

Mac let himself out, admiring everything once again as he left.

Where the hell was all this money coming from? For the first time it occurred to him that perhaps all the men in Jennifer's life weren't social friends. Perhaps she was seeing some of them professionally.

That would explain a lot.

FORTY-TWO

Another day, another letter. This one from the medical school. Formal notification that Mac was to appear before the disciplinary committee to answer charges—in three days. They weren't wasting any time.

The letter was sent out over Professor Law's name, as was all official correspondence from the committee. Law had attached a brief handwritten message: *Mac, I'm so terribly sorry, and disappointed, that it has come to this.* It was signed, *Arthur Law.*

The note had an emotional impact on Mac that he was totally unprepared for. Law was a father figure for most of the students. He was much admired. You instinctively sought his approval. When you failed, you felt the shame of having let Dr. Law down.

Mac tried once again to sort through what he knew and what he didn't know. Jennifer had been a blind alley. The threatening letter which

Mac had taken as hard proof that *something* was going on had been explained—with no apparent link to anything more sinister than Jennifer's belief in Mac's foolishness. And the use of the same typewriter to write the suicide note had also been explained. Based on what Mac was learning about Jennifer's double life, the explanation made sense. Others would accept it. Mac might have accepted it too if he didn't still have that gnawing gut feeling that Austin Delacroix's death was not a suicide.

But Mac now had an unexpected ally in George Williams. Someone who, at the very least, shared Mac's delusional system. George had acted on his belief in a very different way than Mac. George had floated a trial balloon, his wife's life. Could her death have been merely a tragic coincidence? Doubtful. But again, others would believe it had been. Unless George was holding something back, he wasn't going to be of any further assistance. If George told his story to the disciplinary committee, he could kiss his own medical degree good-bye. Regardless of the facts, George had *believed* that his actions would result in his wife's murder. The medical community frowned on that sort of behavior.

Somehow, Mac had to come up with more evidence. He had a hunch how he could do it. The only problem was, like a lot of his ideas lately, the downside risk was pretty big.

The plan was straightforward. Mac needed evidence that Frost, VanSlyke, and Delacroix had been killing patients. Their victims appeared to be culled from cases presented at the ethics seminar. Mac intended to compare the death rate for patients presented this year with the rate for similar patients presented in the past. If the rate was way up, that would provide evidence that something very wrong was going on.

All Mac needed was a list of patient names and diagnoses.

From the logs in Dr. Law's office.

Law's office opened off a fairly busy corridor. The first couple of times Mac walked by there were other people in the hallway, so he didn't try the door. Someone could always happen to walk around the corner just as Mac was entering Law's office. That was a risk he'd have to take. But he wasn't about to walk in right in front of someone, someone he *knew* was watching. He wasn't that stupid.

The other thing Mac wasn't going to do, he wasn't going to break a window or pick a lock. He wasn't sure how many years in jail they were handing out these days for breaking and entering, but he was confident it would be more than he cared to spend.

Mac had noticed that Law's door didn't close

completely on its own—at least not all the time. Sooner or later, Mac figured, he would be able to just walk right in. If not tonight, maybe tomorrow night. If not tomorrow . . .

But tonight the ethics seminar was meeting. Law could be counted on to be gone for nearly two hours. All Mac needed was a little bit of luck. He figured he was long overdue.

On his third pass, the corridor was empty. Mac could hear footsteps, well behind him, around the corner, but he couldn't see anyone. It was now or never.

He gave the door a push. It gave. In an instant he was inside, standing in total darkness.

Find the light switch. That was his first priority. If he was caught standing in the dark, there was no way he could explain his way out of it. *Just go ahead and put the handcuffs on, Officer. I'm all yours.*

Mac had thought it all through, over and over. What did he say if he got caught? He had come by to see Dr. Law. The door was open. Law wasn't here, so now he's leaving. No crime in any of that. Just as long as no one saw him walk in and turn on the light.

Rule number two: move fast.

He entered Law's inner office, the sanctum sanctorum. Once again, he needed to find a light. He couldn't get caught standing here in the dark. There was a lamp on the desk. That would do for starters.

Mac was standing behind Law's desk, in the dark, when he heard the hallway door open. No key in the lock. No warning. Just pushed right open.

Bullocks!

FORTY-THREE

All of Mac's carefully laid plans were suddenly out the window. It had been a calculated decision, not to tightly close the door. Another person, Mac had reasoned, who found the door to Law's office unlocked and entered the same way Mac had, would have no reason to be suspicious of Mac's presence. Assuming Mac wasn't caught in Law's inner office. Behind Law's desk. In the dark.

Mac ducked under the desk, pushing Law's chair aside. The casters jiggled as the chair rolled. To Mac it sounded like thunder.

He heard the door swing shut. This time there was a distinct clicking sound as it closed completely. Mac was trapped, totally and completely. He would never be able to come up with a lie big enough to explain this away.

He heard footsteps. In the inner office now. Stealing a glimpse under the front of the desk, he could make out a pair of feet.

In high-heeled shoes.

And then legs. Nice legs.

Okay, really nice legs.

And then a voice.

"Mac?"

He pulled himself up from behind the desk with as much dignity as he could muster. Then he reached across the desk and turned on the lamp. She had clearly seen him enter Law's office. There was no point pretending he wasn't here.

"Mac, what the hell are you doing?"

"I dropped a quarter," he said.

She gave him a look that could wither vegetables.

"Scavenger hunt?"

"I'm worried about you, Mac." In a tone which implied she wasn't going to waste any more of her time worrying about him. She turned to leave.

"I'm sorry, Karen," he said. "Look, you don't want to get involved in this."

"Somebody's got to, Mac, before you manage to drown yourself."

Mac didn't want Karen involved, but thought she deserved some kind of explanation. So he gave her an abbreviated version. At least she didn't look at him like he was crazy. She even offered to help.

"Why don't you let me jot names down from

one of the logs while you copy from another? That way you can get out of here in half the time—if I don't slow you down any more."

Karen seemed determined, and Mac couldn't afford to waste any additional precious seconds arguing. "Here's the current log," he said, pointing to the book on Law's desk.

They were standing side by side, behind Law's desk, when they heard the key in the lock.

Without thinking, they both ducked under the desk. Mac felt sick that he had gotten Karen involved in this thing. He'd have to say he'd abducted her or something. Polanski would probably buy that.

There was a great deal of loud, metallic banging in the outer office, then the sound of humming. Mac understood what it meant before Karen. Probably because all this was becoming old hat for him.

"Rollo." Mac mouthed the word to Karen, but in the semidarkness she couldn't make out what he was trying to tell her. So he said it out loud, "Rollo."

In the next office, the humming and banging continued unabated.

Karen tried, unsuccessfully, to stifle a giggle. Her laughter was infectious. The whole situation was so ridiculous—like something out of an *I Love Lucy* episode. The two of them trapped under the desk while the janitor cleans the room.

In the TV show, Lucy would probably hand a wastebasket out from under the desk. The janitor would empty the wastebasket and hand it back without missing a beat.

Rollo had worked at the medical school for something like a century and a half. The bad thing about Rollo, he was soooo sloooowwww. Mac and Karen were likely to be pinned down for quite a while. The good thing about Rollo, he was deaf as a post.

Mac figured, might as well pass the time. "Did you know we were having an affair?" he asked.

"I heard it was over," Karen said.

"Wanta fool around a little?"

"You're already at second base."

"I thought that was your elbow."

"No, *this* is my elbow." She gave Mac a playful shot in the ribs.

Mac coughed theatrically.

"Now, turn your head the other way and cough again, please."

"Shouldn't you be wearing gloves, Doctor?"

The sound of the hallway door opening once again was instantly sobering. The office was starting to become a bit overcrowded.

Fortunately, it was just Rollo—leaving.

Alone again, Mac and Karen quickly found the logbooks and began writing down names. They tried as best they could to match recent patients with those from the past as to age, diagnosis, and time of year.

When they were done, Mac insisted that Karen leave first.

"You've done too much already, Karen. I don't want you to be seen leaving with me. If anybody sees you, just act normal. You were looking for Dr. Law. Remember, there's nothing amiss in here. We haven't removed anything. Everything is back where it belongs."

Mac felt a very strong impulse to give her a kiss to send her on her way, but instead just said, "Thanks, Karen."

He waited several minutes, then stepped out into the corridor himself. It was empty.

The door closed slowly behind him. Mac didn't hear a click.

FORTY-FOUR

Perhaps the worst thing about being called to appear before the disciplinary committee was the fact that everyone in the school seemed to know about it. What they knew was that Mac McCall had done something terrible and might be thrown out of medical school. The rumor was pretty unspecific.

The committee had two new student members. One had been appointed to replace Austin Delacroix. The other had taken Mac's spot. When Mac saw Turner Frost sitting there next to Peter VanSlyke, his first thought was that Frost was going to testify against him. Then he realized that Frost was one of the committee's newly appointed triers of fact.

Karen Anderson was there. Mac now thought of her as an unindicted co-conspirator. Despite the setting, Mac had to work at keeping a smile off his face when he looked at her.

The rest of the faces were familiar and mostly

friendly—or at least formerly friendly. He had worked with all of them, students and faculty, when he served on the committee. But today several of them appeared somewhat embarrassed, working hard at avoiding Mac's gaze.

The committee had been meeting for some time before Mac was allowed into the room. He was called only when they were ready to hear his testimony. It was a terrible feeling. The Inquisition.

Professor Law sat at one end of the table, Mac at the other. The members of the committee sat on either side.

"Mr. McCall," Dr. Law began, "the committee has been asked to review reports that you have engaged in behavior inconsistent with your status as a medical student. You have been invited here to respond to these charges."

Law seemed more formal, much stiffer than in their meetings in his office. It was the way he maintained an aura of impartiality during these proceedings—the same attitude he adopted for the ethics seminar—in an effort to prevent his personal viewpoint from influencing others. He was the consummate chairman.

"Mr. Turner Frost," Law continued, "will present the first charge."

Mac had been wrong about Turner. He was up to no good. Working both sides of the table today. But something was really amiss here. "I don't understand," Mac said. "Is Turner testifying as a witness to some alleged misconduct?"

"He is," Law replied.

"May I ask what?"

"You are about to hear."

"No," Mac insisted, "I want to know exactly what this is about before he launches into some diatribe in front of all these people."

Despite himself, Law appeared weary. "It has to do with your having ordered a digoxin blood level on a person who is not your patient."

It was all Mac could do to remain in his seat. He turned to Turner. "Are you claiming to have witnessed such a thing?" Mac's tone was defiant and angry.

Frost looked at Law. Law nodded. Frost shook his head.

Mac, now furious, confronted Law. "I'm truly surprised that you would consider allowing hearsay testimony. That is not the way this committee has operated in the past. If someone has evidence that I did this thing, that person should come here and accuse me, face to face. I don't have to put up with this."

Turner Frost was red-faced but said nothing. He looked to Law.

Law said, "I believe your point is very well taken, Mr. McCall. Until such time as an appropriate witness comes forward, I believe we should set this charge aside."

"Is there anything else?" Mac asked.

Law seemed momentarily befuddled. "There is the issue of your failure to maintain the confidentiality of the ethics seminar."

"You and I have already discussed that, Dr. Law, at some length. I deny that I betrayed the seminar's confidentiality. I did feel strongly enough about certain matters to take them up with the police. You, however, felt equally strongly that I was wrong. The penalty for breaching seminar confidentiality is quite clear. Summary dismissal. You dismissed me. I had no recourse in the matter. I believe that you were wrong in dismissing me, but I accepted your decision without complaint. That matter is over."

Mac wondered if he had gone too far. He understood that Law was only trying to do his job. Mac didn't want to get into some kind of personal war with the professor. That would be a battle which, sooner or later, Mac would be certain to lose.

Law attempted to shift gears. His voice continued even, his tone compassionate. "People have raised concerns about your obsession with certain matters, Mr. McCall. There have even been questions as to your mental stability."

Mac was beginning to understand. At home, worrying all by himself, this whole disciplinary committee thing had seemed insurmountable.

But here, in the light of day, it all looked different. They had *nothing*!

"First of all, Dr. Law, there is nothing wrong with me mentally. Second of all, if I were a raving psychotic, that would not be the business of this committee. This committee deals solely with *disciplinary* matters." Mac's voice rang with righteous indignation. Why shouldn't it?

"You have to understand, Mr. McCall, it is not the purpose of this committee simply to punish. We are here to *help* students who are in trouble. To find ways to keep problems from festering."

"I appreciate your concern, Dr. Law, but at this point I don't really see that we've identified any real problems." Mac struggled to keep his temper under control. "Is there anything else?"

"Well, I hadn't wanted to raise this issue, but there is the matter of impending charges by the police."

That damn letter! Polanski and Mallory must have been talking to Law. "I'm sure you understand, Dr. Law, how prejudicial it is for you to suggest that the police are going to file some unspecified charges. Frankly, I don't have any idea what you're referring to. I do know that I have never committed any crime whatsoever. Anyone who says I did is a liar."

Mac stood up. "If the committee has nothing further?" No one said a word, so Mac left.

FORTY-FIVE

Karen Anderson caught up with Mac half an hour later in the ICU and greeted him with a high-five.

"I never saw Law at such a loss for words," she said.

Mac shrugged. "I didn't mean to thumb my nose at the guy. I don't need him for an enemy."

"You know Law," Karen said, "he never takes sides. So I don't think he gets very much of himself invested in the outcome."

"I guess you're right."

"By the way, what's the story on George Williams?"

"What do you mean?"

"It looks like he's moved into the ICU."

"Oh, that." Mac debated just how much he should tell Karen. "He's helping keep an eye on Maria Valenzuela."

"You think she's in danger?"

"She's exactly the kind of patient who's been

dying unexpectedly. Relentless underlying illness. Very expensive therapy. Her only hope is a transplant. If there *is* a hit squad around here, she's bound to be number one on their to-do list."

"So when are we going to finish our little mortality-rate analysis?" Karen asked.

"We're not going to finish anything," Mac said. "I feel guilty enough already about how far I've gotten you into this."

"I'm really eager to get a look at those charts, Mac, to find out if the current ethics-seminar patients really are dying at a faster rate than the ones from before. I bet it's going to be interesting."

Mac shook his head. "Karen, I just can't let you get any more involved in this. You've already taken too great a risk. You don't want to end up before the disciplinary committee like I did."

"It looks to me like you're holding them pretty well at bay right now, Mac. If I get into any trouble, I'll just have you represent me before the committee. They'll be shaking in their boots."

"Can't let you do it," Mac said with what he hoped was a tone of finality. "I don't even know if I'll be able to pull that many charts. Somebody's bound to want to know what I'm up to. Hell, it's going to take at least a couple of weeks, requesting a couple of charts at a time, trying not to attract any attention."

"Here's the thing, Mac. I'm already doing a chart review for the pulmonary division. I usually give them a list of fifty patients at a time. I can just hand them a list of patients from the seminar. Nobody'll think anything of it at all."

It really didn't seem like too bad an idea. There was almost no way Karen could get into trouble. No one had a clue they were looking for anything. However reluctantly, Mac had to agree with her.

From the long list of patients they'd culled from Law's logbooks, they decided to concentrate on two groups: current patients and patients from five years ago. Mac reviewed the new patients. Karen took all the old patients. They only counted deaths that had occurred in the hospital within six weeks of the patient's presentation at the ethics seminar. They worked separately to avoid introducing bias into each other's calculations, then met back at Mac's apartment to compare results.

Mac felt completely vindicated. Eighty percent of the patients presented at the ethics seminar in the last two years had died within six weeks.

"We've got 'em nailed!" he told Karen. "No way there was an eighty percent mortality rate five years ago."

Karen didn't look quite as thrilled as he'd hoped. "Seventy-five percent," she said.

"You're kidding." Mac's balloon instantly deflated. Statistically, seventy-five and eighty percent were essentially the same number, given their sample size.

"I wish I *were* kidding. I couldn't believe it."

Unless one of them had made some kind of mistake, the mortality rates for the two time periods were approximately the same. That meant that their investigation had provided no evidence against Delacroix, Frost, and VanSlyke. On the contrary, it could be argued that the numbers exonerated the trio.

For the next hour, Mac and Karen reworked the data, trying to find some fatal error. They came up empty. Their little study had discovered nothing.

Then they were done, sitting there on the couch together, suddenly each very aware of the other's presence.

Then they were looking directly into each other's eyes.

Karen smiled.

Mac smiled.

Karen said, "Are you going to kiss me?"

"Probably," Mac replied.

"Soon?"

"Probably."

"Today?"

He kissed her. It's fair to say that she kissed him back. With enthusiasm.

"I guess the rumor about us must have been true," she said.

"Where there's smoke, there's fire," Mac said.

FORTY-SIX

Mac worried about his budding relationship with Karen. It was the kind of thing which could get very serious very quickly. He wasn't sure that Mac McCall represented a very good investment for any woman at this point.

His performance before the disciplinary committee had bought him time, perhaps even enough time to graduate. The only thing they really had against him was the digoxin level he'd ordered without authorization. That could still come back to haunt him, but it was hard to believe you could get kicked out of medical school for that.

Regarding Austin Delacroix's death, he was still at ground zero. He really had nothing but his personal conviction that Delacroix had been murdered. And on all those other deaths, not much more. No real proof of anything. Maybe he should just drop the whole thing.

Maybe he should just quit breathing.

So, in the absence of any hard leads, he was going back to the beginning. Like he'd told George Williams, *chercher la femme*. Only this time, it would be a different *femme*.

Mac decided not to call ahead, trying to avoid another elaborately plotted seduction scene. He had gotten the impression that Eleanor Delacroix's relationships with men were pretty unidimensional. That impression was about to be fortified.

The front door of the Delacroix town house was in plain view from where Mac parked his car, which was why Mac happened to see Peter VanSlyke leave. VanSlyke walked straight through the door without turning back to talk to anyone, as though he was letting himself out. Mac wondered if Peter had received the four-star reception.

He waited until VanSlyke had driven off, then went to the door and pushed the doorbell. There was no answer until he pushed a second time. Then Eleanor appeared at the door in some kind of fancy bathrobe. Which raised the very definite possibility that VanSlyke had received the *five*-star reception.

"Mac, this is a surprise," she said. "I'm afraid I was taking a nap."

"I'm sorry to bother you, Eleanor. There were a couple of things on my mind that I wanted to

talk to you about. I would have called, but—"
this needed to be phrased very carefully—"I
didn't want you to feel like you had to go to
any trouble."

She stepped back from the door. "Come on
in. It's no problem."

Mac could smell alcohol on her breath. There
were glasses on the table in front of the couch
where Eleanor, in Mac's experience, liked to en-
tertain her male guests.

"I had friends in last night," Eleanor apologized, "and it's Cook's day off. I'm afraid I
haven't had a chance to clean up."

"No need to apologize, Eleanor. It's my fault,
dropping in on you like this."

"Would you like anything? A drink?"

"No thanks. I can only stay a minute."

They sat on the couch. As she moved, her
robe opened this way and that. Mac could be
pretty certain that there was no long flannel
nightgown underneath.

Mac wasn't sure how to begin. There was an
awkward silence.

"What was it you wanted, Mac?"

"I guess you know that Jennifer and I are no
longer together."

Eleanor nodded. It seemed like everyone in
the Western Hemisphere had heard the news.

"And even when we were together, that Jennifer wasn't what you'd call faithful."

Eleanor nodded encouragingly. Mac could tell none of this was hitting her as a startling revelation. He might as well be telling her that George Washington had died.

"Anyway, I was wondering if you might have any idea who she might have"—how to put this?—"you know, been unfaithful with?"

"Mac, first of all, I don't know why you think I might have that kind of information. Second of all, if I did, it wouldn't be the kind of thing I'd do, tell you who's been sleeping with your old girlfriend." This was a very stern Eleanor Delacroix speaking. She had rules. A sense of propriety.

"I'm sorry, Eleanor. I know it's a pretty weird question to ask, but it's important." Might as well go for the whole enchilada, Mac decided. "What I really want to know—and I wouldn't ask if it wasn't terribly important—is there any chance at all that Austin and Jennifer were having an affair?"

Eleanor abruptly stood. Mac thought she was going to ask him to leave. Instead she said, "I think I'll have that drink now. Anything for you?"

Mac shook his head. He watched in silence as Eleanor crossed to the bar and fixed herself something with a lot of gin in it.

When she returned, she said, "You're asking a lot, Mac."

"I know, Eleanor. I'm sorry."

"No, you *don't* know. You're asking far more than you realize." She took a long drink from her glass and weighed things over in her mind.

As he thought about it, Mac was surprised by her reticence.

"Austin's dead," she said. "And when he was alive, we had problems. I'm not denying that. But there's such a thing as privacy. There's such a thing as respect for the dead."

Mac waited. Eleanor seemed more reflective than angry. She truly wasn't certain how much she should reveal.

Finally she said, "I guess I can tell you this, but I need you to promise you won't go blabbing it around."

Mac nodded, thinking this was an awful lot of build-up for a question that, when he had the answer, he wasn't certain what he was going to be able to do with it.

"It wasn't a mental thing," Eleanor said. "It was definitely a physical thing. The doctors all agreed on that." She took a deep breath and turned her eyes away before she said, "Austin was impotent. Always has been. He kept that from me before our marriage. I thought he was just being a gentleman. Frankly, I thought he was sowing his oats elsewhere. You know, he was one of those guys who always talked a good game." She hesitated briefly, staring into her drink.

"Don't misunderstand. Austin liked women, and they certainly liked him. I wasn't the only one he disappointed. You'd be surprised . . ."

Mac raised his eyebrows at that, but Eleanor shook her head. "No, I'm not referring to Jennifer," she said, then fell silent.

"I'm sorry, Eleanor. I, of course, had no idea."

"No one did," she said. "The whole thing was very difficult for both of us."

Mac rose to leave. He had intruded enough, surely for the last time.

"I appreciate your talking to me, Eleanor. I know how difficult it was, but it's very helpful to me in sorting all this out."

He reached over and touched her shoulder. She remained seated on the couch, not looking up.

Mac said good-bye and let himself out, much as he had seen Peter VanSlyke do only a few minutes earlier. There was much to think about.

If Austin Delacroix was impotent, he certainly did not have an affair with Jennifer. But if they hadn't had an affair, why had Jennifer claimed they had?

Mac let his mind travel back to the beginning, back to the day of Austin Delacroix's death. He traced all the events as they had occurred, all the way through his recent visit with Jennifer.

By the time his car pulled to a stop in front of Jennifer's apartment building, Mac thought he had it all pretty well figured out.

FORTY-SEVEN

He pressed the button next to her name at the front door of her apartment building.

"Yes?"

"It's Mac."

There was a long pause. "I don't think we have much to talk about."

"I think we do," Mac said.

"Like what?"

"Like the fact that you *did not* have an affair with Austin Delacroix."

Another long pause, then the sound of the buzzer releasing the door that opened onto the lobby.

Jennifer was waiting for him at her apartment door. "What makes you think Austin and I *didn't* have an affair?"

"Doesn't matter. You know you didn't, and I know you didn't. What we need to discuss is, Why did you tell me you did?"

She turned away from the door and walked

back into the apartment, then sat down heavily on a couch. Jennifer didn't look like she was about to volunteer anything.

"It was that gasp you made, Jen, that finally told me everything. That day Polanski and Mallory came by with the suicide note. You covered by saying that you couldn't believe Austin would kill himself over an internship. But the truth is, when you looked at that supposed suicide note, you instantly realized that your typewriter had been used to type it. And as soon as you realized that, you knew that Austin had not committed suicide.

"More importantly," Mac said, "you also knew the person who wrote that note was the person who killed Austin Delacroix."

Jennifer was hearing every word, but made no effort to respond. She certainly wasn't protesting anything Mac said.

"Which one was the killer, Jennifer. Frost? VanSlyke? Or were they equal partners?"

Still nothing from Jennifer. Her gaze never strayed from the carpet.

"Your biggest mistake, Jennifer, was all this." Mac made a gesture with his hand to encompass their surroundings. "There's no way you could afford all this. No job in the world. No amount of credit anyone would be likely to extend to you. You even had cash to pay the rent on our apartment. To my own discredit, I have to admit

I was so relieved to have the damn rent paid that I didn't let myself look at it very closely."

Mac studied her. She looked totally defeated.

"I'm worried for you, Jen. Blackmail is a serious crime. Besides that, the authorities might decide to charge you as an accessory after the fact. An accessory to *murder*, Jen.

"But what scares me most of all is these guys you're blackmailing. They're murderers. That's *why* you're blackmailing them. What makes you think they're gonna let you get away with that? What makes you think they won't just decide to get rid of you when the time is right?"

Jennifer's head came up for the first time. "You don't have to worry about me."

"Somebody has to. Why did you write that stupid death threat? Didn't you know I'd go to the police?"

"I wasn't sure. If you didn't, the letter would have served one purpose, to get your nose out of all of this."

"You know me better than that, Jen. It only convinced me that I was right."

"If you did go to the police, I figured it wouldn't lead them anywhere, except maybe back to the suicide note—if they managed to make the connection."

Mac chewed on that for a couple of minutes. Then he began to understand her convoluted thinking.

"You needed to put pressure on *them*, didn't you?" The expression on her face told him he was right. "Were they balking at paying your price?"

"They didn't believe I was serious."

"And you sent me the note, knowing I would go to the police. You knew the police would check the death threat against the suicide note. It was your way of reminding the killer that you still had power over him. Warning him that you weren't afraid to use that power."

"I wanted to be taken seriously."

"Who is it, Jen? Who are you blackmailing?"

"Sorry, Mac."

"Look, Jen, if you go to the police now and tell them everything, I bet you can get out of this. You should probably hire an attorney and try to cut a deal in advance. It would be plenty embarrassing, but at least you wouldn't have to go to jail. You could move somewhere—someplace where no one would know about this. You'd still have your whole life ahead of you."

"What kind of life, Mac? As a nurse? Go back to not having anything and owing everybody? Or should I marry some rich guy and let him own me?"

"You can do whatever you want, Jen. That's not the point."

"It *is* the point. Why do you think I got into this in the first place?"

318

"You're in danger, Jen. Can't you see that? They're not going to let you blackmail them forever. They're *killers*!"

Somehow, he had to get through to her.

"What about all the others who have died, Jen? What about all those patients? Hell, what about all the other patients who are going to die if somebody doesn't stop them?"

"There won't be any more killing, Mac. That's part of the deal."

"And how are you going to monitor that? You're not in the ICU anymore. How are you going to know if somebody dies who shouldn't?"

Jennifer didn't have an answer to that. Clearly, she had told them there couldn't be any more deaths. She had used that to assuage her own guilt.

"I can't help you, Jen, if you won't let me." Mac felt his own frustration mounting. "I presume you have that typewriter hidden away somewhere you think is safe?"

Jennifer nodded. "With a letter telling everything. They wouldn't dare harm me. If they do, it'll all come out."

"How?"

"Don't worry. It will."

"Sooner or later, Jennifer, they'll figure out a way around that, or they'll decide that leaving you alive is just too great a risk. Then they'll kill you. You should not have any doubts about that."

"I can take care of myself."

"No, Jennifer, you can't."

Mac stood. There was no way he could help her, yet. Maybe she'd have a change of heart before it was too late.

"Call me," he said, "if you change your mind. I'll do anything I can to get you out of this safely."

And with that, he left.

As he walked out of the luxurious building, Mac couldn't help but wonder how much they were paying her. A lot, if the likes of Peter Van-Slyke and Turner Frost had balked at the amount.

In some ways Mac felt like he was getting closer to the end of all this. He understood more and more of what was going on. In other ways, though, he was still at the beginning. He knew that terrible crimes had been committed, but he didn't have a shred of real, hard evidence which could be used to convict anyone.

There were still a couple of loose ends that might give him the proof he needed. One had to do with Austin Delacroix. Who had killed him—and why? Something had occurred to Mac, something from way back at the beginning. It might explain a lot.

And there was something else, something Eleanor Delacroix had said. When Mac got back to his apartment, the first thing he did was call Karen Anderson.

"I'm sorry to bother you, but I need one last favor."

"I don't know, Mac. It's awfully late and I've got a pretty full schedule tomorrow."

"It's not that, Karen. I just want to look at some more charts."

"Darn."

"I want to check out the mortality rate for ethics seminar patients from fifteen years ago."

"You're one incredibly romantic guy, Mac."

"I wouldn't want you to think I was easy."

FORTY-EIGHT

Stacey Martin felt herself tense up. *You're acting silly*, she told herself. *It's not like he's going to actually talk to you or anything.* Still, she felt herself growing increasingly nervous as he approached. She glanced over her shoulder. There were only the two of them in the hallway—she an insignificant sophomore; he a senior and star football player. Stacey buried her head deeper into her locker.

He came closer. He stopped beside her. She thought she was going to die.

"Hi, Stacey."

"Hi, Mitch." She could hardly bring herself to look at him.

"I was wondering, Stace, do you have a date for the prom yet?"

She was tempted to tell him not to be silly; of course she didn't have a date. She was only a sophomore. She wasn't sure if sophomores were even allowed to go to the junior-senior prom.

But she said, "No." Stacey could hardly hear her own voice, so she gave her head a good shake so there could be no misunderstanding.

"Well, would you like to go with me?"

Now Stacey made herself look at him. Was this a joke? She looked around to see if anyone else was watching, waiting to jump out and laugh if she took him seriously.

"I thought you were dating Jessica." Just about the most popular girl in the whole school. And a senior!

"We broke up."

Stacey still wasn't sure what she should do. Was she about to make a fool of herself?

"Do you want to go or not?" Mitch was suddenly impatient—not used to being kept waiting.

"Sure," Stacey said.

"Good. I'll call you later and set things up." With that, Mitch turned and walked back down the hall.

Stacey's mother was pleased, her little girl going to the big dance. Her father wasn't convinced it was all that red-hot of an idea. He wasn't so sure that his little girl should be going out with a senior. There'd better not be any funny stuff, he said.

It turned out that a lot of the senior boys had asked sophomore girls to the prom, to teach those snooty senior girls a lesson. Instead of feeling insulted, Stacey was relieved, pleased that there'd be a bunch of girls her own age going along.

And then the big day came, and Tom Martin could hardly believe it was his daughter looking so darn grown-up in that fancy dress, her hair all heaped up on top of her head like that. Reminded him of going to the big high school dance with her mom, now more than a few years ago.

They fussed around and took pictures. Stacey had only one request. "Please," she pleaded, "*please* don't embarrass me in front of Mitch."

They had their little talk. Home by midnight. Stacey pleaded for one o'clock. Tom thought eleven was plenty late enough. If there was any problem whatsoever, Stacey was to call them. They'd come and get her.

Then Mitch arrived, all tuxedo and aftershave, playing his Eddie Haskel to their Ward and June Cleaver.

Now, Tom Martin was a big man, a whole lot bigger than this football star and one heck of a lot tougher, having put in his nearly twenty-five years down at the mill. He wasn't about to let this kid come in here, blow a little sunshine in their direction, and waltz out with his daughter no questions asked. He wanted to make certain he had the young man's full attention.

"Hi, I'm Tom Martin," he said. Then he gave

the kid a handshake that brought tears to Mitch's eyes. "Real pleased to meet you."

Tom draped one of his enormous arms around Mitch and firmly gripped his shoulder. Very firmly, so there could be no question as to his seriousness. "We're just real pleased to have Stacey go out with you, because we know how careful you'll be. We know there'll be no drinking or anything like that.

"We'll expect you back here by midnight, the latest. Of course, you're welcome to come back sooner. Bring any friends you'd like. We'll be up. Waiting."

He let go of Mitch and gave the couple a big smile. "Now, you kids have a wonderful time, hear?"

And they did. Mitch and Stacey danced a couple of dances together, but mostly he was off somewhere with his friends, and she was able to be with hers. Which was just fine with Stacey. She had worried that things might get a little heavy, Mitch being a senior and all. She kind of liked the breathing room.

The dance was held in the old high school gym, all decorated with streamers and colored lights. You hardly knew you were dancing on a basketball floor. It was all that beautiful. Like a fairy tale, really.

Mitch and his friends kept going outside. Stacey wondered if they were smoking, which athletes shouldn't do, but it looked like they were having a good time. That was the important thing. Everyone should have a wonderful time.

It wasn't until after the dance was over that Stacey began to worry that maybe Mitch was having too much fun. She had never seen him this boisterous before.

Finally, she asked, "Mitch, have you been drinking?"

"What if I have?" he said, suddenly sullen.

Stacey noticed that the car was beginning to weave. "Please slow down," she pleaded.

When the doorbell rang at eleven-thirty, Tom's wife gave him a big smile.

"You can just wipe that grin right off your face," he told her. "I wasn't worried at all. I put the fear of God into that boy."

When he opened the door, still smiling, he was suddenly face to face with two state policemen.

"I'm afraid we have some bad news," the big one said.

Mitch was killed outright, he said, by the force of the impact. Stacey was alive, but she'd suffered a severe head injury. They'd taken her to the university.

The rest of the night and all the next day, the Martins stayed at the hospital. First at the ICU, then outside the operating rooms, then back to the ICU. Every time the doctors spoke to them, they sounded gloomier than the time before.

On the morning of the second day, one of the residents said something about transplantation. Tom said he didn't know much about transplants, but he said sure, go ahead, anything that might help Stacey. The doctor said no, he was sorry, he guessed he hadn't made himself clear. What he meant was, Stacey's organs might help someone else.

FORTY-NINE

Mac looked at his watch for the first time in over an hour. It was now well past time for him to be able to escape the ICU—if only things would settle down for a little while. George Williams had already wandered in and out a couple of times, prepared to assume the watch over Maria Valenzuela whenever Mac was finally able to leave.

Mac nodded at George. George nodded back. Simple acknowledgment of each other's presence, nothing more. Mac understood that he would never again look at George Williams the way he once had, that the two of them could never again have anything like the relationship they had once shared—no matter how this whole mess turned out.

There was a level on which Mac understood what George Williams had done, but it was not a level on which Mac cared to live.

Maria Valenzuela remained stable. Because of

the respirator she had finally been able to get some rest. She no longer needed to dedicate every ounce of energy she could muster to the exhausting task of breathing. On the other hand, as they had feared, there now seemed little hope she could ever be successfully weaned from the machine.

Throughout it all Maria Valenzuela remained steadfast and indomitable. Mac hoped that he would never have to face a test like the one Maria faced day in and day out, but if such a trial should ever come his way, he prayed he could somehow summon just half her grace and dignity.

Her husband too was holding up remarkably well under the strain, but Mac sensed that Diego Valenzuela was pretty dry tinder. It wouldn't take much to set him off.

When he saw Diego standing in the middle of the ICU, tears in his eyes, staring off into nowhere, Mac placed a gentle hand on his shoulder. Diego handed Mac the crumpled note he held in his hand: *Dearest, I need to see the babies. Tonight. Then I'd like to see Father Patrick. I love you.*

Even his own limited experience in medicine had taught Mac that sometimes patients knew much more accurately than their doctors when the end was approaching. This was the first chink that had shown itself in Maria Valenzuela's well-lacquered veneer of intransigent optimism.

"What the hell do you think you're doing, hanging around here all the time?"

It was more the tone of voice than the volume which wrenched Mac's attention away from Diego Valenzuela. The words had been uttered in a low, guttural growl that you'd expect to be accompanied by bared teeth.

Mac turned to find George Williams and Peter VanSlyke squaring off in a corner of the ICU. It was only a question of who would throw the first punch. George was taller and had a reach advantage, but they would weigh in about the same. Both of them heavyweights.

"Someone ought to shoot that asshole," Diego volunteered. "I hope George kills him."

From the look on Diego's face, Mac figured that Diego meant that literally.

"Just keeping an eye on you, Petie," George said. "Trying to learn all I can about your technique."

"I know what you *think* you're doing," VanSlyke said.

"Oh, what's that?"

It put VanSlyke in kind of an awkward position. He didn't really want to mention that George was watching to see if he tried to kill any patients.

He settled for, "You'd better watch out, Williams, or you'll end up just like your buddy McCall."

"Third in my class," Mac said as he came across the room. "George could do worse."

VanSlyke now turned his baleful glare on Mac.

"Besides," Mac added, "a couple more suicides around here, and I could become *numero uno*."

"You're sick, McCall."

"By the way, Pete,"—VanSlyke hated to be called anything but Peter—"I was sorry to hear about your marriage."

"What's that supposed to mean?"

"I understand that you're seeing Eleanor Delacroix."

Now VanSlyke looked like he'd take a swing at Mac. George Williams edged a little closer, just to remind VanSlyke that there were two of them there. VanSlyke was still considering his next move when there was a commotion at the entrance to the ICU and the entire surgical team entered en masse.

They brought news. A pair of donor lungs had already been harvested halfway across the country. The lungs were now on an airplane, headed here for Maria.

Diego's voice was so choked with emotion he could hardly get the words out to share the news with his wife. Maria had an instant concern which she was unable to communicate with the pidgin sign language she and Diego had created since she had been on the respirator.

Her scribbled note read, "Who is the donor?"

Diego told her what he had heard. A teenager had been killed in an auto accident.

Maria's eyes teared for the first time. "How sad," she wrote. Then she added, "No matter how this turns out for us, please let her family know how grateful we are. Promise?"

Diego promised. Maria had one other request.

"Now I really do need to see my babies. And then Father Patrick."

FIFTY

Ruby caught Mac just as he left Maria's room. "You have a new admission," she said.

"No way, Ruby. It's after seven-thirty, and I'm not on call. I have to go down to medical records to check a couple of charts, then I'm out of here." The charts Mac had asked Karen to pull for him were waiting down in medical records. Every time Mac had tried to sneak down there, some new crisis had arisen in the ICU.

Ruby immediately softened her approach. "I need your help. Besides, you might score a few extra points taking care of this particular patient. That wouldn't hurt."

Mac gave her a look. *This particular patient?* "Okay, because I'm such a nice guy, and because you're a girl, I'll stay for a little while. What's the special deal about this *particular* patient?"

"Her name's Constance Law."

"Any relation?"

"Wife."

If Mac had ever known her first name, he had long since forgotten it. An image quickly formed itself in his mind: the carefully made-up woman lying on her bed the night of the party, her gaze fixed relentlessly on the ceiling above her, the aura of death dispelled only by an occasional fluttering of her eyelids.

"What's her story?" Mac asked.

"Her acute problem is probably pneumonia—she's apparently deteriorated pretty dramatically over the last few hours—but her underlying process is neurologic. A little over six months ago she bled into her brain stem—knocked out her ventral pons. She's been locked-in ever since."

Mac shook his head, instantly understanding what he had witnessed that night at the Law house. It was hard to imagine a condition more psychologically and emotionally devastating than the so-called locked-in syndrome. Patients suffering from the syndrome—usually the result of a stroke—lose their ability to move their extremities; they are unable to speak. The only voluntary motions which are preserved are vertical eye movement and eyelid elevation. EEG examination shows perfectly normal brain-wave patterns. Patients are fully conscious and alert—they are merely locked in.

"Do we know why she had the bleed?"

"Not a clue," Ruby said. "It happens. Often it's young women."

Mac looked at the chart. Constance Law was forty-two. She must be at least twenty years younger than her husband. The thought made Mac cast his gaze around the ICU. "Is Dr. Law around?"

Ruby shook her head. "No one seems to be able to find him. Apparently it was Mrs. Law's nurse who called the ambulance. The ER team has talked with her. They say she doesn't know where Law is either."

It was a strange night which stood a good chance of becoming a great deal stranger. Ironic, Mac thought, that Mrs. Law should be admitted just as he was about to go down to the medical records department. She might delay him, but she wasn't going to stop him.

Mac's patient looked much older and much sicker than when he last laid eyes on her. Then, she had appeared alert. She looked as though she could have talked to him if she had only wanted to. Now she didn't. Her temperature was 103.6 degrees. Her heart rate was 130. Her respirations were rapid and labored. Gurgling sounds emanated from the back of her throat, the result of the accumulation of secretions.

Mac talked to Mrs. Law as he examined her, explaining as he went along, but reasonably certain that he wasn't getting through. When he listened to her lungs, he heard rales and bronchial breath sounds—both consistent with pneumonia. She was a very sick lady.

Mrs. Law's chest X ray showed diffuse, bilateral pneumonia with some suggestion of early abscess formation. When they looked at her sputum under the microscope, they saw organisms that looked like staph. She was quickly started on appropriate antibiotic therapy.

Still, no one could find Dr. Law. Stan Schell, the chief of the neurology service, came by. He was a friend of the family and had helped care for Constance Law when she suffered her stroke, so they latched on to him for advice.

"The big question," Mac said, "is, Should we intubate her?"

"I think we should wait," Schell said, "as long as she's holding her own and we still haven't talked to Arthur. The two of them have probably discussed this, since pneumonia and the problem of intubation are quite foreseeable eventualities with this type of neurologic deficit. They may have a strong opinion.

"It's quite remarkable," Schell added, "the way they're able to communicate through her use of eye movements. He's really quite dedicated to her, you know. I can't imagine what's happened to him."

Schell made a brief note in the chart, one of

those "Kilroy was here" kinds of notes that attending physicians seemed to be able to get away with. Not much information. Just a quick impression jotted down. Maybe four of five lines total. The resident might add a page. An intern was good for two or three pages. Medical students were *expected* to go on interminably. A ten-page note was nothing for a medical student.

Mac wrote his admission note—adequate, but no ten pages—then turned to Ruby. "Do you think you can make it through the rest of the night on your own?"

She gave him The Look.

"Okay, I'll be in medical records for a little while," Mac said. "You can beep me there if you need me, but try to think through the problem first on your own before you call. It's good experience."

The Look intensified.

Mac gave her a smug smile and headed for the medical records department. The patient charts that Karen had requested were set aside, waiting for him.

He didn't spend a great deal of time with each chart. All he needed was a quick and dirty review. Halfway through, Mac was already confident that he was going to find exactly what he had expected. In less than two hours, he was done.

The results were unambiguous. Fifteen years

ago the mortality rate for patients presented at the ethics seminar was less than thirty percent. That was high, but not totally unexpected given the nature of the cases presented at the seminar— and it was strikingly lower than the seventy-five to eighty percent rate that he and Karen had found more recently.

The pieces of the puzzle were now nearly all in place. Mac was contemplating his next move when his beeper went off. He called the operator, thinking, *If you want me at this hour of the night, Ruby, you're really going to have to beg.*

"Mac McCall," he said.

"You have an outside call," the operator said.

Outside call? At this hour?

"Mac"—it was Jennifer—"I need to talk to you."

"I'm all ears."

"In person."

Mac hesitated. He wasn't certain he could handle Jennifer along with everything else tonight. "How about tomorrow? Maybe meet for lunch or something."

"I need to talk to you tonight." Jennifer's voice started to break. "I'm scared."

"Is this about what we discussed before?"

"Yes—I think so—but I can't talk about it over the phone." Then she added, "I'm really afraid, Mac."

"You have to talk to the police, Jen."

"I will, Mac. I promise. But first I need to talk to you."

"Okay. I'll be right over."

"Thanks, Mac. And, Mac, I'm sorry. For everything."

FIFTY-ONE

Jennifer paced the floor of her darkened apartment, repeatedly going back to the window, parting the curtains ever so slightly, and stealing a glance at the street. She could no longer make out the hulking figure in the shadows. She was relieved that he was gone but embarrassed that she had panicked and called Mac. He would use it to try to get information out of her. He would insist once again that she go to the police. There was no way she would do that.

She peeked out from behind the curtains once again. A shudder went through her body. Was there movement? No. Don't be silly. He's gone.

He. From the sheer bulk of the stalker, she assumed it was a man. She had never gotten a good look. First he had followed in a car, then lurked outside her building. She assumed it was the same person. Perhaps she was only imagining the whole thing.

She heard the buzzer announcing someone at

the front door. As she crossed the apartment, she turned on a single lamp.

"Yes?" she said.

"It's me."

She pushed the buzzer, then headed for the bathroom, figuring she would have just enough time to run a brush through her hair and check her makeup before Mac got upstairs. But she no sooner got to the bathroom than she heard a soft knock at the apartment door.

"You must have run up the stairs," she said to Mac as she opened the door—before she realized it wasn't Mac who was standing there.

She tried to slam the door, but he blocked it. She barely managed to form the slightest beginning of a scream before it was muffled by his hand.

He held her from behind, one massive arm across her chest, pinioning both arms and holding her a full foot above the floor. The other hand was across her mouth.

Jennifer tried to kick back at him but couldn't make solid contact. He seemed to enjoy her struggle.

"You're even prettier than I remembered," he said.

Mac's first thought was, Whatever had finally put the fear of God into Jennifer, it was about time. She had been playing with fire for far too long. No matter what her fate at the hands of the legal system, anything was better than simply waiting for VanSlyke and company to exact retribution.

Mac figured it might be best if Jennifer went directly to the district attorney's office, bypass Mallory and Polanski completely. They'd had their chance to crack the case. The DA might be more than willing to cut a deal if it allowed him to show up the police in the process. Then Mac thought, *That's stupid, the first thing she needs is her own attorney*. She shouldn't be relying on Mac for legal advice.

The other thing, more in the back of Mac's mind, this whole business was moving rapidly toward resolution. The facts were about to come out. VanSlyke and company were about to be served their just deserts. And, not altogether unimportantly, Mac was about to be exonerated.

So by the time Mac completed the short drive to Jennifer's apartment building, his mind was completely fixed on the process of unwinding the mess which had preoccupied him for the last several weeks. For whatever reasons, Jennifer had finally come to understand the seriousness of her position. That she was in any immediate, grave danger did not occur to him.

Mac pushed the button beside Jennifer's name at the front door of her building.

"Yes," she said.

"It's me."

The buzzer sounded, unlocking the door, and Mac walked into the well-lighted lobby. The indicators above both elevators showed that they were going up, so Mac figured what the hell, it wouldn't hurt him to take the stairs. Apparently he wasn't the only one to have that idea. Mac heard the sound of someone rushing up the stairs somewhere above him.

The footsteps were heavy, almost felt more than heard, even though Mac was a flight or two below. Their violent cadence disturbed the peace of the otherwise soundless building and set off a warning bell in Mac's brain.

He quickened his pace, taking the steps two and three at a time. There was the sound of a door being thrown open above. Mac was on the landing before it closed. Down the hallway he caught sight of a dark form disappearing through Jennifer's doorway. He thought he might have heard a muffled scream.

Mac pounded the door with his fist, tried the knob. It was locked.

"Jennifer!" No response.

He backed away and threw his shoulder into the door. It felt like his shoulder would break, but the frame gave. One more heave and he was inside—in darkness—the only light coming from the hallway behind him. He wondered if any of the neighbors had called the police yet.

"Jennifer!" There was no answer.

Mac found a switch. A ceiling light went on over his head. He found another switch. A lamp went on in the living room. The curtains were drawn. The apartment felt close. He could smell sweat.

Mac began to slowly make his way through the apartment, searching as he went so that he would always be between the intruder and his escape.

There was a closet near the entryway. He sprung the door open. Nothing. No one.

He slowly entered the living room. Empty. No one hiding behind the couch. The bathroom—empty. No perpetrator behind the shower curtain. The kitchen—empty.

Mac moved toward the darkened bedroom, its door pulled to but not shut completely. He had to be in there, the intruder. Jennifer too—if she was in the apartment.

He gave the bedroom door a kick. It flew open and banged against the wall. No one behind the door.

"Jennifer." He heard motion, maybe fifteen feet away in the far corner of the room.

Mac groped for a light switch and found one near the door. He was half crouched, ready to defend himself, every muscle and sense alert. He threw the switch. A lamp went on beside the bed. They were in the far corner where he had heard the noise.

Beano had one hand over Jennifer's mouth; the other held a knife to her throat. There was already a streak of blood across her neck where he had cut her. Her eyes bulged in terror.

The first thing, Mac thought, was not to panic Beano.

"Looks like we've got ourselves kind of a stand-off here, Beano."

"Come any closer and I slit her throat."

Mac nodded. "I'm fine where I am, but you've got a problem too. How're you getting out of here?"

Beano smirked. "The knife."

"You could kill Jennifer," Mac said, "but not me. You come at me with that knife, and I'll cut your heart out with it." It was the only kind of language Beano understood. Mac could see that he had made an impression.

"I should have run you down when I had the chance."

"So that was you, huh, Beano? Were you working for somebody else or just freelancing?"

"That was personal."

"How about tonight, Beano? Who sent you over here tonight?"

"That's for me to know and you to find out." Beano Smith, erudite and sophisticated as ever.

Mac studied Jennifer. She was terrified. She

had the small cut. But otherwise she was fine, for now. He had to focus on Beano. Then he noticed something.

"You cold, Beano? Looks like you've got goose bumps." Beano knew what he meant. He was beginning to look a little shaky. "You didn't stray off the methadone program by any chance, did you? You look like you could use a fix."

"You got something you want to trade, Doc—for the girl?"

"Sorry. I'm fresh out of narcotics. You're gonna have to find another source."

"You better come up with something, Doc, or I'm gonna cut her." Beano's priorities were quickly shifting.

"You cut her, Beano, and I'm going to let you experience the joy of narcotic withdrawal in the trunk of my car someplace way out in the country."

Beano was getting shakier by the minute. All he cared about now was his next fix. Nothing else mattered.

"Tell you what," Mac said. "I'll just slip over here against the wall on the other side of the bed and get out of your way. All you have to do is let go of Jennifer and leave." As he spoke, Mac moved slowly to his right.

"Don't try anything funny."

"Don't worry. All I want is for you to leave."

Beano began to edge toward the door, still holding Jennifer.

"Huh-uh, Beano." Mac took a step back toward the door. "As long as you've got Jennifer, I'm staying between you and the door. You've got to let go of her."

Mac could tell Beano wanted to get out, but he knew that Jennifer was his only real bargaining chip. Beano was already convinced that Mac wasn't afraid of the knife. Mac edged back to his right as a sign of good faith.

Beano began to relax his grip on Jennifer. She just sort of melted onto the floor.

Beano was alone now, crouching, making sideways, crablike movements toward the door. For a brief moment it looked as though he might attempt some futile gesture like throwing the knife.

"Don't do it," Mac warned him "If you throw that knife, it better kill me, and I don't think that's going to happen."

Beano gave a halfhearted upward thrust with the knife from about ten feet away from Mac. It wasn't worth the effort. Mac took one step toward him, and he was gone.

FIFTY-TWO

Mac followed Beano out of the apartment and did his best to shut what was left of the front door. Then he went back to Jennifer—picked her up off the floor and laid her gently on the bed. Tears stained her cheeks and her makeup was a mess, but she was holding up remarkably well. The cut on her neck was very superficial.

"That creep followed me around this afternoon," she said with a faltering voice. "He was standing outside when I called you."

"In the morning you can call the police and press charges. I don't suppose there's any hurry. The important thing is that you now understand the danger you're in. It's time to put an end to all of this."

Jennifer was suddenly less emotional, more defiant. "I don't think this had anything to do with what's going on at the hospital. This was just Beano trying to get some money for his habit. We don't have any reason to believe this had anything to do with anything else."

Mac couldn't believe his ears. He was suddenly sorry he'd let Beano escape. "Jennifer, this is nuts. We're dealing with killers here."

But Jennifer was going to believe what she wanted to believe. There was no persuading her, which meant that—at least for the time being—she wasn't going to be providing any evidence to support Mac.

He was able to talk her into going to a hotel for now, so he wouldn't have to worry about her. Mac dropped her off, making certain they weren't being followed, then headed back to the hospital.

He found the ICU much as he had left it—with one major exception. Maria Valenzuela's room was empty. There was no reminder left behind to suggest that Maria had ever been there. The cleaning people had been in. There were fresh sheets on the bed. In spite of himself, Mac felt his heart sink.

He had seen this many times before, the first announcement of death. He would come back to the hospital in the morning to find an empty bed. The patient had died during the night. In Maria's case, there was the probability of a happier explanation.

"Maria Valenzuela's in surgery?" Mac asked a nurse.

"Been gone for a couple of hours," she replied.

"The medical students go with her?"

She nodded. "And that pair can stay down there as far as I'm concerned."

VanSlyke and Frost were not universally loved.

Mac made his way down to the bowels of the hospital, looking for VanSlyke and Frost. The operating room, like the morgue, was located in the basement. For reasons Mac had never fully comprehended, it was always cold down there. He felt a chill pass through his body. Then another.

He pushed a plate on the wall, and the double doors that marked the OR's main entrance opened. The long hallway before him provided access to the locker rooms, recovery ward, and central nursing station. There wasn't a soul to be seen. This time of night, only one or two operating rooms would be in use. It wasn't economically sensible to keep the recovery room open with so little going on, so any patients requiring extended postoperative recovery services were generally taken to the ICU.

Mac walked the length of the hall and back, as far as he could go in street clothes. All he wanted to do was make certain that VanSlyke and Frost were down here. Then he would simply wait.

Finally he found a circulating nurse.

"What room is Maria Valenzuela in?" Mac asked her.

"She the double lung?"

Mac nodded.

"She's in OR-2."

"Are there some medical students in there?"

"There's about a thousand people in there. Some of 'em are probably medical students. Some of 'em are probably a busload of hockey fans from out of town."

"Is there a dome over OR-2?"

The nurse nodded, and Mac was once again looking for a stairwell. It made sense that they'd do a double-lung transplant in one of the domed theaters. Mac figured he could pick VanSlyke and Frost out from above about as easily as from the floor of the OR. Once he'd located them, it would simply be a matter of waiting.

One floor up, he found the door marked OR-2. The viewing area inside was dimly lighted. And of course it was cold. There was one person already there, watching. A dark figure in surgical scrubs who turned as Mac came in. Karen Anderson.

"Mac! You're not on call. You should be home asleep." Then, after an appropriate pause, she added, "Alone."

He smiled. "It turns out I can't sleep alone anymore." At any other time he would have taken more notice of how sexy she looked in her OR scrubs.

She came over to give him a hug, pressing her body against him in the dark and whispering into Mac's ear, "Wanta fool around? Double-lung transplants make me hot." She gave his ear a nip for emphasis.

"Maybe later," Mac said. "How's the operation going?"

"They're really just getting started, but everything seems fine so far."

Mac leaned over the glass that formed the ceiling of the operating room and stared down at the scene below. The nurse had been right. There was quite a crowd down there. Maria's chest was open. It looked like they were about to remove the lungs she had been born with—a necessary step before new lungs could be implanted.

Mac studied the faces behind the masks. There were some he could make out, some he couldn't. He couldn't identify either Frost or VanSlyke.

"Where are the Golden Boys?" he asked Karen.

"We came down here together, but it was pretty obvious we weren't all going to be able to get into the OR. I came up here to watch; they must have gone back upstairs."

"How long ago was that?"

"A half hour or so."

Mac sank back into his own thoughts. Going over to Jennifer's tonight, he had once again felt confident that the lid was about to be blown off this whole thing. But Jennifer had let him down. Not for the first time.

Mac *knew* what was going on, but like George Williams had said, there was a big difference between what you knew and what you could prove. Mac needed proof.

One other thing had been bothering him—those charts that he and Karen had reviewed. Mac had looked at the most current charts and at those from fifteen years ago. There had been a dramatic difference in mortality rates. Karen had told him that the rate from five years ago was essentially the same as the current rate. He had only Karen's word on that. He hadn't actually reviewed those charts.

What if Karen was lying? What if she was involved with VanSlyke and Frost? Her finding that the rate of death for ethics-seminar patients was the same five years ago as it was today exonerated Frost and VanSlyke.

But Mac had another theory which accounted for everything without implicating Karen. How to prove it?

"Want to let me in on what you're thinking, Mac?" Karen had been staring at him for several minutes now.

"Same old, same old," Mac said.

"Did another patient die?"

Mac shook his head. He wasn't ready to say anything about the adventures of Jennifer and Beano yet. "I guess I'm just a little distracted," he said. "I think I'll wander back up to the ICU and see how everything's going."

He gave Karen a peck on the cheek as he left. He didn't want to believe she was involved, but Mac's judgment—where women were concerned—hadn't exactly been perfect of late.

FIFTY-THREE

The ICU was in late-night mode. Lights were dimmed. All visitors had pretty much gone home. The staff now spoke in hushed tones. The only discernible noise was the sound of modern medicine at work. The whoosh of respirators, the gongs and chimes of various monitors, the occasional whirring of a telemetry device as it spat out an EKG strip.

The only unusual sight, the one thing that Mac had never before seen at this hour, was the chief of neurology, Stan Schell, sitting hunched over a chart at the nursing station. Mac quietly took a seat beside him, not saying anything until Dr. Schell looked up.

Then he said, "How's Mrs. Law doing?"

Schell shook his head. "Not well. She's going to need a respirator, and the last thing in the world I want to do is put that woman on a respirator without her husband's consent. But if I can't get hold of Arthur, I don't see what else I can do."

Mac wasn't about to offer any advice to the chief of neurology. Schell wasn't really even talking to Mac. It was more like he was thinking out loud.

"No trace of Dr. Law?" Mac asked.

Schell shook his head. "I finally called the police and asked them to keep an eye out for his car. We really need him to make this decision."

Mac wandered over to the far corner of the ICU, where Ruby was writing in a chart. "Sounds like Mrs. Law isn't doing so well," he said.

"No response to the antibiotics so far. But it's still early innings."

"Have you seen Frost or VanSlyke?"

"They've both been around. VanSlyke was in with Mrs. Law for a long time. I guess he knows her pretty well."

"Has she had any rhythm problems?"

Ruby gave him The Look.

Mac shrugged and headed off for Mrs. Law's cubicle. There didn't appear to be any improvement in her respiration. Her temperature was still elevated. Her blood pressure was on the low side.

Mac listened to her lungs and noted that she wasn't moving air very well. Her skin was clammy. She didn't seem to be aware of his presence, but her level of consciousness was very difficult to judge because of the locked-in syndrome.

There was a strong odor of penicillin at the bedside, which wasn't unusual in patients receiving an antibiotic of the penicillin family. Mac saw the empty plastic bag of nafcillin still hanging from a pole at the head of her bed.

Still, the odor did seem unusually strong. Mac began poking around the bedside, following his nose. Then he found it, in the bedding beside her left arm.

Mrs. Law's nurse was busy charting narcotic meds when Mac caught up with her. "When did Mrs. Law get her last dose of nafcillin?"

She looked at her watch. "About a half hour ago."

"Any problems?"

The nurse shook her head. "Why?"

"Anyone around when she got the nafcillin?"

"Just that jerk medical student."

"Could you be more specific?"

"The big blond one."

Gotcha! Mac thought.

The next hour flashed by in an instant. Mac was certain he wouldn't be able to convince everyone and get things organized in time.

Ruby was no easy sell. "Misery loves company, Mac. You're just trying to get me thrown out of here along with you."

"You're not taking any risk at all, Ruby. We're talking one extra antibiotic dose—which really isn't even extra—and then just carefully monitoring the patient. How could you get into any trouble?"

"Why do I feel like you're trying to sell me a ticket for the *Titanic*—it's just a short cruise, world's safest ship. What could go wrong?"

Schell was easier to convince than Ruby. He was intrigued by the whole idea. "Why not?" he said.

Once Laura Rubenstein and Dr. Schell were on board, things moved quickly. Mac had to be certain that everything was documented by the others. For too long he had been the only true believer. With any luck at all, that would soon change.

Then they were done, and the clock which had been moving so swiftly suddenly ground to a screeching halt. Two hours passed during which nothing happened. Not a sign of Peter VanSlyke. For all Mac knew, Peter had gone home to bed.

Finally Mac threw Ruby a wave and left the ICU. There was nothing more he could do. His presence could only queer the game.

Then he waited. Twenty-five minutes. He walked to the cafeteria, but he wasn't hungry. He went down to radiology and pulled some X rays, but he couldn't concentrate.

When Mac finally allowed himself to go back to the unit, he still didn't see any sign of Van-

Slyke. Laura Rubenstein and Stan Schell were standing at Constance Law's bedside.

Ruby gave him a weary shrug. "Sorry, Mac. Nothing." She poked around in the bed with her hand, then shook her head.

"Was he here?"

"Showed up right on time," Schell said. "He stood by the bedside for the entire infusion. I thought you were really on to something."

Mac sniffed. There was an unmistakable odor of penicillin in the air. His hands searched the bed. Nothing. He pulled up the edges of the mattress to have a peek underneath. Nothing. He looked under the bed. Then he noticed the wastebasket at the head of the bed. It had a plastic liner. There were some paper towels thrown in on top. There was fluid at the bottom. It reeked of penicillin.

"This time he bled the line into the wastebasket," Mac said. "All we need to do is get the fluid in the wastebasket analyzed and draw a nafcillin blood level on the patient." It was all very clear. Mac finally had his proof. He said simply, "We got him."

FIFTY-FOUR

A nurse said she had seen VanSlyke heading up the stairs outside the ICU. He could have been going any number of places, but Mac had a pretty good hunch where he'd find him. How appropriate, Mac thought.

The tower steps were darker than Mac remembered. And colder. There might still be ice up there.

He made the climb in as much silence as the rickety wooden stairs would permit, promising himself this would be his last trip up here—ever. He dimly recalled having made a similar promise once before.

Each time he made the climb, the superstructure seemed less secure than the time before. As always he hugged the cold brick wall, avoiding the open well in the center of the tower that grew deeper with every upward step he took.

He was especially cautious as he climbed the final steep flight of stairs which ended at the floor of the tower's highest stage. When Mac poked his head through, he saw Peter VanSlyke standing at one of the giant portals in the sides of the tower's summit. A bitter wind whipped around inside the tower.

VanSlyke turned as Mac pulled himself through the opening in the floor. "What are *you* doing here?" he asked.

Mac didn't say anything, just walked to another opening maybe ten feet from where Van-Slyke was standing, well out of VanSlyke's reach. He was bigger than Mac. A couple of inches taller and perhaps twenty-five pounds heavier. Mac needed to be careful.

Finally Mac said, "I just wanted to be the one to tell you. It's come to Jesus time."

"What's that supposed to mean?"

"It's over, Peter."

"What's over?"

"Your little game. Everything. The killing."

"Is this supposed to be a threat? Am I supposed to be afraid?"

"You know which piece gave me the most trouble?"

VanSlyke gave a shrug to indicate his indifference to whatever Mac was going on about.

"Austin Delacroix," Mac said. "He developed a conscience, didn't he?"

VanSlyke was giving Mac a hard stare now.

"Delacroix killed Havlicek because he thought

that Havlicek had Alzheimer's. Havlicek was supposedly incurable. Then it turned out not to be Alzheimer's at all. Havlicek was probably suffering from an acute depression. Delacroix had killed a guy who had a treatable illness.

"Austin was devastated, wasn't he? He tried to get a digoxin level on Jan Havlicek to prove he had been killed. Then he tried to get a digoxin level on Annie Williams. Austin was going to expose the whole thing. He was going to confess and take you with him. So you murdered him."

"Prove it," VanSlyke said.

"You'd be surprised how much I can prove—with Jennifer's help. Oh, don't worry, Pete. Jennifer's fine. Just a tiny little scratch on her neck. Beano botched the whole thing. The police haven't picked him up yet, but I imagine he'll be pretty talkative when they do. When Jennifer and Beano get done talking, you'll be up for one count of murder and one of attempted murder—minimum."

Mac felt his muscles growing tired. It was freezing in the tower. He needed sleep. Despite his acrophobia, he took a seat on the ledge. Just sitting made him feel better. He tried not to think how far down it was to the pavement below.

VanSlyke fixed a baleful glare on Mac. Only the keening wind disturbed the silence.

Mac focused his attention back on VanSlyke. "If a patient gets presented at the ethics seminar, do you know what his chance of dying in the next six weeks is? Eighty percent. Can you believe that?

"I did a little study, compared the current mortality rate with five years ago. I figured, you know, there'd be a big jump and that would provide evidence of what you guys were up to. But the rate from five years ago was about the same as now. Fifteen years ago, though, now that was a different story. Only about thirty percent died back then. Why do you suppose that was, Petie?"

VanSlyke's expression didn't budge. He didn't appear to be in a sharing kind of mood just now.

"What I needed to find," Mac said, "was some constant in the seminar which extended back a few years but not to the beginning. As soon as I saw what that was, the rest was easy."

VanSlyke was becoming increasingly agitated. He now looked like he might explode at any moment. He repeatedly clenched and released his fists.

"It was something Eleanor Delacroix said which first put in my mind the idea that her hold on you and Austin might be more sexual than intellectual. Didn't that bother you? You were just part of her current crop of lovesick little schoolboys."

VanSlyke had begun to edge closer to Mac, ever so slightly.

"Constance Law was playing you and Austin against each other, wasn't she? The two of you, competing for her favor. I'm sure she'd played that game many times over the years. And to poor Austin—with his handicap—the whole thing must have seemed terribly unfair. That may have helped spark his conscience a little at the end. Made him feel a little less uneasy about dragging you and Constance Law down with him.

"And speaking of Constance Law, that was a pretty clever idea. Instead of *giving* her some deadly drug, just deprive her of a lifesaving antibiotic. Unless you got caught in the act, it would be impossible to prove you'd done anything. Unfortunately, you got caught in the act. Lots of witnesses."

Mac slowly rose to his feet and began to move away from the gaping portal and the vast expanse of empty space beyond.

"Don't worry, Petie, we've given her all the antibiotics you thought she didn't get." Mac paused, crouching down a little to lower his center of gravity and prepare for the charge which was sure to come. "Why did you try to kill her? Because of her illness, or was it because of the little game she'd played with you and Delacroix?"

Suddenly VanSlyke lunged, reaching out with both hands and grabbing fistfuls of Mac's shirt. His grip was unbreakable. It was more likely the shirt would tear than that his grip would loosen.

Mac took his cue from VanSlyke. With one hand he grabbed VanSlyke's tie and shirt, with the other, his belt. They were two sumo wrestlers. The winner would be the one who wasn't thrown from the ring. The loser's career would be over. Forever.

The struggle began. Both men tried to maintain a very broad stance. VanSlyke tried to force Mac closer to the edge. Very soon both men teetered on the brink of eternity.

"Hey!"

The shout came from the opening in the tower's floor where the final flight of stairs poked through. Mac and VanSlyke both turned toward the voice and saw Turner Frost scrambling toward them.

The next thing Mac knew, he was falling.

FIFTY-FIVE

"Look," Turner Frost said, "I told you that I would be happy to tell what I know, to help in your investigation. But if you're going to start talking to me like I'm a suspect, then I want to have a lawyer present."

Polanski said, "Like I told you, you are not now a suspect. We'd just like you to answer a couple more questions."

"How was it that you happened to go to the tower?" Mallory asked.

"I was looking for Peter," Frost said. "A nurse told me he had gone up into the tower."

"How did she know he had gone there?"

"I don't know."

Polanski jumped in again. "Did you know that Mac McCall was up there?"

"No, I didn't."

"Did you know," Polanski asked, "that McCall was accusing you, Peter VanSlyke, and Austin Delacroix of killing patients?"

"I knew that he thought patients were being killed. Everyone knew that. I didn't know that he was suspicious of me."

Polanski zeroed in for the kill. "Did you take part in a plot to kill patients, Mr. Frost?"

"I certainly did not."

"Were you aware that anyone else was deliberately causing the death of patients?"

"I was not."

Mallory said, "Would you please tell us one more time exactly what you saw when you first arrived at the top of the tower?"

"Like I said, they were fighting. More like *struggling*. They had hold of each other. They were standing very close to the edge."

"What did you do when you arrived?" Mallory asked.

"I yelled at them. They stopped struggling for a second or two. Then they went right back at it."

"Then what happened?"

"I was walking toward them . . ."

"Walking?" Polanski asked.

"Okay, running, scrambling. I was trying to get to them as quickly as possible."

"Why?"

"Why? To prevent from happening just exactly what did happen."

"Then what happened?"

Frost took a deep breath, then let it out in a

sigh. "They were both close to the edge. There was ice all over the place. All of a sudden it looked as though they were both losing their balance. It looked like they both were going to fall. I just grabbed blindly, trying to save somebody if I could."

Polanski leaned down very close to Frost's face. "You're sure you *grabbed* somebody. You didn't by any chance happen to give somebody a push?"

"No. I did not give anybody a push. And that's the last question I'm answering without having my lawyer present."

Mallory looked like he was going to zero in for one last attack, then backed off. "Okay," he said, "that's all for now. You can go. But just so you'll know, we're going to go talk to your buddy right now. If he can't confirm everything you've said, you'll be hearing from us."

In the interrogation room down the hall, Mallory led off. "I think your buddy Frost is about to crack," he said. "If he does, and you're still denying everything, he could work a soft deal for himself and you could go away for life."

"What am I supposed to be admitting to?"

"That you and Frost gave the guy a little push. That you had planned to kill him."

"Look, I told you guys, I hardly ever even talk to Frost. I thought he was involved in the murders. When I saw Turner climb up into the tower, I thought that *I* was the one who was going to die."

"Tell me again," Polanski said, "how you happened to go up into the tower in the first place."

"I was looking for VanSlyke."

"Why?"

"To tell him the game was up."

"Not so you could be judge, jury, and executioner?"

"No."

Mac couldn't believe these guys. He'd just cracked the case of the century for them, and they were still trying to pin something on him! It was like he'd become their favorite suspect and they couldn't let go of the idea that he was guilty of *something*.

"You guys find Professor Law yet?" Mac asked.

Polanski and Mallory shook their heads.

"Mrs. Law still alive?"

"Last we heard," Mallory said.

"You going to charge her?"

"Even if we had witnesses," Mallory said, "or any other kind of evidence which might have a chance in hell of standing up in court, no prosecutor's ever going to file anything—not unless she makes some kind of miraculous recovery from her stroke."

Mac shrugged. "Nothing the state could impose would even approach the imprisonment her own body has already subjected her to. And at this point there's virtually no chance at all that she'll ever improve."

"I guess you can go," Mallory said. There was more than a trace of regret in his voice. "You're still not off the hook on the VanSlyke death. At the very lest there'll be a coroner's inquest."

"The guy tried to kill *me*," Mac protested.

"Whatever."

What was Mac expecting, a warm handshake and a chorus of thank-yous?

The city Mac stepped out into was still gripped firmly by the icy winter night. It would be a couple of hours yet, at least, before the first rays of sunlight began to pry away the night's hold.

Mac should go home, take a hot shower, crawl into bed. He had earned it. And he would—soon. It was almost over.

Almost.

FIFTY-SIX

As Mac entered the hospital he noticed a light on in a first-floor window over at the medical school. He tried to call up an image of the floor plan in his head. Was that Law's office? Mac thought it probably was. Perhaps Dr. Law had finally materialized, and that part of things would now come to a close. Or maybe it was just the police, ransacking Law's office the same way they'd gone through Mac's apartment. Sooner or later there would be a warrant issued, or a subpoena. They'd want to see those log-books if nothing else.

The ICU was still in nighttime mode, the morning bustle yet to begin. Mac found Karen at Maria's bedside. She threw her arms around his neck.

"Oh, Mac, how awful!" Then she stepped back to look him over. "You're okay?"

Mac nodded. "I was lucky."

"You could have told me what was going on."

"I'm sorry. You were down in surgery. Things started to move pretty quickly. Then I was essentially in police custody." He looked over toward the bed. "How's Maria?"

"So far, so good. Everything seemed to go well in surgery. Her numbers look pretty good. If no technical problems turn up from the surgical point of view, then it's just a matter of watching for infection and rejection."

"Is that all?"

"I see the events of the evening haven't altered your basically sarcastic personality."

Mac smiled. "Sorry. It would be nice to see something go smoothly for once. Maria deserves that."

He gave Karen's hand a squeeze and wandered over to the nurse's station where Laura Rubenstein was sitting.

"How's Mrs. Law doing?"

"Mac! Where the hell have you been?"

"It's my night off, remember?"

"I suppose, now that you're such a big celebrity, you're gonna be wanting a night off every week." Good old Ruby.

"Any change in Mrs. Law?"

"Nothing positive. I'm surprised she's still with us. She looks septic. I imagine her blood cultures will be positive for staph."

"She's gotten all of her antibiotics?"

"As far as we know—unless VanSlyke has a buddy in the pharmacy filling her IV bags with saline."

"How about her husband?"

"Vanished from the face of the earth."

"I saw a light on when I came in that I thought might be his office."

"We've called. No answer. Same thing at home."

Mac wandered over to the medical school—more out of restlessness than anything else. He wasn't quite ready to give in to the fatigue that was pressing in on him, but he wouldn't be able to hold out much longer.

The door to the outer office was closed. Mac started to knock, then—on a nostalgic impulse—gave it a push. The door yielded.

A single light was on, the lamp on the professor's desk. Professor Law was seated there, dimly lighted, a gun in his hand—pointed at Mac.

Mac entered and closed the door securely behind him. He stood in the outer office, staring at Dr. Law. The professor stared back, gun in hand.

"Everybody's looking for you, Dr. Law."

If Law heard him, he showed no sign of it. The man was suddenly old and tired and defeated. No light remained in those famous blue eyes.

"Your wife is very ill, Dr. Law. Pneumonia. There's a question of whether to intubate her, put her on a respirator."

Something stirred deep inside the man. "She wants to die," he said. "She doesn't see why she should be treated any differently."

"Differently?"

"From all the others who died." Law collapsed back into himself momentarily, then said, "Do you know what she's done?"

Mac nodded.

"I owe you an apology, Mac. You were right. Right about everything."

"Not about *everything*. I was sure wrong about Ralph Perkins." That was the digoxin level which had nearly cost Mac his career.

"Did you know she'd been taking lovers?" Law asked. "From among the medical students?"

Mac didn't think it was necessary to reveal that he had figured that out. No reason for Law to worry that that was common knowledge.

"She told me everything," Law said. "At first I didn't believe it. I thought she just wanted to make me angry—so that I would kill her." There were tears now, streaming down his cheeks. He looked at the gun in his hand as though noticing it for the first time. "This gun is hers. It was in a drawer. I had no idea . . . She wanted me to shoot her."

Law began eyeing the gun with new fascination, as though he saw in it a solution.

"No one will blame *you*, Dr. Law. None of this is your fault."

"But it's *all* my fault, Mac. Don't you see? It was through me that she got involved with the seminar in the first place. It was through me that she gained access to these . . . these . . . boys."

Mac moved closer, trying to get within reach of the gun.

"What made them believe that they had the right?" Professor Law asked. "Who were they to decide who should die?"

"We'll never know," Mac said, mainly just to keep the conversation going.

"I should have seen what was going on. It was right there. Right under my nose. Why didn't I see it?"

"They were very good at it. Nothing was obvious." Mac thought he might just be able to grab the gun. He had to be so very careful.

"You saw, Mac. You recognized what they were up to."

"I was just lucky," Mac said.

He slowly reached out and was able to take the barrel of the revolver firmly in his right hand.

"Let me have the gun, Dr. Law. Please."

Law released the gun and hung his head, bringing his hands up to cover his face. He began to sob, probably not for the first time in the last twenty-four hours.

EPILOGUE

Mac had taken yesterday off. He didn't really ask permission of anyone. He just called Ruby and told her that he needed to try to get some rest. She gave him the expected grief, *they don't make medical students the way they used to*, and so on. "See you tomorrow, Ruby," he had told her.

Mac had forced himself to come in today but was trying very hard not to get involved in patient care. Patients deserved a whole lot more focused thought than Mac would be able to give them at this juncture. Perhaps tomorrow, or the day after, Mac could begin to get on with the rest of his life. Today he just wasn't quite ready.

He had tried once again to talk some sense into Jennifer. Now she wasn't certain she should even press charges against Beano, open that can of worms. With VanSlyke dead, she figured maybe she'd just let the whole thing drop.

Mac didn't like to think of Beano getting away with anything, but—on the other hand—he was his own worst enemy. Sooner or later, probably sooner, Beano would do himself in.

Stan Schell, the chief of neurology, had taken the responsibility for Arthur Law out of Mac's hands. Together, Schell and Law had made the decision not to place Constance Law on a ventilator. She died a few hours later.

Mac couldn't help but wonder what might have happened if Constance Law had remained healthy—if she hadn't suffered the stroke. Over many years during which her participation was the only constant, hundreds of murders had been committed without the slightest suspicion being raised. If she had remained in charge, would the conspiracy still have unraveled the way it did?

Mac hadn't seen Turner Frost since they'd come down from the tower together in the wee hours of yesterday morning. So when Turner walked into the ICU, Mac rose and offered his hand. It was the commission of an unnatural act, behaving civilly toward Turner Frost.

"I think I was a little too shaken yesterday morning," Mac said, "to properly thank you for saving my life. And I owe you an apology—for thinking you were mixed up with Law and VanSlyke."

Turner's hand had the feel of an uncooked salmon fillet. Mac released it quickly and had to consciously resist the urge to wipe his own hand on his trousers.

"It was just a fluke," Turner said, "that I happened to save you instead of Peter. You were the only one I could reach. If I could have gotten to Peter, they'd be holding your funeral tomorrow instead of his."

Good old Turner. Mr. Warmth.

Mac had tried to be gracious, but he didn't feel any obligation to go on and on about it. So he changed the subject.

"In a way, I would have liked to have seen Constance Law answer for her crimes," Mac said.

Not surprisingly, Frost disagreed. "No, it's better this way, to just be done with it once and for all."

"It's more convenient this way," Mac said. "I'm not sure it's really better."

Turner shrugged and wandered off without further comment. Mac walked over to the other side of the ICU to check on Maria Valenzuela. Karen Anderson was standing at her bedside. Maria's eyes were closed.

"How's she doing?" Mac whispered.

"Just great," Karen said. "We may be able to get her off the ventilator soon. So far, no complications."

Mac slipped an arm around Karen's waist, and she responded by putting an arm around his. Someone might see them. Mac didn't care. He needed a little human warmth and reassurance right now.

"Strange," he said, "that she doesn't have a clue about anything that's happened."

"I hope she doesn't learn about all of this until she's out of the hospital," Karen said. "Still, at least now she's safe. We don't have to worry that somebody's going to kill her because she's too expensive to save."

"I wish I could believe that," Mac said.

Karen threw him a questioning look.

"Don't forget that little case study we did," Mac reminded her. "That seventy-five percent fatality rate among ethics-seminar patients five years ago wasn't caused by VanSlyke and Delacroix. They weren't around in those days. Someone else was killing those patients."

"So you think that somebody else may *still* be around here killing patients?"

"Maybe," Mac said. "We know they *were* here, five years ago. Maybe they're still here; maybe they've gone on to some other hospital. Maybe they've started their own little ethics seminar somewhere halfway across the country, training a whole new generation of Peter VanSlykes and Austin Delacroixs. Who knows?"

"So what are we supposed to do, Mac?"

"In the short run, we can take another look at Law's logbooks, see how far back the killing goes. But in the long run," Mac said, shaking his head, "I haven't got a clue."

Maria Valenzuela awakened and saw them standing there. Mac and Karen instantly removed their arms from around each other.

Maria looked bright-eyed and alert. So far this brave young woman had sailed through the post-transplant period without the slightest hint of an unfavorable headwind. Now, for the first time, she could realistically plan for a future *with* her children—instead of planning for their future without her.

Maria signaled that she wanted something to write on.

Karen found a clipboard and held it while Maria tried her best to scrawl a legible message.

The first line she wrote said, "When do I get to see my babies?"

On the second line, Maria drew a little heart and wrote, "And what's going on between you two?"

INTENSIVE FEAR
FROM ROBIN COOK

☐ **COMA.** They call it "minor surgery," but Nancy Greenly, Sean Berman, and a dozen others, all admitted to memorial Hospital for routine procedures, are victims of the same inexplicable, hideous tragedy on the operating table. *They never wake up again.*   (159535—$5.99)

☐ **BRAIN.** Martin Philips and Denise Sanger were doctors, lovers—and desperately afraid. Something was terribly wrong in the great medical research center, and they had to place their careers, and their lives, in deadly jeopardy as they penetrated the eerie inner sanctums of a medical world gone mad with technological power and the lust for more. . . .
        (157974—$5.99)

☐ **GODPLAYER.** There have always been many ways to die. But now, in an ultra-modern hospital, there was a new one. The most horrifying one of all. "Impossible to put down . . . a crescendo of action to a smashing finish . . . don't miss this one!"—*San Diego Tribune* (157281—$6.99)

☐ **FEVER** The daughter of a brilliant cancer researcher becomes the victim of a conspiracy that not only promises to kill her, but will destroy him as a doctor and a man if he tries to fight it, in this terrifying medical nightmare. "Gripping, vivid, believable!" *The New York Times Book Review.*
        (160339—$5.99)

Prices slightly higher in Canada